PANDORA'S BOX

LUKE CHRISTODOULOU

VINCI

BOOKS

Vinci Books

vinci-books.com

Published by Vinci Books Ltd in 2026

1

The publisher and the author have made every effort to obtain permissions
for any third party material used in this book and to comply with copyright
law. Any queries in this respect should be brought to the attention of the
publisher and any omissions will be corrected in future editions.
A CIP catalogue record for this book is available from the British Library.
Paperback ISBN: 9781036712624
The EU GPSR authorised representative is Logos Europe, 9 rue Nicolas
Poussion, 17000 La Rochelle, France contact@logoseurope.eu

By Luke Christodoulou

Murderous Greece

Pandora's Box
Achilles' Heel
Beware of Greeks Bearing Gifts

Greek Island Mysteries

The Olympus Killer
The Church Murders
Death of a Bride
Murder on Display
Hotel Murder
Twelve Months of Murder

Dedicated to every work of art
born from a creative mind in quarantine

Chapter One

ELAFONISOS ISLAND, GREECE

Summer, 2004

Crimson blood formed rivulets along her trembling hands as she ran barefoot on the golden sand beach of Kontogoni Bay. Droplets fell, forming a short-lived trail under the limited scarce moonlight. There were too many clouds for this time of year. As if the sky knew what had taken place and wished to protect its stars from viewing the horrendous crime. Soon, the blood mingled with the crystal-clear waters of the Aegean Sea and swam out to the dark horizon. The saltiness nested in Melpomene's nostrils as the chilly sea breeze attacked her sweaty face. The warm blood upon her pale skin cooled as she speedily made her way through the bay, hoping that no eyes would be open at such an hour. A Christian girl of only seventeen, she had never been out at four past midnight. The serenity of the exotic beach scared her. Only the waves and the rustling of majestic palm trees provided the soundtrack to her getaway. Her hands felt tired. The cupboard box she was carrying grew heavier as her strength diminished.

Leaden, silent houses stood along tenebrous streets. With the bars and taverns closed, sun-kissed locals and sunburnt tourists were tightly tucked in their beds enjoying carefree slumber. Melpomene sighed with relief. The small fishing port was just ahead. She crept in the shadows, avoiding any light escaping from the blue metal lampposts. The box shook slightly.

'Shhh, my lovely, shhh. Not now!'

The white fishing boat danced upon the calm waves. The girl with the ripped pink pyjamas tiptoed along the wooden dock, the planks screeching as she made her way to *Saint Demetrios*, her father's boat. Just the thought of him, made her spine shiver. With care, she placed the box in the boat, untied the nautical knot and took the keys out of her bloody jeans pocket. She formed the sign of the cross on her body, prayed and placed the key into the ignition. With a roar, the engine came to life and running without lights, Melpomene made her way out of the port and into the open waters. Mainland Greece was less than two kilometres away. She was minutes away from freedom. Off Elafonisos Island that was heaven for all, but her. 'The most beautiful hell...' she whispered as she looked back at her island for the last time. Her bronze hair danced upon the strong wind. The box between her feet rattled again. Cries broke the silence. Melpomene lifted the lid and stared down at the weeping baby. The dark corners of her mind gave birth to ideas that terrified her.

'If I throw her overboard, she will depart this Earth. The Lord would welcome her. Why leave her alive to suffer like I have?'

She looked down at the deep unfriendly waters of the open sea. Just then, she saw the light coming from Saint

Spiridon's church. A lone building of worship on the small uninhabited island.

'I can't. My Saint, please give me strength.'

The clouds above her scattered and the full moon shone upon the waters.

'It will be just you and I, my lovely. Just you and me. I will be the best mama and I will protect you and feed you and always be by your side.'

Melpomene kept all her promises from that night. As the boat reached Pouda beach on the mainland, Melpomene picked up Pandora, wiped her cold tears, placed a soft kiss on her forehead and dashed away into the night.

Chapter Two

Summer, 2019

'You cannot be serious, mum! Moving again?'

Pandora blew a strike of blond hair that had escaped her high ponytail away from her tanned face. The sound of her teeth grinding echoed in the low-ceiling rental apartment. Melpomene bit her lip and turned her gaze towards the cross hanging on the wall. '*Lord, give me the strength to survive another tantrum.*'

'Mum? Mum? Are you praying?' Pandora raised her voice. 'I'm not a demon you can banish, you know.'

Melpomene could not help but laugh. A short quiet laugh, yet still a laugh. 'My lovely, you know that we must go where mama finds work.'

'All nurses that I know of work in a freaking hospital.' Pandora fell back on the worn-in brown sofa.

'I am a carer, baby. I look after old people that need someone who has medical knowledge. It has been three months since Mrs. Toula died. We cannot stay here any longer. I need to work. I stayed here for you to finish your school year. Now, we are moving on. I have found a new client.' Melpomene paused to catch her breath. Her high-pitched voice ran marathons when she had much to say. As if all the words floating in her head came out in one long sentence, an unstoppable flowing river of thoughts.

'Where to?'

'The exotic seaside village of Parga!'

Pandora sat on her wicker stool. A round lime pillow provided her with comfort. She was pleased with the reflexion in the oval mirror glued on the wall opposite her. She placed her red lipstick on last and stood up. Barefoot, with her black high-heels in hand -the ones she saved for months to be able to buy and had hidden well in her cupboard, she crept towards her bedroom window. Her gaze ran from the clock that struck midnight to the figure built out of pillows under her beige sheets. 'Markos, here I come,' she whispered and out the window she fled. Seven-teen-year-old Markos was waiting for her. He stood by his black Honda Civic enjoying an Assos cigarette. His eyes widened as he saw the beauty in high heels, a short red skirt and a jean jacket running awkwardly toward him. The dim light from the streetlights above made her hair shine and Markos smiled at the idea that his girlfriend wore a halo. 'My saint,' he joked and pulled her into his strong bare arms. Markos never skipped gym. 'Please, no church stuff,' she replied and laid a loud kiss on his cold dry lips. 'I have enough of that at home.'

Markos stroked back her hair and squeezed her face between his hands. 'I'm so glad you texted. I've missed you.'

'Well, you know how my mum gets...' Pandora paused and breathed in enough air as to work up the courage for the next words. 'I had to see you. I am moving.'

'Moving?' Markos took a step back. If the circumstances were different, Pandora would have laughed at his sorrowful puppy eyes. 'Where to?'

'Parga.'

'That's hours away.'

'I know. That's why tonight is so special.' Pandora moved back into his embrace. Her right hand ran between his legs. 'We will probably never see each other again. I want you to be my first.'

The boy shivered as he felt the bulge in his ripped jeans growing and Pandora's fingers caressing him. 'Let's go,' he said, and the two teens leapt into the running vehicle. He drove over the speed limit with the music booming. As deafening as the radio was, both could hear their beating hearts pounding away under their youthful chests. The seafront road was quiet as always on a weeknight. Soon, the park by the cliff came into view. The moonlight danced around in the stubborn olive trees and the majestic cypresses. Markos parked the car by the rusty swings with the chipped red paint and switched off the loud engine. For a minute, both sat in silence, unable to look at each other. Their eyes were focused on the sea and the dark horizon.

'So...' Markos swallowed the lump inhabiting his throat. Pandora leaned in for a kiss. Neither spoke again. Both did their best to suppress meddling thoughts and live in the moment; both with their young minds on porn videos that they secretly viewed at nights on their cell phones. Soon, two clothesless bodies lay as one in the narrow space provided by the Honda's back seats. With shaky hands, Markos placed on the condom that had been living in his wallet for the last six months or so and smiled at the naked body before him. He entered her slowly. She was warm and wet. Pandora bit her lower lip and put her arms around him.

'I can't believe this is happening. My God, this is perfect,' she said and closed her eyes, truly lost in the moment. Her mind was miles away from the packed suitcases standing side-by-side in her living room.

Chapter Three

PARGA

Summer 2021

The little fishing boats danced upon the warm clear waters, gently pushed by the fresh morning breeze. Arianna finished the first half of her day's run always on the same spot. Parga's short pier. A strip of cement cutting the small town's bay into two. The police captain jogged up to the edge just in time for her favourite moment of the day. She sat down quickly, not minding the dirt attacking her black leggings, and gazed to her left. The sun, dressed in all its majestic rays, rose from behind the tiny islet occupying the next bay -the popular one, the one you could swim in. Arianna took off her designer sunglasses and embraced the newborn light. She counted to ten and then succumbed to her nemesis. 'Filthy habit.' She placed her thin cigarette in her mouth and lit it with a blue lighter that she had *borrowed* from a co-worker back at the station. A short-lived cloud of pale smoke scattered in the wind before her as she smiled at the waves below. '*We start off small, grow, make an impact and vanish forever.*' She chuckled as she finished her cigarette. '*You're a right-up philosopher, Arianna!*' She stood up and jogged to the empty green bin at the end of the pier. She threw in her bud, ran around the three-meter metal anchor on display in the small-town square and dashed through the narrow roads that led uphill to her house. The one she inherited from her late mother. The one that came in handy when she had divorced and left Athens to return to her roots with her then ten-year-old boy.

The garden gate squeaked as she slammed it closed and walked through her prize array of rose bushes. She bent forward to smell a large yellow rose and streaks of pitch-black hair escaped her ponytail, sticking to her sweaty face.

'Timothy? Timmy? You up, boy?' she called out as she entered the house. 'Come down and have breakfast with your mother.'

A grunt came from above, followed by a 'Jesus Christ! School is in an hour. Let me sleep.'

'Okay, okay. I'll shower first and dress for work. Then, breakfast together!'

The seventeen-year-old was all she had. Him and her job. The only things Police Captain Arianna Kontou cared for. She knew that she spent too many hours at the station. She knew that the move to her maternal village had cost her son a father. A one-visit-a-week father that is. Timothy spent the Christmas and Easter holidays with him in the metropolis of Athens, while his father always came and stayed in the touristy village for a couple of weeks, end of August.

Timothy had grown into a fine young man. Tall, masculine, with deep dimples and a smile that brightened even her darkest of days. He was kind, polite and eager to help. It was no wonder he was school president and captain of the football team. She remembered that day fondly. He came rushing into the house, throwing his schoolbag to the floor and leaving -as always- the front door swinging from its hinges. 'Guess what, ma? We are both captains now!'

Across town, Ophelia gathered up her silver hair into a bun and picked up her green garden hose. The warmth of the sun embraced her as she took small weak steps out of the shade of her twisted olive trees. She witnessed the same view for the last eighty-six years and yet it still amazed her. The castle on the hill lost in pure bright green, the two bays of turquoise waters, the colorful houses lined up in a row, the sandy beach, the islets occupying the shiny waters, and the glorious Greek sun that welcomed her every morning. Her old wrinkled hands trembled as the cold water rushed powerfully through the hose and loudly leapt out to cool down colorful geraniums baking in the dried dirt. Her mind trembled more than her hands as once again her two tenants were yelling at each other. Old Ophelia shook her head. 'Just the two of them. Religious lady. Highly recommended nurse. One spoke calmly, the other not at all. No man with them! I thought, oh bless me, oh the luck. Nice, quiet mother and daughter to have stay with me and avoid the awful nursing home!' Ophelia mumbled to herself as she made her way to the fuchsia bougainvillea that grew on an arch made by her late husband above their garden gate. The yelling grew louder and then suddenly stopped. A minute later, a red-faced Pandora stormed by her. 'Morning, Mrs. Ophelia,' the youth said without turning her head. Pandora slammed the gate behind her and rushed down the stone sidewalk. 'Good morning, child.'

Melpomene stood by the open window with her eyes fixed on Pandora. 'That girl will be the death of me...' A deep sigh escaped her dry lips. Melpomene held back her tears. She held them back well. After everything she had been subjected to, she knew not to cry over insignificant things. 'If only trying to discipline a teenager girl wasn't so damn hard!'

'What's that, dear?'

'Oh, Mrs. Ophelia, good morning. Nothing. Just talking to myself, hoping Jesus will hear me and show me His light.'

The old lady nodded in agreement. 'Amen to that.'

'I hope we didn't startle to you. I will have your breakfast and pills ready in a minute.'

Ophelia dropped the running water near the trunk of a sweet-smelling lemon tree. 'No rush, dear. I still have the anemones to do.' She scratched her nose and rubbed her lower back. 'And you can't startle me dear. I've lived through a world war, a civil war *and* the Junta!'

'With schools closing today, I have to live through an entire summer with Pandora!'

Ophelia looked up. 'Last exam today?'

'Yep. And tonight, all the seniors want to gather and party.'

'Oh, I see...'

Melpomene's thumb ran along her short colorless nails as her right hand clenched into a loose fist. Her left hand scratched her long neck. 'I know you think I am too strict, but...'

Ophelia waved her hand. 'Not my place to judge, dear.'

'But I am a single parent. A religious parent. And underage girls should be kept under a watchful eye from...' Melpomene paused. She controlled her tongue. Her mind pulled back the lingering adjectives and *perverted*, *sex-hungry*, and *filthy* were devoured by the darkness.

'From?' Ophelia asked as she trudged towards the pipe. She turned off the water just in time to hear Melpomene's low-pitched voice. 'From teenage boys.'

Ophelia wiped her wet hands on her *gardening* apron. The oldest of her cooking aprons that still had some mileage to go was newly appointed as a gardening apron. She sighed deeply as she walked up to the window. 'You know, dear, I have four children and eleven grandkids. None alike and definitely none living the way I lived. Our children are not destined to repeat our mistakes.' Ophelia looked up and stared straight into Melpomene's weary eyes to check if her point had reached its destination. She let it sink in for a while and added, 'they will make all whole new ones!'

'You're implying that just because I had a baby as a teen, I fear my daughter will suffer the same?' Now, both her hands had formed strong fists. Her nails dug slightly into her skin. Ophelia could not see from where she stood how her words had affected her house nurse. 'I fear because I know the cruelty of the world.' Her harsh tone did not go by unnoticed.

'Again, I am not judging, dear. I had my first at fifteen.'

'At your choice,' Melpomene mumbled.

'What's that, dear?'

'Coffee time, Mrs. Ophelia. Cherished coffee time. Come on in. I will have it ready in a jiffy.'

Chapter Four

Pandora's eyes followed the hand of the clock as it journeyed round, conquering the seconds. The old faded-brown clock hung right above the whiteboard and just below the deep crack that had spread like lightning on the bare wall. Their teacher had taken all her posters down for the summer. Pandora counted all the stains left behind from the overused Blu Tack. 'Thirty-six,' she whispered as she played with the corners of her exam papers. Chemistry was her favourite subject. She had finished the exam half an hour ago. She had completed all sixteen questions and gone over them twice. Yet on her wooden chair she remained. Pandora never raised her hand in class, nor took part in any extra-curriculum activities. She hid her test marks from her friends well. Popularity over academic success.

She looked to her left and held back a giggle. Her two best friends looked puzzled. Both of them hated chemistry. Nefeli chewed on her golden locks while Iris flicked through the four-page test trying to find something vaguely possible to solve. Timothy was the first of the *cool kids* to stand up.

Up to that moment only *nerds* had left the well-lit classroom. Pandora's sea-blue eyes followed him as he passed his test to their teacher with the permanently bored expression. Her eyes fell upon his behind. Pandora bit her lower lip gently. She wished she could bite into Timothy's. '*You're one fine specimen, Timmy.*'

Pandora counted to ten and rose from her seat. She winked to her friends and mouthed, 'I'm bored. I'm going for a smoke with Tim.' She handed in her paper and her multiple bracelets rattled. She avoided her teacher's eyes. Pandora knew that judgmental look well. The good-hearted teacher had tried before to talk sense into the girl. She would have none of it. Popularity over academic success. The paper dropped from her hands and she dashed out the door. The dark quiet corridor welcomed her. The head teacher, a small plum woman with thinly framed reading glasses sat on a crooked nose, stood in attention with her index finger placed on her steady lips. 'Ssshh!' The whispery sound echoed toward Pandora. The head teacher opened her eyes wide and nodded to the exit. Pandora gladly left the building. A smile spread on her face as the sun rays sailed around her and warmed her. She was no longer a pupil. She was no longer a child. She was a step away from sweet eighteen. '*I am a woman.*' A woman carrying a pencil case. Pandora looked to her left. An old green trash bin held papers, empty cans of soft drinks and various chocolate wrappers. Now, it held a purple pencil case full of pencils, a cracked ruler and an abused eraser. With her hands free of bondage, Pandora walked with haste toward the back of the boys' toilets. Timmy was still there. He was surrounded by teens enjoying his camping story. 'I'm heading out there as soon as possible, man. No more alarms and exams and... Hey, Pandora.'

'Hey, so who has a light?' She placed a cigarette on her lips and walked toward him. He extended his strong arms and a flame came to life from his prized Zippo. The silver one his uncle bought him at last year's fair and told him to hide it from his mother. 'I will kill you, you little shit, before my sister kills me. You know that, right?' his uncle said as he held him in a headlock. Timothy laughed. 'I don't know. Mum is pretty fast.'

Arianna ran down the empty hallway and pushed the door to her right with her body. The ladies' toilets were empty. Logical as in the Parga's police force of eight, only she and the front desk secretary were women and she saw Pauline on her fast exit from her corner office. A must needed journey to the spotlessly clean lavatory. 'God, I hate these days. Lord, you owe me a menopause, soon!' She checked her trousers for any unwanted stains. She felt more flooded that she actually was. She pulled out a lengthy piece of toilet paper and just then, her phone vibrated in her jean's right pocket. It was her police partner, Adrian. The only Lieutenant that she had found a pleasure to work with in her two-decade career. She held the screen a good foot away from her eyes and mumbled the text message. 'Robbery... Angelica's bakery... money from the cash register... Where are you, boss? I came to your office... For fuck's sake, can't a woman even have five minutes in the toilet anymore!'

Adrian stood by the main entrance an inch away from the door. If it was winter, he would be waiting for her in the police vehicle. Now, he stayed safe near the strong air-conditioning unit blowing out essential cold air. Outside, as the day moved on, the ferocious June sun settled in the sky and burned all below it. Adrianos -only his grandmother used his full name- was born and raised in Metsovo, a village nested in the snowy mountains of Epirus. Unlike the majority of Greeks, he and the sun were never friends. His skin, used to his native icy weather, suffered during the summer months as he patrolled the coastal Ionian village. Each pore cried out sweat and begged for cool air. Adrian would walk into the small station and switch on the air-conditioning first thing in the morning. If it was already turned on, he would still pick up the remote control and lower the temperature, sure that none of his sun-worshiping colleagues would have chosen a suitable number. He chose sixteen degrees Celsius. The lowest it could go. For a thirty-two-year-old bachelor, living on his own, Adrian took care of himself well. He never ate junk food. He shopped from the organic corner shop and cooked his every meal. He ironed all his clothes perfectly; his black boots were spotless, and his blue car shone brighter than a night star. A straight *A* student, his stockbreeder parents had big dreams for him. A doctor or a lawyer. Something important, according to them. Something in the city, away from the hardships that their everyday life entailed. He shocked them a week before graduation with his plans of not attending university, but that he was going to head down to Athens to enrol in the Police Academy program there.

'You can't be serious, son,' his father said, while his mother covered her mouth and took a step back; her hand searching for the kitchen chair behind her. 'A cop? And cut parking tickets? A bright mind like yours?'

'Officer's School, dad. It's a university-lever institution. I want to follow that with a master's degree in forensic science. I want to use my bright mind to solve crimes.'

It took his parents a few years to truly accept his decision, but his happiness persuaded them. And soon, they had something else to bother him about. At twenty-eight the questions came. Marriage. Kids. The dream of every Greek mother. To see their children married with kids.

'Let's go, partner,' Arianna said as she walked past him and pushed the glass door open. The heat invaded in and Adrian made a dash for the police car. He had already put the key in the ignition and switched on the cold air. Arianna shivered as she sat shotgun and opened her window slightly. 'So, another major crime in our metropolis, huh? Money taken from the bakery register!'

Adrian smiled as he placed his foot on the pedal and sped out of the parking lot.

The police vehicle descended the narrow road that ran all the way to the beach. One of many snake-like roads running down the hill that loaned its slope to the good folks of the town. Angelica's Divine Goods was the last in a row of shops just meters away from the picturesque promenade of Parga. Along the esplanade, only taverns, bars and ice-cream parlours survived. Law of the tourist village. Nearer to the sea, the higher the rent.

Angelica's nickname, if it may be called as such, was *larger-than-life*. A six-foot tall, energetic sixty-year-old stood by the shop's closed door. Red high heels and a black dress trying desperately to cover her curvy figure were the only items on her body. When Mrs. Angelica baked, all bracelets, rings, pearls and watches were removed and placed on a velvet pillow in a safe at the back of the store. Her purple hair stood steady even as the wind picked up. In front of her well-decorated store window, her employee, a petite girl from a near-by village, sat behind a table selling bread.

'Good morning, Angelica. How are...'

Angelica waved her hand. 'Screw good mornings, Ari. Get your gun out and get in there!'

'What?'

Adrian's eyes widened. Girl selling goods outside on the pavement. Mrs. Angelica guarding the closed door. He sighed deeply. 'You have him locked in there, don't you?'

'Of course, I do! Tried to put his hands in my till! I hit him over the head with my grandma's rolling pin and tied him up!'

Arianna rushed into the shop. 'Stay outside, Angelica!' A bearded man in his late fifties sat on the white and violet floor tiles with his hands tied up behind his back to the table's leg. A cloth was forced into his mouth. A thin rivulet of blood came out of his thick hair and got lost in his bushy eyebrow. Arianna looked back at Adrian. 'It's that drunk homeless man you picked up last week for harassing guests at the Lichnos Hotel.' Arianna shook her head, and her right hand tapped the box of cigarettes sneaking from her trousers' pocket. 'Tend to him, Adrian. Get him to the hospital for a check-up and stay with him. I'll deal with Angelica.'

Adrian saluted her. 'On it, boss.'

Minutes later, Adrian escorted the man with the dirty Rolling Stones T-shirt and the ripped blue shorts, out of the deliciously smelling shop. Adrian had left a five euro note on the counter and took a sausage roll and a bottle of water for the accused man.

'...you can't go hitting people, Angelica. He could have been dangerous. Call us! The police will deal with...' Arianna was lecturing Mrs. Angelica on safety.

'And let him take whatever he wants?'

'Err, boss? If I take the car, how will you be getting back?'

Arianna tapped her two legs and returned to her conversation. 'Did he ask for money from the register or for food?'

Adrian took the homeless man by the arm and walked toward the car. *'Yeah, I'm a real crime fighter.'* He smiled as a few shop owners gave him a thumbs-up. One even clapped. He rolled his eyes. *'When will we ever get a good twisted case for me to solve?'*

Chapter Five

The following morning

The waves crushed upon the rocks strategically placed to protect the long promenade from getting wet. The sound travelled through the darkness. Only a black cat creeping along after a summer cockroach was there to witness the majestic blue as the first rays of light came from the sky and sea's meeting point. Light spread out and dark shadows diminished or were pushed back into corners behind the colorful row of houses. Another day under the glorious Mediterranean sun. Another day in Greek paradise.

Hector, the town's priest, was sleeping supine inside Holy Mary's chapel on the islet that bears the same name. His phone's alarm clock woke him from his slumber with divine sounds of Byzantium choirs. He looked up and it took him a while to focus and remember that he was in church. He quickly gathered his belongings and his black kalimavkion fell and instantly covered his thin body. The priest needed to gain weight, but he never managed such a feat. He rushed outside, pausing only to gaze at the horizon and thank the Lord for the view of the aurora. 'Must get back to shore before anyone wakes up,' he muttered as he rowed his small wooden boat, struggling with the unusual-for-the-bay strong waves. Minutes later, Hector tied his boat to a bent wooden post and scratched his long black beard, happy that the promenade seemed deserted. Gossip in rural Greece travelled faster than the speed of light. He climbed a few large rocks and hopped over the one-meter wall that served as a barrier between the Ionian and the pavement. He dusted his black clothes and made his way by the square that connects the two main arteries of the village. His green eyes were fixed on his dirty hands. Dirty thanks to dust gathered from the large rocks. As he went by the landmark anchor, his eyes turned and nested in their corners.

Father Hector froze on the spot.

His mind was unable to process the tremendous image opposite him.

A twisted naked corpse was tangled on the huge metallic anchor. Every bone in the woman's lifeless body seemed out of place. The skin was severely bruised and had turned shades of purple. Blood had dried in the multiple cuts that cracked the tormented body. Blond hair, stuck together by blood, hung, covering the woman's face.

Hector's hands trembled. He was unsure as to how to proceed. He wanted to scream louder than ever before. He felt his blood rushing faster around his veins. With one hand upon his beating heart, he took a few reluctant steps forward. He wanted to see the face. He ducked and looked under the bloody mass of hair.

He fell backwards and yelled for help.

The face was unrecognizable. All its features were gone, beaten into a pulp of human skin.

Lights came on in the residences above the cafes and taverns. Mostly their owners lived there. Though, some had moved to bigger houses, mansions even, after the tourist boom and had rented their previous homes through Airbnb. Mrs. Angelica was down first in a shiny pink robe. 'Oh my...' Her hands held back her renegade hair as she ran up to her nephew. 'Hector? Hector? Are you okay? What the hell is going on?'

Hector would always correct his auntie's poor choice of worlds. But this was not the moment. He held out his phone. His hands shook similar to the jasmine branches behind him that rode the morning wind. 'Call... the... police.'

'Not an ambulance?'

Hector's eyes never left the twisted figure. 'Does she look alive to you?'

By the time Police Lieutenant Adrian Metsovitis arrived at the scene, many had gathered around. A mixture of a crowd; locals and tourists. All stood at a distance in clear shock.

'Who is she, Hector?'

'Did you check?'

'I'm calling my daughter.'

'Who would do such a thing?'

Their voices turned into background noise and sounded like a constant buzz ringing violently inside Hector's mind. He remained sitting with his legs spread out forward on the rock paved road.

'Stay back. And be quiet!' Adrian's strong voice brought silence as the sun crept out from behind the islets occupying the bay. Light fell upon the dead woman thrown upon the historic landmark. Completely naked but for a torn bikini top hanging from her left shoulder.

'Dear Lord!' Arianna's voice came from behind Adrian as he had squatted and was placing on his rubber gloves. He carefully moved forward toward the body. His eyes scanned every inch of the ground. His mind went into overdrive. *'Where's the blood? She was carried here. Put on display. Why? By whom? Who is she?'* Adrian lifted the woman's hair and bit his lips. He took a step back and avoided facing his boss. He placed his hand upon his stomach, closed his eyes and breathed in as much fresh air as he could. At least his stomach was near empty. He had had no time for breakfast. After the phone call about the crime, only a glass of water that sat on his nightstand travelled down his oesophagus. Yet, he could feel last night's pastitsio swimming dangerously upwards.

'Recognize her?'

He pointed towards the hanging hair. He shook his head. He watched as Arianna copied his moves. She held up the bloody hair and remained there starring at the remains of what was once a human face. Adrian played with his fingers. He wished he could have been as calm as her. 'Get all these people out of here.'

Arianna stood and gazed towards the sea. She taped her palms upon her thighs and sighed. Adrian and two fellow officers were instructing the crowd to return to their homes. Adrian looked back at his captain. 'Err, boss? Shouldn't we call the coroner?'

'Huh?'

'The coroner.'

Arianna nodded. 'Of course, of course.' She pulled out her phone and flicked through her long contact list. D. Dr. Jacob Petsas (coroner).

Arianna walked when she spoke over the phone. She hated using the line land in her office. Too restraining for her. She wandered around the anchor, explaining the crime to the coroner. As she placed her phone back into its nest, her tired eyelids raised her long eyelashes. The woman was holding something. Arianna stepped closer. The edge of a brown jewellery box was visible in the mass of tangled arms. The morning wind pushed her hair in front of her eyes as she bowed to don her rubber gloves. Another step closer. Close enough to smell. Arianna breathed through her mouth and gently tried to raise the victim's right arm by just an inch as to dislocate the object. The box fell from its owner with its decorated lid open. Arianna was prepared and grabbed the box as it departured from the corpse's cold embrace. She was not prepared though for the open lid. Dozens of pieces of torn paper flew out and scattered in the wind. Arianna's loud gasp made the crowd turn around. Everyone moved to catch one of the pieces flying around them and crawling among their legs.

Adrian stopped one with his foot. He picked up the tiny paper.

WWW.PANDORASBOX.WEBS.COM

The address was typed on the thin pink-shaded paper.

Arianna approached him as he read. His attention fell to the box in her hands. 'Let's bag this,' she said as she looked down at the paper pinched between his fingers.

'Oh my God! That's Pandora's! That's where she keeps her rings! Mum, mum, is that Pandora?'

All eyes fell upon Iris. The short-haired teen, dressed in blue pyjamas slightly hidden by her beige robe, squeezed her mother's hand. 'Are you sure, baby?' her mother asked.

Iris nodded and swallowed the lump growing in her throat. She took a few reluctant steps forwards, her eyes fixed on the body. 'It's... it's Pandora! That's her bikini!'

Chapter Six

Maria heard rattling coming from the dark corners of her bedroom. Her phobia of rats made her weak spine shiver and she sat up immediately forcing her peach sateen sheets to slide from her naked body. The shadow was too large for a rat. She chuckled. The shadow was too large for a human.

'Where are you off to, dear? Going to eat one of your unhealthy breakfasts before your megaera of a wife wakes up and torments you?'

Jacob Petsa, *her* friendly giant, rolled his eyes as his left foot was ready to creep out of the door. 'How the heck can you sleep through an entire phone call literally taking place by your ear and yet hear me leaving?'

Maria smiled. 'Because you know *how* to whisper. You have no clue *how* to tiptoe your overweight body. And the bloody door squeaks as it has been *only* four months since I told you to oil it with some WD-40! Two more months to go before you actually do it.'

'Megaera is the wrong word for you.'

'Bitch?'

Jacob held his large round belly as he laughed. A strong laugh with bass. Maria loved the sound. 'You said it, not me. I meant it is wrong from a mythological aspect. Megaera was the Erinya that caused envy and jealousy, and forced people into committing crimes...'

'La la la. Stop! It's...' Maria leaned over and checked her phone lying on top of her Linda LePlante book on her nightstand. 'It's not even seven o'clock yet. No lesson, I beg you!'

Jacob ignored her pleas. If he started a sentence, he always finished it. Maria knew this well. A trait she hated during every argument during their thirty-four years of marriage.

'...especially infidelity. You maddening me about my weight and forcing me to eat your crappy vegan rabbit food is your crime, not mine. If you wish to be a female mythological beast, you could be Charybdis as you suck all the joy out of my life like a whirlpool.'

Maria fixed up her hair. Even with the air conditioning on, the back of her neck was covered in sweat. 'Where are you off to then, my hero, my Odysseus?'

'Parga. Dead woman. Murdered and... listen to this, thrown on that anchor they have in that little square you love.'

'I hate your job.'

'Love you, too, light of my life. Bye.'

A Hellenic police medical examiner of thirty years, Jacob knew the drill well. He dressed as he went along the dark hall, avoiding *junk* Maria had gathered over the years. Junk to him, of course. He would not dare utter such a word about Maria's tall vases overflowing with fake flowers and bamboo sticks, her colorful wooden cabinets or her floor lights. Fifty-two seconds. That is how long it took him to brush his teeth, enjoy his morning pee, splash some water on his face and run his sausage fingers through his thinning grey hair. He knew because he timed himself. Coffee making was a ritual for him. He was a firm believer that it was a ritual for all Greeks. If he met a Greek that did not drink coffee in any of its varieties, he considered him a *lesser Greek*. A ritual of course, that took longer than fifty-two seconds. It was June. Coffee was a Frappe. November to April, strong hot Greek coffee. May to October, strong cold Greek Frappe. Easier to take with you, too. With his coffee in one hand and an entire loaf of eliopsomo in the other, he rushed toward the kitchen door. Maria had baked the bread with olives the night before. He had no time to cut it and share. Maria would have to do with the three slices of village bread that sat on the counter, envious of the aroma spreading around the large kitchen from the freshly baked goods placed by their side. They were on their fifth -and most likely last- day of kitchen residency.

The stark glare of the rising Mediterranean sun invaded the kitchen through the half-open curtain as he was about to step outside, reminding him to pick up his shades. 'Bye, babe,' he shouted and closed the door behind him. Maria watched from above as he entered his spotlessly shiny Alfa Romeo. '*If only he kept the house as tidy and clean.*' She waved and blew him a kiss from afar.

She truly did hate his job.

Chapter Seven

Melpomene found herself running again. It could not be true. It just couldn't. It was surely a mistake. Or some cruel person's sick twisted joke. There was absolutely no way her mind could accept a world where Pandora was no longer a part of it. Her feet ached as they made contact with the rocky path. Her thin slippers offered no protection. Her robe's furry belt danced upon the wind that dried her running tears.

'Mrs. Melpomene, wait. Stop! I can drive you down there...' the young police officer begged her to return. He slammed the gate close and punched the hood of his police car. The last ten minutes replayed in his mind.

He had messed up.

He had parked outside and had taken his time to exit the running vehicle. He had wiped his sweaty palms on his brown trousers and had enjoyed a slow deep breath. An old lady who had been watering her plants was staring at him. He had waved and opened his door.

'Good morning, ma'am. Is Mrs. Melpomene awake?'

Ophelia had limped towards him, dropping the garden hose at the feet of a blossoming lemon tree. 'What happened?'

'Is she inside?'

'Haven't heard neither of them. Ring the bell, laddie.'

Leventi had walked slowly up the wooden steps and had stood on the porch. He had rung the bell and stepped back. Ophelia studied his mannerisms. Nothing good was about to departure from his trembling lips. He had tapped the doorbell again.

'Coming.'

The officer had exhaled all the gathered air trapped in his lungs and rehearsed his lines.

'Is that you, Ophelia?' Melpomene's voice was heard as she rattled to unlock the door. Ophelia always exited to the yard from the kitchen's side door.

'It's officer Leventi with the Hellenic Police.'

It was as if all color left Melpomene's body at once, leaving her a lifeless cartoon character in a film from a different era. Her jaw had dropped, yet no words came out from her mouth.

'It's about your daughter. Pandora?'

Melpomene had tilted her head. 'Excuse me?'

'You need to come with me...'

'Why? You said this is about my daughter.'

The officer's fingers tapped upon his side. He had scratched his nose. 'A young girl has been found...'

'Pandora? Pandora?' Melpomene turned away from him. She rushed to her daughter's door. She pushed it open and quickly switched on the lights. A small cry left her. She ran back to the police officer. 'Where is my daughter?' she screamed.

'The body on the anchor might not even be...'

'Body!'

An animal-like yell came from deep inside her guts and Melpomene leapt out of the house and down the steps.

'*Fuck!*'

He had messed up.

Down by the bay, Hector had managed to pick himself up, physically and emotionally, and sat on the rock wall, allowing Angelica to stroke his hair.

'Oh, no. It's her mother!'

Angelica's words brought complete silence to the already quiet crowd. The sight of Melpomene running along the promenade was one that would remain carved in the vaults of their minds for years to come.

Her cries made Arianna shiver as she turned and prepared to face Melpomene. 'Let me handle this,' she said as she placed her hand on Adrian's arm. He was ready to step forward and prevent the mother from approaching any further. Arianna breathed in a large amount of air and kept it in her lungs. She could taste the sea's saltiness floating around in the breeze as it settled on her tongue and crept up her nostrils. She loosened her hands and focus on Melpomene's feet. She was drawing nearer.

'Is that my baby? God, no. Please. Not my Pandora. No, Lord, no.'

Arianna embraced Melpomene and squeezed her arms around the shaking woman hard. 'Let me see her, Arianna. Let me close.'

'I can't,' Arianna whispered in her ear as she felt Melpomene push her slightly forward. 'That's not her hair! Arianna, that's not her hair. My Pandora is blonder. She's blonder.' Melpomene yelled and pointed to the corpse tangled on the anchor. 'Look. Look!' Tears fell freely from swollen eyes. Salty droplets that landed on the rocky path and lived shortly under the scorching sun that had yet another heat wave in store for the folk of Parga town. That is when she noticed the yellow bikini and fell to her knees.

Iris took two short steps forward. Nefeli stood behind her with her head leaned on her friend's broad shoulders. 'I dyed it for her yesterday. She wanted a different look for the graduation party. She was with us all evening yesterday.'

'It was meant to be honey brown, but it did not take to her blond hair,' Nefeli added, wiping her eyes.

'I want to see her! Now!' Grief and stress gave way to anger.

Arianna raised her palm toward the girls, requesting their silence. 'Melpomene, we will run a DNA test, don't worry.'

'Why? Why won't you just let me see her?' Melpomene screamed.

'Cause her face is unrecognizable.'

Arianna knelt by her. Melpomene placed her head upon Arianna's chest and wept like never before. 'It can't be my baby. It can't be. Find my Pandora, Arianna. Find her. That... that piece of meat is not her! It can't be her! I want my baby. Please, Oh, God, it hurts. It hurts so much. I can't! I can't believe my baby is gone. She can't be dead. I need her. Jesus, it hurts. I can't...'

Chapter Eight

THE PAST I

Demetra watched at the downpour plummeting onto her window. She sat in the back seat as her father drove into the vast parking lot. Thunder used to scare her, but not anymore. The darkness used to terrify her. Her vivid imagination used to picture demons and monsters lurking in her bedroom. Many small daily things managed to awaken and unleash her fears. She was after all, only an eight-year-old girl. Yet, all that changed overnight. A new word came into her life, scarier than anything her mind could cook up. Cancer. Such a small word. Just two sounds side by side. Can-cer. She had never heard it before until the night her mother sat her down on their living room sofa and tried to be brave. She failed. Demetra had noticed the change in their household. Her father was quieter and paid more attention to his wife. Her mother was paler, weaker and grew fond of wearing bandanas. And now, her mother fought back tears to tell her that she had to go and stay at the hospital for a while. Her father could not even bear to listen to them talk and disappeared upstairs. A thud gave away the punch he threw at the defenceless wall.

Demetra remembered that night well. It was the last time all three of them were under their roof, their home.

Her father struggled to open his black umbrella and rushed around towards her. He forced a smile as he opened the car door. 'Come on, sweetie. Let's go see Mummy.'

Demetra's pink trainers stepped into a shallow puddle. She did not notice. Her eyes ran up the tall building in front of her. It was the tallest building the young country girl had ever seen. It was also the ugliest. Grey, dull, monotonous with small balconies. It did not impress her. She was expecting more from Thessaloniki. It was, after all, the town her parents met and fell in love during their studies at Aristoteleio University. Her father promised to take her to the White Tower later. Maybe that would be better looking.

'Come on, Demetra. It's pissing down.'

The young girl was trying to read the difficult words on the sign above the entrance with the old creaky wooden door. 'Theogeneio Anti-cancer Hospital,' she muttered. She had no idea what Theogeneio meant, but she did like the anti-cancer part. She smiled. Her mother was going to be okay. She had cancer and this place was anti-cancer. Simple thoughts born from hope in an eight-year-old mind.

Inside, dark tiles welcomed her wet feet and a strong scent of detergent nested up her nostrils. Curious by nature, Demetra's eyes travelled around as her father talked to the young lady behind the reception desk. All art was featured in the same exact brown frames. All paintings were the same size. And annoyingly to Demetra, all hung up crookedly.

'Come on, pretty one. Let's go up to Mummy.'

She followed behind him quietly with her eyes fixed on

his back. She did not want to see more. Two open doors revealed too many sickly-looking people lying in beds made with sheets that had seen better days. Tired nurses checked temperatures and scribbled down on overused charts hanging at the end of old metallic beds. 'Third floor,' her father said as the elevator doors screeched open. Demetra took him by his hand and stepped inside. She had never been in an elevator before. She looked at herself in the mirror. Her hair was ruined by the rain. She had tried to mimic her mother's favorite hair style.

The long corridor seemed to grow before her adolescent eyes. She felt like her animated heroine Alice, lost in a strange world, a world where she should not be. She was walking but the corridor never came to an end.

'Honey, are you okay?'

She nodded to her father. She floated by his side. Her legs were jelly. Was her mother as sickly-looking as the people behind the glass window to her left?

Unfortunately, her answer came soon, and it was a yes. Her mother looked the same and even worse. Her skin had crawled inward, and her bones were visible. Her face had never been so pale before. Once a Mediterranean beauty with shiny olive-oil skin, now her mother resembled the ninety-year-old from whom they rented their home.

The strange machinery around her mother confirmed that she was indeed in a weird hospital wonderland. Nothing was normal. Nothing was correct.

A large warm smile spread out on her mother's face. A beacon in the night that drew Demetra close. She missed that smile. Her mother tapped the bed. 'Hop on.'

Her father stayed by the door.

'How was school?'

The question pulled her out of her daze. She missed retelling her days to her best friend.

The next twenty minutes felt like the old days. Those magical days when the three of them lived a normal life together.

Her mother coughed as she laughed. The cough caused her pain. Demetra could see it in her eyes. Her mother sighed and stroked her hair. She looked straight in her eyes.

'Baby, you know how much I love you, right?'

Demetra nodded and touched her mother's cold hand. 'And I would do anything, anything, to be with you always. To go home with you. But...'

Another deep sigh. Her father had left. She saw him wiping his eyes as he dashed down the unusually long corridor with his packet of cigarettes squeezed between his fingers.

'But, baby, I can't. I won't be coming home with you, my sugar eyes.'

'Mum? Are you... are you going to die?'

'Oh, Lord!' Her mother looked up at the icon hanging above the doorway. 'It looks like it.' She struggled with the words. Each syllable burned her throat. 'But I will still be with you always. Watching from above. Your guardian angel.'

'I don't want an angel. I want my mum.'

'Look.' She pointed to the icon. 'The mother of us all. Mary, mother of Jesus. She will make sure everything will go right in your life. And I will be by her side, making sure of it. You will grow up to be a beautiful, smart, caring young lady and I will be so damn proud of you. And you will study, and you will travel, and you will meet a boy and fall in love, and get married and have amazing little children of your own and every single second I will be looking down from Heaven and smiling widely at all that you have become...' The tears could not be held back any longer.

'Mum, you're hurting my hand.'

'Sorry, my sweet. Here... come into my arms.'

Demetra cuddled up and closed her eyes. Her mother caressed her hair and sang to her. Saint Marina's lullaby. Just like the old days. Demetra closed her eyes and drifted away.

Her father awoke her as he quickly picked her up. 'Don't open your eyes,' he whispered in her ears. She did not obey. His eyes were swollen. She looked over his shoulder. Her mother was still. Motionless, sunk into her pillow with closed eyes. She had never seen a paler person before. All the lights on the machinery around her had disappeared.

'It's just the two of us now.'

Chapter Nine

The yellow police tape danced in the wind; its end snapping every now and then when a small gust blew by. The anchor sat in the middle of the newly set up ring. Adrian had unravelled the shiny warning around three lamp posts that had been around since fascists ruled the lands, and a seal statue. The statue was younger, an eighties child, yet still featured the same decay that all metallic creations must succumb to when placed near the salty sea. Unfortunately, it featured the same amount of pigeon droppings, too. Adrian, a born perfectionist, tied the tape around the cleanest spots he could find.

'Coroner's here.'

Arianna's voice made him turn as the last piece of dancing ribbon was wrapped around the post nearest to the Ionian. Jacob Petsa came down the rocky path between the Italian ice-cream parlour and the sports cafe. Huffing and puffing, he was wiping some renegade crumbs off his shirt as he approached. Police Captain Arianna Kontou had worked with the medical examiner before. She was just an officer back then and was mesmerized by the profession-alism of the famed coroner. Dr. Petsas had worked on at least two infamous cases that shocked Greece's small society. The Olympus Killer and the Church Murders were cases that left a permanent imprint on the small country. They were the two cases with the notorious record of highest body count by a serial killer and Dr. Petsas worked on both. She welcomed him with a firm handshake.

'Be strong, my dear. It's a man's world you're entering. Never show weakness.' The words of her female mentor all those years ago in police academy stuck with Arianna more than any of her lessons. Words that defined her posture and handshake for all the years to come.

'Captain!' Jacob nodded and offered a flatline smile. 'Talk me in,' he continued as he let go of her hand and approached the body. 'My... my!' an audible whisper left his thirsty lips as he titled his head and walked around the body.

'Son,' he raised his voice. 'Don't bother with the tape. We need to set up a tent. We must collect evidence first and then move the body.'

Adrian stood up straight and looked at his symmetrically perfect job. 'Yes, sir,' he replied. Both words colorless; carrying no emotion at all.

As the Captain began to fill in the coroner, Adrian marched over to his fellow officers. They had a police tent to set up. He hoped the unused forensic marquee that sat in the back of the police warehouse collecting dust was high enough to encompass the entire landmark. The three men walked off in unison. All three avoided turning their heads to their left. Melpomene wept uncontrollably in the hands of the town's women. All mothers themselves, they placed a hand on Melpomene and bit their lips. They did not even wish to try to comprehend the pain of losing a child. It was a lingering thought in the back of every parent's brain. A terrifying *what if* scenario. Not my boy. Not my girl. God, no, please.

Adrian might have avoided his left, but to his right, his eyes fell upon the first two walking away from the crime scene.

'Excuse me? Mrs. Angelica? Father?' Both turned toward him. The priest's face still ashen from his morning shock. 'Father Hector, you will have to come to the station ASAP for your testimony. You were the first here.'

Angelica nodded. 'I'll feed him something sweet and bring him by.'

Chapter Ten

Greece needed to have had its own Einstein. Too many theories needed equations. At what speed does news travel in Greek villages and how much does the speed accelerate according to the village's population size and how tragic the news was.

An hour.

That's all it took for every single resident of Parga to be informed of Pandora's tragic demise.

An hour and three minutes.

The time for Parga's bronze-skinned residents to type in Pandora's Box in their preferred search engines.

Another minute later, shock and terror nested in their minds and hearts. The box emptied out its dark secrets and left no hope to be held.

Mayor Phoebe Katsimiha was an excellent driver. An avid automobile fan from a young age, she never used a driver. Today though, was not one of the days where she would prove to the close-minded old folk of her town that women drivers were equal and even better than their male counterparts. She slammed on the brakes and with the thick tyres screeching on the hot asphalt, she *parked* her beloved Range Rover over the ground's white lines which she had respected vigorously during her entire term as mayor. The large vehicle took up space from three parking spots. Phoebe leapt out of the car and rushed up the newly restored side steps that connected the parking lot to the town hall. Flushed, without an ounce of makeup and with her hair just as it were when she awoke in her beach villa, she had many reasons to avoid the main entrance. Her short heels tapped along the path running alongside the old, weather-beaten wall. Not that the signs of its decay were visible. Phoebe was a master of cheap solutions. Jasmine and Ivy plants were planted during her first month in office. Now, three years later, they covered the majority of the eighty-year-old wall.

Sweat dripped down her neck as her natural brown hair left no room for her skin to breathe. Phoebe never dyed her hair as her devout strict Christian image resonated with her voters. Even though her priest husband had died over seven years ago, only black covered her body. But just like politician's promises, looks can be deceiving.

Phoebe unlocked the back door and dashed up the marble steps. Her heart was bounding hard underneath her heavily clothed chest. Soon, with her office door locked behind her, she turned on her strong air-conditioning unit and removed her black knitted cardigan and shirt. In a tight tank top, she stood in the cold flow with arms spread out wide.

'How the fuck did that young girl know? How? Why? Why? Why?' Her thin fingers met and formed fists. She exhaled and started counting backwards from ten. By four, there was a knock on the door. Her hands reached for her cardigan. 'Who is it?'

'It's me.'

A step above a whisper, she knew the voice well. Her hands dropped the clothes onto the large mahogany desk, and she rushed to the thick wooden door. With trembling hands, she turned the key and let the tall, fair-haired man in. She locked the door again and turned to face the town hall's lawyer. The forty-year-old man, ten years her senior, stood opposite her with an ashen face and watery eyes.

'You look worse of than me, Atlas! I texted you to come because I need comfort. Did you see the website?'

Atlas squinted his eyes and took a step back. 'Have you?'

Phoebe waved her arms. 'Of course, I have! I pressed on my photo! Our beloved mayor, a modern-day Pharisee! How the hell did she know that I had an abortion at seventeen? And was forced to marry my priest of a husband as punishment! Atlas, she knew every detail! You have to do something. What do you always call it?' She snapped her fingers three times. 'Damage control. Yes, that's it. Damage control.'

Atlas sighed and walked over to the desk. He rested against it and stared at the floor. Phoebe placed her hands upon his cold cheeks and raised his head. She stared straight into his dark green eyes. 'What's wrong with you? I'm dying over here.'

She could see the lump travelling down his throat. 'So, you only clicked on your photo?'

'After seeing what I saw, I was no mood in reading other's dug up gossip!'

Atlas scratched the back of his head. 'I am on her site, too.'

Phoebe took a step back, run her fingers through her

hair and left her palms stuck to her head as she shook it. 'Please, don't tell me that...'

He raised his phone to her eye level.

'Atlas Georgiou, our mayor's secret lover.' A small animal-like cry escaped her quivering lips. She snatched the phone right out of his hand. 'The married lawyer indeed gives it his all when working late at the town hall. Among his many services, screwing the mayor upon her luxurious sofa is one of his most valuable contributions...'

'Helena is going to kill me. My marriage is over.' Atlas slid down the desk and sat on the ground.

'We will deny everything!'

'How can we? There are nine entries on that blog. Nine people of our town with their shit put on show. It only takes one to admit it's true and we are all fucked. And some are so obvious...'

'Ours is not!'

'And you think the police are not going to interrogate us all? The girl is dead and look at all that she knew. Are we going to lie to the police too? Add criminal offence to our list of sins?'

Another cry departured from Phoebe's lips. Louder this time. Stronger. Her prized vase met the south wall and scattered in fragments across the office.

Chapter Eleven

Officer Leventi sat up straight in the not-too-soft office chairs offered by the police department. His sweaty palms hovered above the keyboard while his mind was still stuck in the morning *fuck-up* as he referred to it by. Newborn sweat partied on his rather large forehead as his heart accelerated to beats unreached by it before. The captain topped the list of people that scared him the most, while Lieutenant Adrian topped the list of men he looked up to, envied and wished to be. Now, both towered over him and were focused on his every move. The 19-inch screen opposite them was displaying Pandora's website. Arianna breathily read the short but to the punch intro. The intro was in the center of the page, between a photo of a sinisterly smiling Pandora and an image of mythological Pandora opening the box given to her by the father of the Gods, the almighty, light-ning-bearer Zeus. The beautiful woman knelt above the opened gold box while spirits and demons escaped it. The Greek words for anger, sickness, hate, lies, violence, pain, misery, and wrath were written on their elusive ghost-like figures.

'Well, well, well... welcome to Pandora's box. A site where all the juicy gossip living underline in our small town comes to thrive on the surface...'

'Girl has a way with words,' Adrian commented, placing his hands on the dusty desk and leaned in closer.

'...and live as truths and not dark secrets. Many profound and pompous characters walk among us, yet we have been deceived. Filth covers their every step. Sex, lies, drugs, and even murders, ladies and gentlemen. So, buckle up and keep with us for one hell of a ride. Happy reading! Just press on the pics and enjoy! Yours, Pandora. XXX.'

'Scroll down.'

'Yes, Captain.'

Arianna's eyes ran along the rows. Each row with three photographs. Three rows with photographs either available on Google from town events or weirdly angled snaps, most likely from Pandora's cell phone as Adrian had stated.

Arianna whispered the names as they flashed before her. She controlled her relief when she reached the end. Not her, nor her son were on the list.

A tenth box existed by itself in a fourth row. A blank box with the words *Melpomene -Coming soon- Shock doesn't even describe it!* written underneath it.

'Press on the priest,' Adrian said. 'He will be here soon.'

The mouse's cursor floated over to a smiling Hector. From the local newspaper, it was a photo from the opening of the church museum in 2015. His wife, dressed in a violet floral spring dress, stood proudly by his side. Their four children were lined up by height behind their mother. Two girls and two boys.

Officer Leventi's index finger pressed down, and the

picture grew. The photo faded to the background and red letters came into focus. Arianna placed her elbows on the desk and her head in her hands. Leventi pushed his chair back slowly as to give the two more space. He was suffocating between them. He wheeled back until he banged into the cherry-wood credenza behind him.

Adrian was a fast reader. His eyes sped along the sentences. Yet, he held back his shock until his captain had finished reading. Arianna always took her time and always read aloud. Even if just in a whisper, she needed to hear the words for them to truly resonate with her.

'Father Hector, our beloved priest. A loving husband? Yes. A caring father? Yes. A benefactor to our town? Yes. A laughable cliché? Yes. Why a cliché, Pandora, you may ask. Well, because our priest enjoys blowjobs from fifteen-year-old boys!' Arianna stood up straight. 'This can't be true. This is just awful ramblings of an attention-seeking teenager girl who has seen one too many episodes of Gossip Girl.'

'It says to press here for proof.' Adrian's hand landed on the mouse. Soon, another photo appeared. Arianna gasped while Adrian shook his head. The photo was from inside Saint Mary's chapel. On the front row of stools sat Father Hector with his black clothing pulled up to his waist. His black boxers were around his knees. A teenage boy knelt between his legs with his tongue out while he held the priest's erection.

The teenager's face was not visible. However, the darkish blue hair and the neck tattoo of a pirate flag left no doubt.

'That's Apollo. George and Tina's kid.'

'He's like fifteen. My God.' Arianna placed her hand above her mouth.

Adrian's pupils rushed to their left corners. He was often

impressed by his captain's cool on any given circumstance. Even today at the murder site, she remained professionally expressionless. '*She is probably worried about her boy.*'

'Your Timothy did not attend Sunday school, did he?'

The cold look he received made him regret every word spoken. He tried to form a sentence, yet the lump of remorse was not leaving his throat.

'What? Why would your mind even think that? Go there?'

'I'm sorry, boss. I just...'

'Just nothing.' She raised her palm. 'No, he didn't. But even if he did, he knows better and tells me everything. A predator like this stands no chance with my Timmy. He has a good head on his shoulders...'

'I know, boss. I'm truly sorry for mentioning it and clearly upsetting you.'

Arianna waved her hand and turned her head back to the screen. 'I fear to continue. These people are our neighbours, our friends. We have to, though...' Arianna let loose a deep sigh. '...open every single one of these.' She turned back at officer Leventi. 'I want everything opened and printed out for me. Everything. Every word, every photo.'

'Yes, Captain. On it.'

'And Adrian? I want you to find out from headquarters who the tech guy in charge of our area is. I want to know everything about this webpage. When it was built, when did it go live, from where, all the details we can get.' Adrian nodded slightly the entire time she spoke. His eyes still. 'Also, get them to make the site private. Visible only to us. Or as we will print it all, take it down completely. Though...' She tapped her finger on the keyboard's corner.

'Though, what, boss?'

'Though I prefer the idea of making it private as the coming soon section intrigues me.'

Adrian scratched the back of his head. 'Yeah, but the girl is dead.'

Arianna kept her eyes on the screen and clicked on the mayor. 'Yes, but we haven't established if she was the one that made this page. What if this is her killer's work?'

'Gotcha.' He processed his thoughts. 'If you think about it, she could have been killed for these secrets, yet leaving the box with her makes no sense. That box was placed there for all of us to see. A murderer that wished for this information to be known.' He paused. Arianna did not comment. 'I'll be on my way, then. Phone the tech department. Anything else needed to be done, Captain?' He waited for her to shake her head. She was heavily preoccupied with reading about the mayor's affair. 'I'm off then.' Adrian began to walk away, before stopping and googling his eyes at officer Leventi sitting carefree in his chair, watching the Captain. Adrian nodded to the computer on the empty desk in the corner of the room. 'Yes, yes,' he whispered as he sprang up. 'Copies coming, ASAP.'

Chapter Twelve

Her home carried the same divine aroma that lingered permanently in her store. At the bakery or at home, Angelica baked and cooked with the same passion. Only difference was the clothing. Angelica used most of her income on expensive clothing -though not all designer brands made clothes up to her size, make-up, bags, jewellery, shoes and of course, on trips to the beauty salon for her hair and nails. She covered her age better than her overweight figure. Dressed for the governor's ball, she baked and served her customers. In the privacy of her home kitchen, Angelica danced about in just her knickers and a plain T-shirt, mostly covered by flour and stains from a variety of jams, made by her own hands, used in her delicious pastries.

Her rushing out in her nightgown to find Hector sitting before the brutal crime was a stretch for her. She felt guilty of thinking more of her appearance rather than the poor dead girl on the anchor.

'Give me a minute to get dressed.' She placed two mini

sausage rolls and a chocolate stuffed donut in front of Hector. All three sat in the middle of the white porcelain plate, steaming slightly, revealing their heat. 'Shouldn't you call your wife?'

Hector had leaned forward to take in a whiff of the ghostly lines rising from the freshly heated goods, yet the Greek coffee Angelica placed on the table came out victorious in the odour battle. He yearned for a sip and his stomach rumbled gently, craving for a bit. It had been days since he had eaten properly. Alone in the chapel at nights, he punished himself with the lack of food and water. 'Hmm? Err, yeah, why not? Or maybe a bit later? Surely, they are all asleep at the moment. Why worry them further?'

'*Further?*' Angelica nodded and left for her half an hour of preparing to leave the house. 'Eat and get your head straight. The police will want to know every detail. You, my dear Hector, might help them catch a killer. Poor girl. Poor mother. I can't even imagine!'

The hot beverage wet his lips and travelled down his dried throat. He took a considerable chunk out of the donut, looked down at his slightly paunchy waist and picked up his phone. 'Pandora's box, dot webs,' he mumbled the words as he typed them in. His eyes widened by the second. 'Holy Mary, mother of Christ! That's me.' He clicked on his photo. Reading, he sprang up, knocking the wooden chair to the floor. He clicked to reveal the next photo. Panic kicked in.

'My life is over.'

He looked up to the empty staircase. Angelica's singing of old tunes travelled down. He turned to leave; his hand even reached out for the door handle. *And go where? Escape to where? I am going to get arrested anyway. But I can't face them.*

Everyone will hate me. If I run though, they will think I had something to do with the murder. It will fuel worse gossip. Oh, Lord.'

His inner thoughts spread wildly inside his tormented mind. Father Hector fell to his knees and prayed. For forgiveness, for strength, for guidance, for death. Father Hector asked for it all.

Twenty minutes later, Angelica found him there on her kitchen mat with his head against the door. 'What's wrong, Hector?'

'Check the girl's website. Read me. Then you will know,' he replied through quiet sobs. 'You are on there, too!'

Angelica's face took the position that most faces in Parga took that dreadful morning. Dropped jaw, mouth opened in shock, eyes widening, skin shading away its color, fading to pale as if the circulating blood forgot to pass through there.

'Fuck!' Only one word managed to escape her twitching lips.

'So, what's your sin? So many confessions and you have always been a saint.'

Angelica was carefully dabbing the corners of her eyes with a blue tissue. 'You're one to speak.'

Hector did not reply. He laid his tired face into his opened palms and wept.

'If you must know, this little bitch just revealed to the whole world that I run poker and roulette nights above my shop.'

'Do not bad-mouth the dead, my dear.'

'She just ruined you, Hector!'

'I ruined me.'

'How the hell did she get photos from inside my shop?'

Father Hector looked up. 'Why did you do it? You hate gambling. Waste of money, you always say.'

Angelica was pacing up and down with clenched fists.

'Yes. Waste for the gambler. Not the house! I don't care if others wish to lose their hard-earned money! Which I take! Easily! And buy my lifestyle. You think all this is from the bakery? God! I can't believe we are discussing my little mishap when you fucked a kid, for crying out loud!'

Father Hector stood up. 'Now, wait here, Angelica. It was one consensual fellatio. It was a stupid moment of weakness. Don't you dare go and over generalize on me!'

Angelica slapped her already red cheeks and squeezed them to release air carrying gathered tension. 'We live in Parga! It only takes one mistake to be finger-pointed and gossiped about for the rest of your life. And you do realize that everyone on that list is now a murder suspect, right? And the deepest and darkest of secrets will be on top of that list.'

'What are you implying here?'

She raised her hands. 'Nothing. Just warning you before your interrogation. The person who wrote your sins for all to see was found butchered and tossed like an annoying bug. Found by you. Oh, the police are going to have a field day.'

'Thanks for the cheering up, my dear. Now that the police will shut down your bakery, maybe you should consider taking up motivational speaking!'

Angelica picked up her car keys. Multiple key chains rattled as they were forced to gang together. The Eiffel Tower, the Statue of Liberty, I love Mykonos hit against sayings by Paolo Coelho burnt into oak wood.

'Let's go get this nasty business done with.'

Chapter Thirteen

'God damn it, Phillip, pick up for once in your life!'

Eva limped as she walked up to her butchery's closed door and gazed outside by placing her index finger upon the metallic blind. The streets were empty due to the early hour of the day and the tragic news going from door to door, mouth to mouth. She placed her right hand upon her heart. She half-expected a mob with torches ready to burn her shop down and light her up upon a huge stake, one capable enough to hold her weight. Eva watched the dust floating upon the ray of light invading from the gap she had created. She brought her iPhone back to her ear.

'Hello?'

Phillip's morning voice made his husky voice a bizarre undertone of a sound.

'Phillip, open your eyes and sit up straight.'

'What...err... Eva it's...'

'I know how fucking early it is...' Eva paused as she wiped her forehead. She realized that the humane thing to do was to inform her business partner of the death in their small town and then rant about the website. '...you know Melpomene? The nurse that lives with Grandma Ophelia?'

'Aha.' More of a question than an answer.

'Her daughter was murdered.'

'What? Pandora? She's Jason's and Jimmy's classmate, isn't she?'

'That's the one. Now, listen here. We have bigger problems on our hands.' Eva could hear Phillip's wife inquiring about the early phone call. 'Phillip, concentrate. The girl has a webpage where she wrote about us.'

'Us?'

'About our illegal meat trades. Go to pandora's box, one word, dot webs, dot com and see for yourself.'

'Are you pulling my leg, Eva? Is this one of your weird prankish jokes that I never get?'

'Fuck, Phillip. Just check it out and get your skinny ass down here. I'm at the butchery. I'm scared.'

Eva let go of the blind, allowing it to swing back into its proper position. Darkness returned to the butchery. Eva took a deep breath and with difficulty, slid down the wall and sat on the cold ground. She rubbed her large hands on her jeans. Curse words followed as a few tears fell freely and slithered along her round rosy cheeks. 'Even big girls cry sometimes.' She whispered her granny's line and smiled in the darkness.

Across town, Phillip had forced the darkness back and watched it shrivel into shadowy patches behind furniture. He dragged the burgundy curtains with him as he headed to his high backed armchair by the balcony. A view of the entire town spread out among the green surroundings and embraced by the turquoise Ionian Sea. Yet, his eyes were focused on his phone. He was muttering Pandora's intro.

'What does it say?' His wife sat up straight on their king-sized bed. 'Speak up!'

'Chef Phillip Phillipou. The Cypriot who married into our village and opened the most successful restaurant in the area. ALL GREEK TO ME. A restaurant with a promise. Everything on the menu was raised and produced in Greece. Catchy, huh? Even patriotic, you may say. Yet, we have all been deceived as we devoured his delicious dishes. In cooperation with Eva's Fat Cow Butchery (read more about her illegal imports by clicking her photo), Chef Phillip stocked his restaurant with cheap Albanian meat and minced meat that... well... was not from the 'normal' animals you would expect (sold and made of course, in Fat Cow Butchery).'

Phillip turned toward his wife. Both starred at each other in shock, unable to speak. Their eyes said it all. Their dark secret had surfaced.

Their highly successful restaurant would not welcome another customer ever again.

Chapter Fourteen

THE PAST II

Out of everything that happened on the day of her mother's funeral, Demetra remembered the night the most.

The day went as gloomy as a funeral in the land that gave birth to tragedy could go. Cars gathered round Saint Nicholas's grand metropolitan church and over a hundred people all dressed in black -some youngsters wore dark blue jeans and a black shirt, walked slowly up the marble steps and entered the house of the Lord with bowing heads and crossing themselves as they stepped inside.

The ceremony went on for a full hour. Demetra did not understand a single word. She sat on the large stalls, next to her sobbing father, with her feet hanging well above the carpet. It suddenly went quiet. She heard her father struggling to speak. Did she hear well? She stood up as he asked her to. She gazed over to the coffin on the table opposite her. She hoped her mother would sit up and turn and smile at her. She missed that smile. She missed the warmth of her embrace. She missed her flowery scent. Her little heart hurt like never before. She wanted to scream and run out of the temple, but her ordeal had no end. Everyone passed before her and her father, offering their condolences. Demetra scratched her arm and looked down at her feet. She did not wish for anyone to see her cry. Her pain was hers and only hers. Her tears were not for public consumption. It took another entire hour before she followed her mother to her final resting ground. Demetra liked the shady spot below the tall oak trees. Her mother would have approved. 'Goodbye, mummy,' she whispered and threw the flowers in her hands above her mother's coffin as it was lowered into the earth. Her father knelt in the mud (it had been a rainy night) and cried out how much he was going to miss her.

Time seemed to move slower than usual back at their house. Demetra waited patiently until nightfall came and she asked her father if she could retire. He was listening to the priest's wife telling him that he should sign Demetra up for Sunday school. The church will do her good in these difficult times, the short woman had advised. Her father agreed. Demetra repeated her question, louder this time. Her father just nodded. His red eyes were fixed on the priest's wife. 'Go, my dear. Go shower and lie down for the night. It has been a long day,' her aunt said. Demetra was relieved to be alone at last. As she turned on the shower and the water fell on her face, she silently screamed and finally, her tears fell. After the cathartic waterfall, she dried herself and wore one of her mother's T-shirts to bed. The pink one that she used to love to wear around the house.

Hours later, the house went silent.

Demetra was slightly awoken by the screeching of her door. Noises of footsteps grew louder. She felt her father lie down by her side and his arm fell upon her. He brought her close and kissed her on her forehead. His breath smelled of smoke and alcohol. He stroked her hair and repeated, 'It's just the two of us now.'

Through tears, he kept on repeating the line.

'It's just the two of us now.'

Demetra prayed and it seemed Holy Mary answered her prays as her father, after an hour of weeping in her ears, gradually fell asleep, his head upon hers.

'It's just the two of us now,' Demetra said and closed her eyes.

Chapter Fifteen

Arianna exited the narrow back door by her office, the one mostly used by the cleaning lady when she emptied her red bucket of dirty mop water. The heat carried that sea dampness that she despised. The moisture that enjoyed settling on your flesh, making your skin all sticky and clogging up your pores, leaving your body defenceless against the menacing heat waves of the Greek summer period.

A cigarette quickly landed on her lips and as soon as her right hand fulfilled its duty of lighting the menthol stick, it went for her phone. Multiple missed calls from the Mayor, one from the coroner, none from Timothy. Not even a message. 'That boy never listens!' He was the first she called.

'Hey, mum...'

'Don't you *hey mum* me, mister, I said...'

'I know, I know. I'm home. I'm not going anywhere today.'

She blew out a thick cloud of aromatic smoke. 'You're not going anywhere for days. Not until I solve this mess.

The whole town is going to go mental with these revelations.'

Timothy did not reply. She could hear him breathing loudly.

'Relax. Watch a movie or listen to that noise you describe as music. I imagine I won't be home till late. And remember...'

'Talk to no one. Be home, alone! And remember, mummy loves you. Got to go.'

Arianna pulled her hair back into a ponytail. She decided on finishing her cigarette before calling back the medical examiner. '*I deserve thirty bloody seconds to myself.*'

She rubbed her aching chest and flicked the burning bud away from her. As with guns, she was an excellent shot. The dying cigarette landed beside all its predecessors. In the tall, deep ceramic pot with the pink geranium. The blossoming plant did not seem to mind. It also welcomed without complaints, Arianna's water after it had lost its chill, the deformed ice cubes from her Frappe and generally any leftovers from anything the Captain was drinking to accompany her smoke.

Coroner Jacob Petsas always began with what he had to say. He picked up his phone and saw the Captain's name light up on his screen. 'Captain, I have collected everything I need. Just called to let you know, we were going to remove the body. It has been done now. The girl is in the van, headed to the morgue for the autopsy. I will send you the results as soon as possible.'

'Thank you.'

'My intern will run a DNA test comparing it with hair provided by the mother, as you requested.'

His tone implied a question.

'Yes, and call me with the results. I just want to put her mother's mind to rest. The face is unrecognizable...'

'I see, I see. Anyway, we both have loads of work on our hands. Catch you later.'

Arianna lowered her phone. Just then, the door behind her opened. *'Weird, it is not cleaning day.'*

Adrian stood in the door frame. He placed his hand above his eyebrows in an attempt to block the strong sun rays. Even shadowy, Arianna could see the worry on his face.

'Problem with the techs or did the priest make a runner?'

'Neither.' He stepped outside. 'Techs are on it. The page has been made private and all attempts to view it are going to be registered. They confirmed that the page went live from Parga and by the password, I would say its Pandora's. PandoraIrisNefeli2021. Sound familiar?' Arianna wet her lips with the tip of her tongue and nodded. 'Father Hector is in room B, by the way,' he continued.

'So, let's get to him then.'

Adrian did not move.

'What's wrong?'

'Officer Leventi came to me as he did not find you in your office. He printed out everything from the page. Most are crimes that need investigating but look at this.' He passed her one of the pieces of papers he was holding. 'Read about Stephanie Mitropanou.'

'The math's teacher? She had my Timmy last year.'

Adrian nodded and watched as the Captain read the page. 'Holy flying fuck. What the hell is wrong with this town? We need to drive out there now!'

Stephanie Mitropanou lived on the outskirts of town. She was not one for much unnecessary interaction. A widow at only thirty-two, she kept to herself and avoided socializing. Her teaching job and raising her two children was all that kept her going after losing her Greg in that awful bus collision high in the unforgiving Pindus mountains. If only he had parked just a meter further down.

Her small farmhouse in the middle of the meadow behind Parga's hills came into view as Adrian turned off the main road and the police car's wheels came into contact with the dirt track, causing a large cloud of dust to erupt behind them. Arianna was still shaking her head. 'I still can't believe it.'

'Doubts will fade away soon.'

'You trust the writings of a seventeen-year-old girl?'

Adrian shrugged his shoulders. 'It's not my belief that there is evil in each and every one of us, but... more of a gut feeling with this case. Everything on the list seems plausible. The words shock you at first, but then...' He coughed with his mouth closed and scratched his nose. 'Then you bring the people mentioned in front of your mind's screen and analyze them, and strangely it all makes sense.'

Arianna starred right at him. 'You're a weird one, Lieutenant. But I get your drift. Yet, with the same logic, everything could be gossip. Scenarios born in a young girl's mind from bits and pieces heard around town.'

'Then why is she dead?'

'Unlucky encounter after the senior party?'

Adrian frowned. The idea of the murder being a random act did not appeal to his gut feeling. 'And the murderer kept the body for hours? And why put it on display?'

'Sick people do sick things. I've heard and seen it all.

Sometimes it's better to not even imagine what killers might do, even for hours, with their victim's corpses.'

Arianna rubbed her right pocket. She felt her packet of menthol cigarettes. But now was not the time. They had reached their destination. A lanky, fair-haired boy stood on the front patio, scratching the back of his head.

'Good morning, Mrs. Arianna.'

'Good morning, Zak. You're up early on your first day off school. Is your mother in?'

'Err... no. She... err... popped into town. Supermarket day.'

'At his time?'

'Fresh veggies, she always says.'

Adrian whistled and nodded toward the side of the house. His mother's car was parked in the shade provided by the bungalow.

'Can I come in for a glass of cold water? This heat has dried up my throat,' Arianna said and walked up to the front door.

'Now's not a good time. The house is a mess...'

Arianna walked inside.

'I... I have my girlfriend with me Please stay out here. I'll bring you your water.'

'Quiet, kid,' Adrian ordered. 'Sit over there and stay completely still. Got it?'

Adrian kept his eyes on the teen and his ears by the open door.

The house was dark. All curtains were closed shut. Arianna placed her hand upon her firearm and headed to the stairs leading to the basement. She flicked on the lights and walked up to the locked door. She knocked. 'Stephanie? It's Captain Arianna Kontou. I know you are in there. Don't make this any worse than it has to be.'

Silence.

Arianna placed her ear upon the door. She could hear racket from inside. 'I can hear you. Open up now before I break down this door. One. Two...'

'You have no right to be here. Do you have a warrant?'

'Three!'

Arianna kicked at the door. The old hinges creaked as the lock broke, and the door swung open. 'Oh, my Lord...'

The stale air of the dark room carried the smell of rotten food. A young pregnant girl, obviously in her last trimester, lay on an old metal bed with her right arm chained to the bed post. Arianna could see her trembling wide eyes through her messy hair. Her mouth was covered by thick gray tape. The girl rocked violently back and forth.

'Stephanie, how could you? She is your daughter for crying out loud!'

Stephanie Mitropanou stood still. Tears fell from her eyes as she bit her lip until it bled. 'A daughter I raised properly for eighteen years and as soon as she goes off to the city to study, she gets knocked up! The father is a boy she met in a night club! She doesn't even have his number! I will not have her parading around town like this. Like a common slut...'

'And this is better?' Arianna approached the tormented girl, always with her eyes on Stephanie.

'I was only going to keep her here until the baby was done breastfeeding. Then, she could go continue her studies and I would announce that I had adopted a baby. Say that now my own were grown, I missed being a mother.'

'Yeah, how very motherly you are!' Arianna peeled off the tape with care.

'Thank you. Thank you. Save me, please.'

'Where's the key, Stephanie?'

The woman did not reply. Arianna stood up and pulled out her gun. She aimed it at the distraught woman. 'Where... is... the... key?'

Stephanie placed her hand in her apron's pocket. She pulled out the key and threw it on the bed. She then took steps back and sat down on the ground to weep.

'I'm sorry...'

Arianna helped the girl stand up and with her arms around the teen's shoulders, she escorted her out of her prison. 'Fuck you, mum.'

Upstairs the bright light from the open door made the poor girl's eyes sting. Yet, she did not pause. She picked up her pace. She wanted to be free. As they exited, Arianna turned toward Adrian. 'Well, this secret on the list is definitely true!'

A scream of pain came from the house. Arianna passed the girl to Adrian and ran back into the house. 'Stephanie? Stephanie?'

A shadow moved in the dim-lit kitchen and fell to the ground. Stephanie sat with her back against the cupboards. A round pool of blood covered her once-white apron. A sharp kitchen knife lay on the tiles amongst blood drops. Arianna ran and knelt by her. Her hands picked up a checkered kitchen cloth and she quickly covered the woman's slit wrist.

'This is Captain Kontou. I am requesting an ambulance to Mitropanou farm, off the highway at the 5th kilometre height. Please, hurry.'

Chapter Sixteen

Arianna still sat on benches in the same way she always had. Feet on the bench, bum on the backrest. Her mum told her off as a child ('You're going to fall off and break your head'), her teachers as a teen ('Your dirty feet are where others are going to sit, miss Kontou') and her husband as a young adult ('Seriously? That's no way for an adult to sit. Get down. People are looking at us'). Now, outside of the three-storey hospital building, she sat as she wished and placed yet another cigarette in her mouth. Adrian walked out of the sliding doors and sighed as he left the cold hospital air behind him. The midday heat was no laughing matter. He put on his shades and approached his boss. 'All paperwork, done. The girl is fine by the way. Baby, too. She is expecting a healthy baby girl.' He leaned forward and tilted his head. Arianna knew the gesture well. He was expecting her news.

'Mother is fine as well. She did not cut too deep. They never do.' She released another cloud of smoke. 'The boy is seventeen but will be eighteen in a couple of weeks. He is in my Timmy's class. No need for social services. I left him in the car. We will question him after the priest and then get Leventi to take him to his uncle's.'

'You never smoke this much.' His pupils rushed to their corners as he searched for a non-lingua response. 'If you don't mind me saying so, Captain.'

'Too many thoughts. Unfortunately, this poison calms me.' Arianna stood up and leaped off the green wooden bench. 'We are going to need more officers. I will call local HQ in Preveza. You and I are on the murder case and we will arrest the priest, too for his sexual crimes as he is the one who discovered the body. We will interrogate the mechanic as well as it is a murder allegation. But the rest on the list will be investigated by others more qualified in illegal businesses. The mayor and her lawyer are not crimes. We will pay them a single visit for a chat to gather details, but that's about it.'

'Grandma Ophelia?'

Arianna raised her hands to the cloudless sky and then, finished her cigarette in one long drag. 'Get Leventi to pay her a *friendly* visit after he drops off the kid.'

Ophelia took off her reading glasses. It took her a while to open Melpomene's computer and visit Pandora's website. She sighed deeply after reading about her past and shook her head. She looked behind her. Melpomene had locked herself in her bedroom and had screamed and cried since her return home. Ophelia was informed of the morning's tragic events by the ladies of the village that helped bring Melpomene home. Melpomene had thanked them and asked them to leave her to mourn in solitude. Of course, as

Greek women they stayed another half an hour and gossiped with Ophelia over coffee and freshly baked biscuits with a strong cinnamon scent. Thankfully, none of the ladies mentioned her *sin*. She at least got the privacy to read about what the little rebel girl had written about her. So, now, her secret was out in the world. Ophelia surprised herself. She expected to be more shocked, more worried. Neither shock, neither worry managed to make an impact. 'So, what if they all know?' Ophelia even felt relief. 'Secrets are not meant to be taken to the grave. I have had enough with overthinking things in this life, never mind taking issues with me to the other side.' Ophelia mumbled to herself (something she often did and enjoyed) as she made her way to her go-to place to relax. Her garden. She was on all fours among her plants pulling out unwelcomed weeds when she heard the car park outside her gate.

'*Who is it now?*'

Her heart skipped a beat -or probably two, when her eyes spotted the police vehicle and the goofy-looking officer approaching her premises. '*They wouldn't arrest me. Would they? They have no proof... Silence, you old bag. He is here for Melpomene. He is the young twat that told her about her daughter's death so bluntly.*'

It took her a good moment to manage to stand up. She wiped her hands upon her clothes and nodded to the officer. 'Officer Leventi, right? Melpomene is inside. She might need a minute. Don't think she is up for a talk right now. Maybe you lot could give her more time. Losing a child is a hellish suffering...'

'I'm here for you.'

'You can't arrest me based on what a dead girl wrote. You have no proof...'

A wide smile brightened the young policeman's face.

'Mrs. Ophelia, I am not here to arrest you. But I will need you to confirm the story.'

'Do I like senile to you, son?'

'Mrs. Ophelia, we need to check out each story and confirm the stories. Up to now, everything investigated was the truth. There are more serious crimes for the police to investigate. I highly doubt anyone will charge you.'

Ophelia trudged up to her rattan-made garden armchair and fell back into it. 'My husband was a very sick man, young man. He suffered daily. He was twelve years older than me and the love of my life. He gave me forty-six blissful years of marriage. Then, cancer, Alzheimer's and arthritis all came together. A mighty gang attacking my Jason. We spent more time in hospitals, than in our home. Pills, and pills, and pills... He couldn't dress himself, feed himself, go to the bathroom... He begged me daily to put him out of his suffering. Did I agree to such an act? Only God, Jason and I know the answer to that question. Now, if by retelling my man's hardships to a foolish teenager, made her believe that one night, after a day of throwing up and violent, painful shaking, I placed my pillow over Jason's sweet face and listened to his last breaths, then that's the dead girl's problem, not mine. You can also take away from this, whatever you wish. But laddie, I watch my police shows and there is no way I am admitting to something that will open a case against me.' Mrs. Ophelia took in a much-needed deep breath. 'Coffee, officer?'

The officer departed defeated. He tried not to feel that way though. He received no confession, yet his gut knew better. He returned to the station to inform Captain Kontou about his talk with Granny Ophelia.

Ophelia returned to her home with a heavy heart. Her body, mind and soul were attached to her husband's memory. She could not ever forget him. He was in her thoughts daily. He was her everything. And she did everything for him, in life and in death. He was her rock, her constant and she was never the same after she placed that pillow on his face as to block the little oxygen that still managed to reach his infected lungs. Her loss came after decades of happiness and blissful marital life.

Ophelia stood in the hallway listening to Melpomene's cries. Every loss is painful and there should not be a comparison. But Ophelia knew well that Melpomene's loss was much more severe than hers. The loss of a child. The unexpected loss of your child. The unexpected violent loss of your murdered child.

'How do you live with that? What do you say to that? Lord, give me strength.'

Ophelia's knuckles hovered by the door for a minute before knocking twice. She did not receive a reply, nor did she expect one. The knocking was just kind warning that she was entering the darkened room.

Melpomene was curled up on her bed. Her ashen face turned to Ophelia and she stared at her through wild, mangled hair. In her shaky hands, she held childhood photographs of Pandora.

'I... I can't even speak right now.'

'That's fine, dear. I'm not here to talk.'

Ophelia wobbled towards the grieving mother, sat down beside her and hugged her gently.

'I can't believe she is gone...'

The words came out among sobs.

'All that energy, light, mischief, attitude, beauty...butchered!'

Chapter Seventeen

A folklore anecdote enjoyed by many Greeks is one that explains how God sat and decided where each group of people would get to live. Each narrator would add any ethnicities they liked as they retold the 'tale'. God set the French and the Germans in central Europe, the Egyptians by the Nile, the Brazilians in the Amazon jungle, the Swiss on the Alps and so on. God was quite pleased with himself when he finally had distributed all the lands of the planet to his finest creation, humans. Until an angel (Archangel Michael in most narrations) pointed out that He had forgotten a tribe. 'Which one?' God inquired. 'The Greeks, my Lord.' God was saddened by the fact. 'But I have no where left to place them,' he complained. 'Well,' said the archangel, 'What's that little corner there? You haven't placed any humans there.' God looked down. 'But... err... but that little piece of paradise is mine. I was saving that for myself.' God then exhaled and reluctantly said, 'Okay, okay...the Greeks can have my piece of heaven on earth.' And that is how the Greeks ended up with the best land on the planet. Rich, lush lands surrounded by thousands of majestic isles nested in a quilt of multiple shades of blue.

This joke lingered in Arianna's mind as she starred outside from her office window. The town of Parga welcomed the morning summer sun and the Ionian Sea rushed to embrace the cosmopolitan seaside village with its multicoloured, Italian-influenced little houses. 'Perfect paradise, yet filled with so much deceit, pain and death.' Arianna placed her hand upon her heart. It had accelerated its beats once again. Lately, her heart had been playing tricks on her. At first, she thought they were minor stress attacks. Then, the arrhythmic beats came even late at night when Arianna rested, all nice and cosy, in her queen-sized bed with a hot-cocoa and a good murder-mystery movie. 'I really need to book an appointment at the docs.'

The characteristic knocking on her door pulled her out of her thoughts. Two sharp knocks, a second apart.

'Come in, Adrian.'

Arianna watched the handsome thirty-two-year-old man walk into her office. She enjoyed watching him walk. She had tried in the past to pinpoint what it was about it that she found mesmerizing. Was it the manly military pacing? How his upper body remained so stiff while he made his way?

Her eyes left his legs and focused on the papers in his right hand. She had already gone over his and Leventi's notes late last night. She had them email her everything.

'So, it looks like everything the girl wrote is fact.'

'Sure does,' he said and sat down in the comfortable armchair opposite her. 'Good morning, by the way.'

'What's so good about it? Our small town is being shredded to pieces. People can't take multiple blows like this.

Their brains' designated gossip area is in overdrive. And all eyes are on us!'

Adrian, a man of few words, nodded.

'Any update on the mechanic?' Arianna asked as she poured half-a-cup of filtered coffee. Caramel flavoured and scented. 'Coffee?'

'No, thank you, boss. I don't drink hot coffee during our seven-month summer. I had my frappe on the way over.' He leaned forward. 'The mechanic's phone rang each of the four times that I called him. He never answered. The neighbours said he is on vacation with his wife and kid. Barcelona. I am hoping he will see my calls and get back to me today.'

'And say what? Hey! Yeah, I heard you all know about how I murdered my wife's ex. Yeah, it's true...'

'News has surely reached him. I hope he doesn't do a runner.'

Arianna scoffed. 'And go where? Jonas gets lost on his way home. Never mind managing to survive undercover in a foreign country.' The Captain sat on and took in a deep breath. 'I can't believe how many crimes can take place in such a small town. A village by most people's standards. And I am the one in charge for maintaining the law. A dead teenage girl should be the worst thing.'

'A dead girl *is* the worst thing.'

Arianna released the long-kept deep breath. 'I mean, the only bad thing. Not all this. A package of dreadful deeds. A death where the suspect should be a rapist or a jealous boyfriend, not half the freaking town!'

The station's secretary's voice could be heard from the hallway.

'Come in!'

The secretary's rosy cheeks and bent smile appeared

through the slightly opened door. 'Oh, good morning, Adrian,' she said and quickly turned towards her boss. 'You have to get to the church quickly. Apollo's father attacked Father Hector. No one intervened. As soon as I received Angelica's call, I sent all officers on their way in an alarm. Thankfully Leventi was nearby...'

'Freaking town,' Arianna mumbled and leapt up. 'Come on.'

Adrian drove in silence, his eyes shifting from the downhill road ahead towards his Captain. She looked troubled. He had always admired her manner, her professionalism. Would the pressure of such a tangled, complex case squash her down? Was this really the case that would break her? He could not accept such a fact, yet Arianna's twitching fingers and her dead look outside the windscreen, caused turmoil in his gut and mind.

The stone-built church of Saint Nicholas came into view as they turned off the main street. Its octagon of a bell tower stood proudly above the roof tops. The clock on it informed them that it had just turned eight o'clock. As with all incidents (minor or major) in small towns in Greece, a crowd had gathered. Adrian turned on the police vehicle's lights and siren as he made his way to the church yard. He parked next to Leventi's aged vehicle. The car had not yet come to a complete halt and Arianna had opened the door and jumped outside.

Arianna came face to a scene she felt was dragged out of a black and white Greek movie. The protagonists all stood still. Alexander, Apollo's father, stood tall, huffing and puffing, with his fists clenched. Steps in front of him,

Leventi stood with his firearm at eye level. Behind him, Angelica knelt by a heavily wounded priest. Blood oozed from his mouth and head. His eyes were closed, but Arianna could see his lips slightly moving as he tried to reply to Angelica's manic cries for help.

'I'm fine,' he managed to say and crimson blood ran out of his opened mouth and dyed his thick beard.

Arianna approached the father with a steady pace. 'Lower your gun, Leventi,' she said as she got closer. 'Let's all try to relax here,' she raised her voice. Many villagers stood behind Alexander. All agreeing to his actions, but one. His son Apollo begged his to stop yet did not dare go near his manic father. Apollo's blue hair shone under the summer sun and Arianna was momentarily mesmerized by the halo that seemingly glowed around the boy with the many piercings and tattoos.

'He forced himself on my boy, Captain. A servant of the Lord, for fuck's sake. Apollo is underage. Arrest him or watch me kill him.' The large tall man spoke loudly as if giving a speech. The crowd reacted with applause and even cheers. He, then, took two steps forward and slightly bowed as to reach eye level with Arianna. In a heavy breathless whisper, he said, 'what you would do if the filth's cock was in Timothy's mouth, eh?'

'Alexander, the priest came into the station...'

'Because of the girl's murder! I bet he raped poor Pandora and tossed her body as yesterday's trash. He is a monster!' Again, the crowd applauded their fellow villager.

Arianna took in a much-needed deep breath and continued. '...we have opened a case against him as Apollo is underage. You can always come in and press charges. Form a stronger case. We would like to hear Apollo's side to all of this. As for Pandora, the murder is under investigation. You cannot just go around and take the law into your own hands, Alex! Now, back off before you do something you will regret for the rest of your life. Your kids need a dad at home, not a father in prison.'

The sound of the deafening ambulance sirens echoed in the air. Arianna walked up to Alexander who seemed to be calming. His chest remained still, and his face had returned to its normal sun-kissed color. She placed her hand on his broad shoulder. 'I get it. You had to show that you did not accept it. People saw you beat him. Your pride is safe. But you and I both know he did not force Apollo to do anything. Please, please, relax and come with the boy to the station. Right away. The priest will be punished by the system for sexual acts with a minor and he will surely lose his job when the church hears about all this.'

'Dad, come on,' Apollo's soft voice came from behind.

The tall man nodded. 'If you release him, Captain, without punishment, I will find him,' he belted out as he starred at the gathered crowd. 'Come on, son. Let's get out of here.'

Behind Arianna, paramedics provided first-aid to the wounded priest.

'I deserve it,' Father Hector said as the paramedics lifted him up on a stretcher. 'We need to get him to the hospital. I suspect he has a fractured arm, and we must take a better look at his lungs. I don't like that sound in his breathing,' the woman in red said quickly as they rushed the priest to the ambulance.

'Of course,' Arianna replied and wiped her forehead.

'I'm coming with him,' Angelica said and rushed into the ambulance without waiting for confirmation.

Chapter Eighteen

'Apollo and his father are here.'

Once again, Adrian interrupted her quick *secret* cigarette break. She took in as much she could master with one drag and killed the bud in a large clay pot featuring dark purple milkworts.

'Be there in a sec.' She did not turn to face him.

Once again, Adrian wondered about his Captain. She did not seem her usual self. Too much stress showing. His Captain hardly showed her emotions. At work, at least. Once again, he worried if his words could be interpreted as overstepping the line. 'You okay, boss?'

'Fine, fine.' She waved her hand as to dismiss such a ridiculous notion. Of course, she was fine. She was Captain Arianna Kontou and no case of hers was ever left unsolved. 'Let's get to the interrogation room.'

Apollo sat awkwardly on the hard chair. He watched the steam from the hot coffee travel up and vanish before reaching a great height. He kept his eyes away from those of his father's. He could not bear his disappointed, judgmental look any longer. He tried to pull his mind away from the cold, unfriendly, colorless environment. *'The steam is just like me. Forced to stay low. If I seek greater heights, I will vanish. Lost in despair and oblivion. Very deep, mister philosopher. But like the steam, I am also hot. Hot and fabulous.'* Apollo's lips travelled inwards as he tried to control a giggle. *'My inner voice should have a stand-up show.'*

The sound from the door opening made him jump and brought his mind back to the low-ceiling room with the three white walls and the one with the infamous mirror. The one we all know from countless detective shows. Apollo swallowed the lump in his throat and moved his gaze from the newly brewed coffee to his brand-new Adidas sneakers. *'God, I love them. Wish I was shopping right now.'*

'Gentlemen,' Adrian nodded and sat down opposite Alexander while Arianna sat down opposite the young teen. Her eyes focused on the duo's hands. Alexander's knuckles were red, sore and bloody while Apollo's pale fingers came into full contrast with the black nail varnish that he used.

Alexander placed his hand on top of his son's. Not a sign for affection but to stop his nervous tapping on the table's surface. 'Arianna,' he addressed the woman he respected. A woman that to him and most of the town's population of four thousand represented everything Greek to them. A strong loving mother, a fierce law enforcer with a tremendous sense of fairness and a moral compass that worked better than a Swiss clock, and a person that loved her town and participated in all things communal. 'I'm sorry for all the commotion and especially for the difficult spot that I put you on. I could not just let the paedophile believe he could get away with anything.'

'You're lucky you did not kill him. Think about your family with you in prison.' The veins in her neck danced around as she spoke. 'I called the hospital before entering. He will be fine. He is in a lot of pain...'

'Good.'

'Dad!'

'Silence, you. You've done enough.'

Arianna stayed concentrated. Her nails ran along her hand's skin and even dug slightly. '...yet he requested we do not charge you with assault. He says he deserved the beating, and he accepts his punishment. He merely asks for your forgiveness.'

'Pfff.' Alexander crossed his arms upon his strong chest and rolled his eyes. 'Let him find forgiveness with God. I hear that they are pals.'

Arianna turned her attention to Apollo. The boy had not raised his eyes for as long as they spoke. 'Hey, Apollo.'

'Hey, Mrs. Kontou.'

She could not see his eyes, but she did spot the sweet smile forming on his pale face.

'Apollo, would like to give us your take on things?'

'My take?' He raised his head and looked straight at her. His hairless baby face would easily fool you into thinking he was only a boy of twelve. Thirteen tops. Yet he was weeks away from his sixteenth birthday.

'Did you and the priest meet often?' Adrian asked.

'Oh. Err, no. Of course not. It was just that one time.'

'Did he approach you in church? Invite you to meet up?'

Apollo shook his head. 'No, sir. I...' Apollo looked at his father. 'I went to see him. I waited for a moment when he would be alone.' He could see his father's face turning red as he bit his lips in an effort to imprison the words struggling to break free.

'Want to try and explain to me how Pandora ended with

a photograph of your encounter? Who took the photo, Apollo?' Arianna asked.

'She did. She was hiding behind the chairs.'

'Why was she there?'

'Oh, it was...'

Apollo looked at the thin red hand on the wall clock as it journeyed around.

'What boy? Speak!' His father's voice shook him.

'It was all Pandora's idea. She dared me to do it. It was a set up. She wanted to test a theory. Dig up some dirt.' He paused and looked down. He could not bear his father's eyes on him. 'She came up to me one day after school a few months back and offered me her help.'

'Her help?'

Apollo starred straight at Adrian. 'I'm thinner, shorter, and shyer than every other kid in school. And look at me. People know I'm gay, a mile away. I live in a small town in Epireus! By most definitions, we are categorized as a village. Can you imagine the shit that I get? I was bullied daily. Pandora is like the most popular girl in school and on social media. All she had to do was talk to a couple of the older boys that were really messing with me and she hung around with me in school and posted us together and that was it. Suddenly, it was cool to be my friend. And all she wanted in return was for me to hit on the priest.'

Apollo exhaled. 'Wow. That felt good to get off my chest. She made me swear that I would tell no one but now she is dead, it doesn't count, right?'

Arianna and Adrian exchanged a concerned look. Their innocent victim was losing innocence points.

'Apollo, you say you got to hang around with Pandora,' Arianna said. 'She gathered up pretty disturbing details about folks here in our small town. Do you know how she managed to discover such dirty secrets? Maybe she made promises to other kids like you in return for gossip?'

Apollo sat up straight. A streak of blue dyed hair fell before his eyes. 'Bad mouthing the dead is so anti-Greek, is it not?'

'Not if the bad details might be the ones that bring justice to the dead. We all do bad things, Apollo. We are only humans trying desperately to make it through life. Anything you reveal to us about Pandora will be in absolute confidence. Please, Apollo, help us bring her murderer in. Even by bad-mouthing the dead.'

Apollo rested his arms on the table and placed his chin between his fingers. He raised his gazed towards the two officers.

'There was something weird about her. Something off as my mum says. She was obsessed with secrets and real-life unknown stories. She was always investigating people's backgrounds and followed police stories and such. I believe she was only acting like she did as to be popular and get to know everyone. She put way too much time in her social media presence. Any gossip she heard, she wanted to check it up, to look into it. I truly doubt anyone got to know the true Pandora. It was all just an act. The bubbly fun girl that got along with everyone. That one had a dark side to her, and her eyes scared me. But I needed her help and went along with it.'

Apollo was not the only one providing insight to Pandora that day.

Just under an hour after he and his father departed the stone building that housed the local police station, another father and son duo walked through the doors.

Jonas looked nothing like his usual self. No dark bags under his honeycomb eyes, no rough beard, no messy hair and no black oil stains on his clothes and hands. Arianna had never seen him without black nails. Then again, she had never seen him outside of his garage. Jonas was looking healthier due to the nice tan provided by the Spanish sun and was in colorful shorts and a *I Love Barcelona* T-shirt.

His son, on the other hand, was exactly as she remembered him. A skinny-looking teen with restless eyes and restless feet. His lips moved around yet produced no sound. He scratched his thick brown curly hair a lot and observed everything in the room. He smiled awkwardly at whoever he made eyesight with and then shot straight for the floor. He had a smile designed for models in cologne ads. A smile that pulled you in and made you forget about the madness roaming inside his mind. Some specialists called it ADHD, some autism, some Asperger's. The villagers just called him Nicholas. A sweet boy that always wanted to run around to burn off gathered energy. He was one of their own and doctors are always wrong according to the folks in the Greek countryside. The boy was fine.

'Arianna, I came straight from the airport. Dropped the wife and the girls off at home, of course. She sends her love and says you owe her a visit for coffee and her famous biscuits.'

'I really need to stop standing her up. Tell her next week for sure.'

Small town, small talk.

'Hello, Nicholas. How are you today? Did you enjoy your holiday in Spain?'

The teen nodded in reply. His cheeks turned a rosy color and began travelling towards total red.

'He knows he is in deep shit. He has much to say to you, Captain Kontou!'

And much he said indeed.

Arianna opted for her office rather than the small - scarier- interrogation room. She did not want to cause an emotional episode to Nicholas and watch him *switch off* into himself. Once, after a fight with a boy at school, he did not utter a single word for eight whole days.

'Go on, Nick. You got me in trouble, you love me, I am your father, you get me out of it, now,' Jonas said with a sweet pleasant tone to his voice as he sat down in the armchair in front of Arianna's rather large mahogany desk.

Arianna watched Nicholas's Adam's apple journey up and down as he loudly swallowed the lumps gathering in his throat, drowning the scattered words desperately seeking to form sentences with meaning inside of his brain. He did not sit down. His lanky body swayed slightly side to side.

'It's okay, Nick. It's just me. Your mum's friend, Arianna. You used to call me auntie when I came round when you were a kid.'

'And I won't get into trouble?'

'The truth is never trouble.' She pushed out her most genuine motherly smile.

'I lied.' He started to tap his left foot on the ground and his hands kept crossing on his beating chest and then falling to his sides.

'About what, Nicholas?'

'My dad never murdered anyone. I lied that he killed my mum's ex to Pandora.'

Arianna placed her hands on a pile of papers before her and leaned forward. 'And why did you tell such a thing to Pandora?'

The teen bit his lip. He bit his lip hard. Arianna could see the small droplet of blood forming on his trembling mouth.

'Go on, Nick. It's nothing to be ashamed about. Arianna will understand,' his father urged him.

'To have sex with her. I felt like I was the only virgin in our class.'

Arianna tilted her head. She opened her mouth but was still searching for the words. 'Why... err... why would lying to her about such a dreadful thing... err... get her to sleep with you?'

Nicholas was scratching his eyebrows. 'I ... I observe people. It is what I do. And my mind records it all and makes connections.'

'You would be a good detective.'

Nicholas smiled widely at the thought. 'Yes, I would,' he agreed.

'And what did you observe and connect?'

'Pandora was obsessed with secrets.' Arianna heard the same words just an hour ago. 'The darker, the better. She did not trust people. She felt that everyone was not as they appeared. Everyone, according to her, had skeletons locked away. For her, it was a need. To know the true person that she had before her.'

'And what has this got to do with sex?'

Nicholas giggled. 'Connections. I make connections. Simply put, Pandora enjoyed sleeping around. And why not? It's 2021 for crying out loud. Her body, her choice. I can't think of many boys in our year with which she had not hooked up with at one point or another. If you look at the guilty ones on her webpage you will see that most have a son in our year. I realized that she knew a lot of things about everyone and everything. I believed that she knew things about them as they never told on her after she quickly broke up with them. No one knew she was having sex with them all. And these are teens in school. Everyone kisses and tells. But no one said shit about Pandora. No one knew. Not a single boy mentioned being with her. But I saw the full picture and decided to put my theory to the test.'

'And what did you do?'

'I began texting her saying I was depressed because of family secrets I had just uncovered. Of course, she showed interest and questioned me about it. I, then, invited her over one night when everyone was out. You lot had a wedding or something.' It was the first time that he looked over to his father. 'One thing sort of led to another. I kept hinting at what a tremendous secret it was and only spilled the fake beans after we had slept together.'

In contrast to the boy, Arianna found herself lost for words. Nicholas had swung into his chatty mode and there was no barrier for his words.

'Do you believe others knew this about her and lied...'

'No, no, no! Those fools had no idea. Their family secrets were real. But Pandora's love for them was not!'

———

'I can't believe we failed to make such a simple connection! Shit! And I myself have a son in her class!' Arianna slammed her office door behind her. Adrian had entered with a worried expression and turned to face her. He saw the father and son depart, and then heard Arianna's angry voice calling him.

'Only five out of the list have boys in her year. And one has a son in her school but not her year. It's a small town. We only have one school...'

'I hate excuses, Adrian. We should have seen this. The

other four are the priest and we know how that happened. Angelica has a young girl working in her shop. I bet that is where Pandora got her info. And she lived with her mum and Ophelia!'

She knocked her fist on her desk three times. 'I'm going home. I need to talk to Timothy. Get Leventi and go to her classmates. I want confirmation from every little dumbass that slept with her and exposed their families. I will visit her two close girlfriends. Nefeli and Iris. After, I'm done with Timmy, of course!'

'I can go to the two girls as I will be out and about,' Adrian interrupted.

Arianna waved a hand of disproval. 'No need. I also will be as you say, out and about. I plan to go round and check on Melpomene. Mother to mother, I might get something out of her. Maybe even a confession of what her crime was going to be on the site.'

'Do you think her mother's crime is reason to consider her a suspect?'

'It's a terrifying thought but one we cannot exclude.'

'Everyone is capable of murder under the right circumstances and pressure...'

Adrian murmured his last thoughts. Arianna raised her eyes, looking up to the ceiling. 'Unfortunately, Lord knows how very true that statement is, my friend.'

Even though she was dying for an answer, Arianna walked home. The downhill rock-paved path welcomed her as on so many mornings before. First time though with black heels, trousers and a white shirt. Arianna wished she were wearing her trainers. Running always cleared her mind. Yet, now, as she walked, she noticed so much more. The path ran along the old neighbohood of the town.

Smaller houses compared to the new ones built on the outskirts; they housed older couples and unfortunately many widows. The colorful houses also housed an array of Greek flowers and shrubs and the entire scenery was a delight for Arianna's tired eyes. Soon, divine aromas floated through the fresh air and crept up her nostrils. Greek grandmothers cooked lunch way too early. Then again, everything had to be perfectly ready by noon and the invasion of hungry grandkids. Arianna preoccupied her mind by guessing the dish by the smell. 'Mousakka... lamb... rabbit stew... beans...' she whispered as she hastily walked past the open windows.

She reached the main road in a matter of minutes, glad to not have bumped into anyone. Chit chat and questions about the dead girl would only be a delay and frankly, a nuisance. Few cars were journeying along the road, there was no need to press the pelican crossing's button and wait. Arianna stopped for a second, looked left and right, and speedily made her way across. She reached her garden's fence and smiled at the thought that she had not even broken a sweat. *'Getting fit, girl. Keep up your morning runs.'*

She walked up to her front door, keys in hand. She paused for a minute as to listen to the quiet house. 'Good, boy. I said stay home. No visitors!'

She closed the door behind her and called out his name. She knew better than to surprise a seventeen-year-old boy alone at home. No reply. She called out louder and added many Ys to his name. 'Timothyyyyyyyyyyyyy?' Soon, her handsome young fellow appeared shirtless on the top of the staircase. He wore white socks and navy-blue pyjama bottoms. His prized headphones were around his neck. 'Mum? What are you doing home? I thought I heard you, but thought I was going mad.'

'What you listening to?'

'Just playing games with my friends.'

'Get down here. I need a word,' his mother said and walked into the kitchen. 'Make me coffee as I speak.'

Timothy knew better than to reply. He did as she said and listened to her day and her meetings with Apollo and Nicholas.

'Did you sleep with her?'

The question came as soon as he placed the coffee mug on the table. Timothy appreciated her wait as otherwise he would not have been able to guarantee that he would not have spilled the hot beverage.

'No!'

'Why?'

Timothy opened the fridge and picked up the bottle of freshly squeezed orange juice. He brought it to his mouth and drank slowly as his mother kept on talking.

'She slept with everyone else. You're telling me she did not hit on the hot kid of the class? Did you tell her anything about us? The others surely did...'

'The others! I did not! I did not even know they slept with her and they are my best friends. No one ever said hey, I nailed Pandora and that's weird for guys my age. You know, not to brag and all?'

Arianna took a sip from her coffee. Her son's coffee was always the best. 'And I am meant to believe a seventeen-year-old boy that he was the only one that did not sleep with the tall, beautiful, easy blonde?'

Timothy shook his head. 'You have way too much on your mind at the moment.'

'For what?'

'Nothing.'

'Timmy, tell me. What could be worse that everything I have already heard from you?'

'Cheers, mum.'

'That's not how I meant it to sound.'

Timothy pulled out a wooden kitchen chair and sat down next to her. 'Not worse, but different.' Timothy exhaled loudly. 'I... I am... err... not so sure that I like girls.' He dropped the words and tapped his hands on the table as if playing the drums. The time that he was waiting for had finally arrived. He had rehearsed his lines in various ways in his mind.

Arianna sat up straight. Her eyes opened wide in their sockets. She placed her hand upon her son's. 'Not sure?'

He looked straight at her. 'Okay, I'm pretty sure,' he said and chuckled awkwardly. 'Mum, I'm gay.'

Arianna stroked his cheek. Tears were forming in his youthful eyes. 'I love your strength. Thanks for telling me.'

'Wait... You're okay with this?'

'Why wouldn't I be? You're my son. My smart, handsome boy and your sexual preferences changes nothing of that.'

Timothy shook his head in clear disbelief. 'To be honest, this is not exactly how I pictured this moment going down.'

'How did you picture it?'

'With more tension for sure. You interrogating me if I am sure and if I acted upon my thoughts. A proper Greek rant about hard life as a gay guy in a small town and how you will never have grandkids. Not believing me because I am so athletic and manly and...'

Arianna laughed. 'My sweet boy.' She stroked his hair. 'Maybe years ago, I might have reacted like that. But I have seen so much death in my line of work, that I know what is important in life. Also, I have no such misconceptions about gays. I work with Adrian. You can't get manlier than that, can you?'

'Adrian's gay? No way!'

Arianna stood up, hugged her son and kissed him on his cheek. 'I will always be by your side. Always. And we will get through all of this!'

Chapter Nineteen

THE PAST III

Demetra tucked her mother's photograph under her pillow. Three years had passed since her death and Demetra could still hear her voice inside her head. Soothing, cheerful, calming. She could still smell her and feel her warmth. *'Time heals nothing.'*

Her bedroom door opening pulled her out of her thoughts. She turned to face her father. She had remained naked after her shower just like he told her to. He did not come to her room every night. If he did not show, she would dress and sleep peacefully after praying.

'Have you said your prayers yet?' he enquired.

'Not yet, father.'

'Good,' he said. 'Let's say them together.' He knelt by her bed and waited for her to kneel by his side. Demetra sat down on the carpet and looked at him sideways. The strong man next to her never prayed. He had turned his back on God for taking away his wife. Demetra understood that. She also understood though, that her mummy was an angel and if she ever wanted to be with her mother again, she had to be a good Christian and pray daily. Demetra studied the Bible, a gift from her auntie Toula, and went to church every Sunday with the family next door. She was taking no chances of not rejoining her beloved mother and especially wished to avoid ending up in hell with her father. She was old enough to know what molesting meant but she dared not to stand up to him nor report him. '*Honour thy father...*'

'Amen.' Her father's croaky voice yet again returned her to the room and out of her *thoughts-world*.

'Good night, my sweetheart.' He kissed her hair -still a bit wet from her shower, and got up and left. Demetra watched the door close with utter surprise written all over her twelve-year-old face.

The following nights her father never came through her door. He would ask about her homework -something he rarely did, kiss her good night and tell her to sleep. Demetra would then hear the front door open and close. The house smelled of his cologne. He did not say where he went and Demetra did not ask. Nor cared. She was pleased that he went out the entrance door and not in through hers.

A few weeks later, on a rainy night, the kind that carry many lightnings and thunders, the front door opened and closed again after he had wished her a good night. Yet this time she could still hear her father walking about in the house. That is when she heard the second voice. A faint whisper of a woman's voice. Demetra could not make out what it is that she was saying. It took her a while to even realize what her own father was saying. They were both whispering in English. Broken English, the pair of them. Their whispers faded away as they closed the master bedroom's door behind them.

The next morning was a Saturday morning. The only mornings Demetra woke without an alarm. She thanked

God for these mornings often. She sat up in her bed and listened carefully. The house was quiet. She wondered if the mystery woman from the previous night was still there. Her feet landed on her white woolly slippers and her pink robe embraced her as she quickly tied its belt around her petite figure. She rushed to the kitchen. Her father sat alone, coffee in one hand, folded newspaper in the other. A string of smoke rose from the cigarette sitting alone in the glass ashtray beside his empty breakfast plate.

'Good morning, princess Demetra.' He certainly was in high moods. 'Slept for ten hours straight, sleepy head.'

Demetra offered him a smile and proceeded toward the cupboard where she kept her favorite cereal. The ones with the chestnut chocolate spread in the middle. As she opened the fridge and picked up the cold carton of fresh milk, her father spoke.

'I need your help today.'

Demetra raised her bushy eyebrows. 'With what, daddy?' she asked as she made her way to the bowls.

'Shopping. Tomorrow I will be having a barbeque. Souvlaki, pita bread and all that. But I want you today with me at the supermarket. To pick out a few side dishes. You always helped your mother prepare things.'

'That was years ago, and we haven't had a barbeque since the fune...'

'Yeah, yeah. I trust you. Then we can go clothes shopping. Any dress you want. A nice one for tomorrow. A very special friend of mine will be joining us tomorrow.'

'Friend? From work?'

Her father shook his head and picked up his lit cigarette. 'A lady friend I met at the pub. You will like her. She looks like one of the princesses in those movies you enjoy so much. Tall, beautiful with long blonde hair and shiny blue eyes.'

'Does she speak Greek?'

Her father lowered his newspaper and placed in neatly on the kitchen table. He frowned and starred at his daughter. 'Why would you ask that? Have you been eaves dropping on me? Don't you sleep straight away when I tell you to?'

'Relax, daddy. She just did not sound very Greek to me by your description. I don't know why but I thought straight away that she was a foreigner.'

Her father took a while to speak. Demetra went about with filling up her cereal bowl. 'Well, she is from Finland if you must know and yes, tomorrow you will be practicing your English.'

'What's her name?' Demetra asked, her mouth full of chocolate wheat and milk.

'Helka, if you must know. And look at me. Be very careful what you tell her, okay? Our secrets are *our* secrets.'

Demetra nodded. She knew *that* tone well. The tone that usually came after a few whiskeys. The tone that was friends with a slap or two.

'Of course, daddy.'

'And no need to mention your mother. Just talk about your school or makeup or something like that.'

Chapter Twenty

Lunch in Greece. More like a midday feast. Siesta might be a Spanish word and a Latin ritual, but during the summer it was a divine custom followed by many Greeks. As temperature dipped, just a bit, in the evening hours, refreshed locals set about their *coffee duties*. Social visits and mingling were the basis of strong village communities. The men gathered in the coffee shops and the women, having the house to themselves, welcomed girlfriends, neighbours and relatives. No topic was left unearthed. Pandora and her revelations were the hottest subject discussed.

Pandora lingered in Arianna's mind as she walked at a fast pace toward Nefeli's house. To her delight, outside of the house, a blue Golf was parked. Helen's car. The mother of Iris. Arianna knew both the mothers well as their daughters were in Timothy's class from first grade all the way up to graduation. They had met at countless birthday parties and school functions. Arianna's delight was not about seeing her two friends. It was about the fact that she was sure Iris would be there as well. She wanted to speak to both girls simultaneously as to read their reactions to each other's replies.

Helen and Magda sat on the front porch of the two-storey house that oversaw both green blossoming hills and pure blue sea. It was a view that city folk never got used to admiring. That is why Athenian Magda insisted on a house slightly on the outskirts of town. A house with a view was her demand and her husband always made her wishes come true. Madga's loud laughter echoed towards Arianna. Helen was retelling a joke she had heard at the market.

'...and then he lowered his window and asked, did you fart, too?' Helen repeated the punch line much to her friend's delight.

'Good afternoon, sexy ladies.'

Both turned toward Arianna as she opened the white garden gate and walked the pebble-made path up to the house.

Pleasantries and kisses were exchanged, and a chair was quickly offered.

'Tea or coffee, Ari?' Magda enquired.

'Would not think that you would have time to visit us with everything going on.'

Magda placed her hand on her heart. 'How awful.'

'That poor girl. And our girls losing their friend like that. Seeing her... like that!' Helen sighed, closed her eyes and shook her head.

Arianna took in a deep breath. She knew the reaction that would follow. 'Actually, I am kind of here on police business. I need to speak to the girls.'

Eyes opened wide by both ladies. Mouths opened as jaws dropped.

'Before you say anything,' Arianna was quick to add, 'it's

nothing serious. Typical procedure. They are Pandora's best friends...'

'Were.'

'...and surely they will be a help with her whereabouts and associations. I thought better that it is a friendly chat with me, here at home, rather than with another police officer or down at the station.'

Both women nodded in agreement.

'You're right.'

'Thank you for thinking of them. The poor souls have been through hell. They sit in their bedroom all day listening to sad melodramatic songs and crying.'

'I saw Iris smoking in the back yard last night and did not have the strength to tell her off. I hope it is not a habit she will pick up.'

Arianna placed her hand upon her friend's. 'I will definitely go easy on them. Just a friendly chat. Are they in the bedroom now?'

Both women nodded in reply and picked up their beverages to take a sip. Both watched as Arianna entered the house and made her way down the dark corridor. She paused for a second outside the wooden bedroom door. She could hear voices inside. After a guilty look behind her, she quietly placed her ear on the door. She could not make out words; much to her disappointment. Iris's deep voice came to her like a low base line while Nefeli's high pitched giggle mingled with the sounds, making them unclear while the background music provided by Taylor Swift made it impossible to make sense of their conversation.

The cheery girls inside puzzled her. Their mothers had stated their sadness, something most likely true. Yet, the girls inside sounded happy. *'Coping mechanism, life goes on, single moment of joy...'*

'Our bitch has really got everyone startled, huh? Even in death, she is popular and the talk of not only the school, but town,' Nefeli's voice came as the song came to an end.

'She sure has. Cunning Pandora. Now, look at them all panic,' Iris agreed.

The next tune was an upbeat dance hit. Arianna knew she could not stay outside of their door forever. Neither of her friends outside would appreciate such a move. She knocked on the door twice.

'Come in,' Nefeli shouted expecting her mother's head to pop in. The music continued as the door opened. Both girls froze as they saw who walked in through the door.

'Hi, girls.' Arianna flashed her brightest -and friendliest- smile.

'Good morning, Mrs. Kontou,' Iris said while Nefeli rushed to switch off the music. Both stood in the middle of the room, awkwardly side by side. Their contrast always amazed Arianna. Nefeli wore much makeup on her healthy-looking, sun-kissed skin, had different colors shading her eyes, while bright colorful nails matched her yellow trainers, pink tracksuit bottoms and purple tank top. Her long blond hair fell to her bare shoulders. Iris, on the other hand, was probably the palest girl in town. Her hair was shaved off on the left side, while on the right pure black hair hung no lower than her cheek. No sign of makeup, just a nose piercing decorated her face. She wore only black. A perfect match to her black nails.

'*Puberty!*' A thought followed by a short-lived sigh. 'So, what are you girls up to?'

Nefeli took a step forward. She played with her fingers. A sorrowful look settled on her face. 'Not much. Killing time. Keeping our mind off...' She exhaled deeply and her eyes watered up. '...off poor Pandora.' She wiped her eye.

'Staying in, too. We're scared, Captain. There's a killer out there.' Iris added clenching her fists. 'Have you caught him yet?'

'*Him.*'

'We are on a good path. Following many leads,' Arianna said and walked over to the office chair. 'May I sit?'

Nefeli nodded and sat down on the bed. Iris sat down by her side.

'Many leads,' Arianna repeated. 'Your friend left quite a lot for us. And that is where I was hoping you could help me.'

'Us?'

'You were her closest friends. I was once your age. Your mothers and I told each other *everything*.'

Iris folded her legs upon the bed. 'I'm not sure what it is you want us to say.'

Arianna wheeled her chair towards the girls. 'For Pandora to get so much information, she must have needed some help.'

Nefeli sat up straight. 'Nah-ah! She got all that info from the boys...' Iris nudged her. '...from others. We knew what she was doing, but we never assisted her!'

'Nor did she ask us to,' Iris quickly added. 'It was her own private project.'

Arianna forced a smile. 'I am not here to blame you for anything, girls. Relax. I know how she got her info. I was hoping that you two could tell me the why.'

Both raised their shoulders.

'Really? Nothing? A lucky guess, maybe?'

Iris rolled her front teeth along her lips. 'She was just really into all that. I think she just wished to be like an investigating reporter or something like that. She was ecstatic every time she discovered a secret.'

'Hmm. And do neither of you know what the next secret was going to be? The one about her mother?'

Again, both took on clueless faces and postures. 'She never mentioned anything. We knew that she was planning a web page to post all this, but she never said anything about Melpomene.'

Arianna took out her little black notepad and scribbled something down on the first line of a new page. Both girls exchanged looks and then starred at the Captain as she wrote.

'About her whereabouts the day before her murder, you stick to your original statements that she was with you dying her hair and then you went to a beach party? Any details that you might have remembered since then? You were in shock at that moment...'

'No. She was with us until late. Like elevenish. And then she left to go home.'

'And she never showed up... Where did you go, Pandora?'

'Why did she leave the party so early? Timothy said you seniors were planning to spend the entire night together? Did something happen?'

Iris shook her head. 'Most normally stay...'

'Mostly the boys,' Nefeli added.

'But we said to stay the latest until one. We prefer our bed than freezing by the sea and getting eaten by mosquitoes all night, while the boys try to get into our pants.'

'I see. But why didn't Pandora stay and leave with you?'

'She came on her period, I think. She did not bring any swimwear with her. Everyone was diving in. She probably felt left out.'

Arianna nodded and began to take notes.

'Your coffee is ready, Ari.' The voice interrupted her thoughts. Helen stood by the open door.

'Thank you. Just a sec. I will be with you in a sec. Last thing, girls. Did you ever notice, or did Pandora ever mention any trouble by anyone? A boy offended by her...antics? Angry about her finding out secrets?'

Nefeli shook her head. 'No one knew she was going to release a website. Just us. The boys were fools that loved her attention and revealed their family's deeds. How could they be angry at something they did not know was coming?'

'Anyway, they should feel privileged about any attention that Pandora gave them. She was too much for them. She was too much for the world!' Iris added, raising her voice. 'Most beautiful girl, woman, this village has ever seen.'

The coffee with her two friends on the veranda with a sea view was not Arianna's only social coffee of the evening. Arianna found herself outside lady Ophelia's bungalow gazing at the setting sun travelling down to meet the Ionian Sea. In exactly an hour it would spread out majestic orange rays and color the sky and sea. Arianna wished she were at the pier relaxing, letting her mind and soul to take in nature's wonder. Another deep breath. '*One of many taken lately.*' She fixed her clothes and rang the doorbell.

'Who is it, now?' She overheard Ophelia grumble through the open kitchen window. The door opened and Ophelia's face revealed her surprise. 'Really?' she snapped. 'Send that young fool to get a confession out of me knowing well he would fail and now you come along. The big guns! So many crimes, yet outside old granny Ophelia's house you lot come.' She shook her head and exhaled loudly through her nostrils. Arianna smiled widely. She admired the generation of strong Greek women that came before her. She looked down at Ophelia's hands and red apron. Flour rested all around.

'Cooking a pie?'

Ophelia looked her straight in the eye. 'Of course. What would I be preparing? A cake? At this hour? To eat it late and see it sit on my thighs for the next few months. No, thank you.' She wiped her hands on her apron. 'A delicious, warm, nurturing, chicken pie for that poor mother I have in there, crying her little heart out all day.' Ophelia wandered into the kitchen and Arianna followed in silence. 'If you do not annoy me greatly with all this bullshit confession business and stay long enough for it to bake and settle, you might just get a piece.' Ophelia laughed and Arianna could not help but join in.

'You can relax, Mrs. Ophelia. Officer Leventi mentioned your previous conversation. I am completely satisfied with your answers. Honestly, I just want to solve the girl's murder case. I am here to see Melpomene.'

'News?'

Arianna shook her head. 'Just a bit of comfort to offer and maybe even manage a question or two if she's up to it?'

Ophelia placed an ice cold, homemade lemonade in front of her. She had a jug already prepared from the morning. 'Made with my own lemons from my back yard.' The kitchen was hot and the air thick due to the working oven, the lack of an air-conditioning unit and the small lone window that welcomed no breeze. 'Is it really necessary you speak with her? The woman is broken like a swallow with a snapped neck. She is dying inside. Can't your questions wait until...'

'I have already waited too long. Most of the times, details float around in our minds in the beginning but then vanish to the back and are hard to retrieve.' She took a much-needed refreshing sip. She let the ice slip along her dry lips. 'What if she mentions something that helps me catch her daughter's killer? Would it not be a shame to let such info remain unknown?'

Ophelia raised her eyes. 'You know best, Captain. Go into the living room and I'll try go get her for you.'

Two large three-sitter sofas conquered most of the room. The living room was cooler due to its ceiling fan and large windows opened to the west. The sea breeze journeyed unobstructed into the space. The square cherry-wood coffee table housed Ophelia's knitting Above the fireplace were multiple frames with snapshots from moments long gone. Arianna picked up the one with the golden frame. The one with the wedding picture. Ophelia looked stunning. A healthy looking barely adult Ophelia with a smile that overshadowed the sun lingering above the chapel. *'The years go by so fast.'*

Arianna heard footsteps in the distance. She quickly placed the photograph back in place and turned toward the door. An ashen Melpomene appeared. Shaking, she made her way toward the sofa and fell back onto it. Her hollow eyes and blank expression shocked Arianna. *'That's how I would be if I ever lost Timothy.'* A shiver ventured down her spine. *'I'd rather die than live in a world without him.'*

Arianna approached the grieving mother and knelt by her side. 'Melpomene, I cannot even imagine the hell you are going through. I mostly came to check in on you. Let you know I am here for you.'

'And what else?' A weak, fragile voice.

Arianna looked up.

'You said mostly. That means you have more reasons to be here. Just tell me. Did you find the beast?'

Arianna stroked Melpomene's hand. 'No, but the entire force is working relentlessly toward such a goal. I will bring you justice, Melpomene.'

Melpomene sniggered. 'Justice? For whom? Will I get my baby back? No.'

Arianna found herself controlling another deep breath and the sigh that normally followed. 'Melpomene, I do not wish to torment you any more than the hell you are already in. I'll be quick and out of your way as soon as possible. Do you know anyone who for whatever reason would want to harm Pandora?'

Melpomene shook her head.

'Is there any detail, as insignificant as it may seem, that you think I should know? Anything strange or bizarre that happened lately? Was Pandora herself these days?'

Tears slithered down Melpomene's cheeks. 'My angel... So full of energy. I could even say she was happier than ever. Finishing school. Her entire life, in front of her...' She choked but fought to get the words out. 'And that bastard cut her thread. I will never see her marry, have kids. She never even travelled outside of Greece.' Melpomene began to sob, and Arianna sat by her side and took her by the shoulders.

'There, there...'

Melpomene raised her hands towards the heavens. 'And to believe that Parga was good for us. That we finally found a place to call home. Lord, why did you bring us here? Why?'

Arianna stroked Melpomene's back as she built up the courage to utter the next question. 'You are on her list of secrets, yet she wrote nothing about you. The website promises that your secret would have been revealed soon. Do you have an idea of what your daughter was going to write?'

Melpomene stopped crying and sat motionless. 'Who knows? I have no dark secrets in my life like the rest on the list. Nothing of importance. I once told her that when she was a toddler, I stole from a bakery and a local grocery a couple of times. I had no money, you see, and Pandora was hungry. She was really shocked by this as I am a religious person and told her off often, trying to help her grow up a good Christian. Maybe that is what she was going to write about. I can't think of any other sins of mine.'

Suddenly, the doorbell rang, and Arianna's cell phone started to ring.

'I'll get the door,' Ophelia mumbled as she trudged by the open door. Arianna looked down at her phone. The name Jacob Petsa flashed upon the screen. '*The coroner...*'

'I have to take this. Sorry.'

Melpomene did not raise her head. She wiped her tears, said, 'do what you must,' and picked up the Bible that rested on the side table next to the sofa. Arianna dashed outside. 'Hello? One minute, please.' Arianna quickly exited to the garden. Just as she was about to step outside, her eye caught a glimpse of the visitor. The smartly dressed lady with the small specs settled on her Roman nose. The Mayor of Parga.

'Is this a bad time, Captain?' Jacob Petsa's rough voice carried his annoyance.

'I do apologize. I was with the victim's mother.' Arianna replied as she walked over to the edge of the blooming garden. She rested on the white fence and saw the half-sank sun, ready to disappear into the calm summer sea. '*Guess, I will be witnessing the sunset after all.*'

'Fine, fine,' the coroner grumbled as if chewing something. 'I called straight away. Could not wait until the morning and so-called office hours. This couldn't wait!'

'I'm all ears, sir. What did the autopsy show?'

'The autopsy is not what's important here.' A brief

pause followed. 'I can't believe, I, a coroner, just said that. The autopsy results will be faxed to you. It is pretty straight forward with many details that I hope will help you catch the killer. Anyway, why am I rambling about that? Listen to this!'

Arianna paced up and down the long garden, nodding as she went. She listened carefully and bit her lips.

'Thank you, sir,' she said and ended the call. She turned and faced the house. She exhaled gathered air, rubbed her chest and sighed. Her heart beat irregularly once again.

Inside, she could hear the mayor talking to Melpomene, offering her full support and '*blah, blah, blah,*' Arianna thought.

'What a terrible incident, Captain,' the mayor said as Arianna entered the room. 'The killer must be caught!'

'We are investigating, ma'am and we will have results.' Arianna knelt by Melpomene and took her hands into hers. 'Melpomene, there is no easy way to say this, I know you asked me, but the coroner just confirmed that the body does indeed belong to Pandora.'

Melpomene's tears grew in size and formed new rivulets upon her pale skin. She shook her head. 'They do say hope dies last...I believe this is that exact moment. I will never hold my baby again.'

Arianna stroked her hair. 'If it is any comfort, as small as it may be, he did say that death occurred at once. She did not suffer.'

Melpomene looked her straight in the eye. 'How is that possible? Did you see her upon that anchor? All twisted and messed up and beaten and bruised and mutilated and disfig-ured and...' Melpomene let out an animal like cry.

'No, no. Melpomene, my dear, no. That is why I am telling you this. She did not suffer like that. Like what you

are imagining. The coroner said she died from the first...
err... blow to the head caused by a great fall most likely.'

'She fell?'

Arianna did not turn towards the mayor. 'Her injuries
are from a great fall, Melpomene. Her cuts and bruises
came after she died. Chase those awful thoughts away.'

Melpomene looked toward the Mayor. 'She did not fall.
She was pushed. Someone put her on that bloody steel!'

The Mayor starred at her feet and did not say another
word.

'I promise I will get to the bottom of this. Trust the
police. I will bring you justice, Melpomene.'

Chapter Twenty-One

Adrian drove through the dark pine forest that bordered the short wild-domed hills that were the background of Parga. The forest ran for miles across the valley and even conquered the precipitous mountains of the region. Adrian loved driving in the summer. Owner of a strong sense of smell, having his windows down as he drove through the forest at night was a must. The cold air flew through the car, settling on his skin, cooling his sweat-producing pores. The intense pine scent crawled up his nostrils, hypnotizing his brain. His favorite aroma in the world. He switched off the radio and let the forest provide the soundtrack to his drive. He knew well that his colleagues at the station thought he was crazy living out in a log cabin in the middle of the forest and *forced* to drive every day half an hour to work (everyone walked everywhere in the small seaside town), but Adrian would not change it for the world. Adrian turned left and journeyed down an old country road. His cabin came into view. He had set two porch lights to switch on automatically at eight o'clock sharp. A car was parked outside of his house. It was a blue Maserati Ghibli. Adrian whistled in amazement. 'He never said he was rich. Poor car coming down *these* roads...'

Adrian parked his Toyota Auris, easily one of the most common cars in Greece, in his wooden garage. Adrian quickly took his phone into his hand and texted Arianna that he had interviewed all the boys in Pandora's year and all confirmed what Apollo and Nicholas had revealed. A full report would be ready in the morning. As he typed, the short man in the expensive vehicle got out and stood nervously by his ride. He waited for Adrian to approach.

'Hi! Adrian, right?' He extended his hand.

Adrian shook it. 'Nice to finally meet you in person, Mario. Did you find the place okay?'

The man with the blue eyes nodded. 'Could not have been easier with your pinpoint. How did we ever live before Google maps, right?' he said and chuckled.

'I feel bad for you bringing such a beauty along these *streets.*'

The man waved his hand. 'No worries at all. You're worth it. My God, you're so handsome, it's like looking at a Photoshop. I mean, most pics on Grinder are quite tampered with. But you, boy, you're a marvel!'

Adrian laughed out loud. 'Come on. Let's get inside. I brought Chinese. Your profile said it was your favorite.'

'Handsome *and* considerate. I do believe I am in for a real treat tonight.'

Adrian grabbed his bulge and rubbed it gently. 'Oh, you are in for *many* treats tonight!'

The morning sun came in through the white curtain with ease. It was summer and even forests could not stop sun rays from invading the one-bedroom cabin. The light found the two men naked in bed, heavily sleeping in each other's arms. Mario's head rested upon Adrian's broad shaved chest. Suddenly, the alarm set on his cell phone broke the tranquillity of the high-ceiling room. Adrian opened his eyes and smiled at the man sleeping so close to him. It had been months since they first met online. He had been looking forward to this night. Mario opened his eyes slowly.

'Sorry,' Adrian said in a whispery manner. 'I have to get to work. Stay. Please stay. You did say you took days off work. Stay. Netflix and chill. Read one of my books.' Adrian pointed to his large wooden bookcase. Its four shelves featured books from a variety of genres. Adrian, an avid reader, was proud of his bookcase. It was a prized possession not only for the content of its shelves but for the fact that he built it himself with a little bit of help from a YouTube video about being a carpenter. 'I will be back in four hours. I put in for a half day.'

The man caressed his face. 'Wow, you're a morning talker. I didn't have you for the type. Go, Mr. Policeman. I will be here waiting eagerly.' He raised his head and kissed Adrian on the lips. 'Now, let me sleep. You wore me in well,' he said and turned over, covering his entire body with the grey sheets.

The morning drive to work took place with windows closed. Only the A/C could save him now from the menacing heat.

'Good morning. Looking very happy today,' the police station's front secretary commented as he walked in, coffee and box of Bougatses in hand. Adrian realized he had a wide grin on his face. He probably carried it on his face all the way from his bed. His lips quickly transitioned to his usual flat line look, settling above his strong jaw.

'What are we celebrating?' Her gaze leapt across the room and focused on the white box in his large hands.

'*Me finally getting laid this year.*' Adrian continued walking. 'Err... these? Just some fine creamy pies that just came out of the oven as I was getting my coffee. Could not resist. Thought to sweeten everyone up.' He placed the box on her desk and opened it. He picked one up. 'Have one, or even two, and give one to our fine officers as they walk in.' And with a smile, a steamy coffee and a creamy pie, he walked off and headed straight to his desk. The five-page autopsy report of Pandora's lying in the fax machine's tray caught his eye. He looked over his shoulder. The Captain had not yet arrived. Adrian picked up the report and sat down in the first chair to his right.

'Parga's Jane Doe,' he read the title out loud and frowned. He skimmed over the paragraphs with speed. 'Cause of death... instantaneously... last meal, baked beans and Frankfurt sausages...foreign DNA found; woman's hair was under fingernail... many post-mortem hits to the face...' His eyes widened as he read that the victim had previously undergone an abortion procedure and was three weeks pregnant. Just then, the back door opened behind him. Arianna came through, smelling like tobacco. Adrian sprang up. 'The autopsy report is here!' He raised his hand and brought the papers to her eye level. 'I know. The coroner called me last night.'

'*So, that's why you are out there enjoying your morning cigarette and not in here reading your eyes out?*'

'You've read it all?'

'Nearly. I'm at the abortion and pregnancy. This could be our cause.'

Arianna nodded in agreement yet asked. 'How so?'

'What if her overly religious mother forced her to get it done? Melpomene's secret was never revealed on the website.'

Arianna walked into her office, leaving the door open behind her. 'You really have her capable of such an act? Especially since the girl was pregnant?'

'I doubt either knew about the pregnancy at three weeks. It would fit the way of death. Pushed from a great height. They could have been arguing and one thing led to another.'

Arianna smiled awkwardly as she sat down. 'I was with her yesterday. She truly is a broken woman. I just can't see her as killing her only daughter.'

'Moment of rage. Maybe that is why she is so broken.'

'Could be...'

Adrian left the report on the desk. 'Notice the title?'

'What about it?' Arianna's eyes looked down at the autopsy.

'Jane Doe?'

'Well, the coroner performed the autopsy before the blood results came back. The disfigured face left a tiny hint of doubt. But he confirmed that the dead body is indeed Pandora. I was at her mother's house when he called, and I had to be the one to tell Melpomene. Who, by the way, if she is your suspect, why would she beat the face so much after the girl died? Beat to the point of not recognizing her?'

Adrian straightened his posture. 'It makes sense. Either it happened from the fall or maybe the beating took place after the fall when Melpomene saw that she had killed her precious daughter and could not bear her looking back at her.'

Arianna placed her hands upon the desk. 'I like your

theory. Don't get me wrong with all my questioning. Let us roll with this for a minute. Why place her on the anchor then? For all to see?'

Adrian rubbed his chin; his fingers running among his four-day beard. 'That is a tricky one. Hmm, as punishment? A display to God. I'm going with the religious angle here.' He looked at the Captain. 'If not the mother, who does it for you?'

'Well, we do have a list of people offended by her.'

'None though admitted they knew what she was planning. They were oblivious to their secrets having been uncovered. Besides, the killer placed the box on the body. The killer wanted the secrets to be out. Again, this would go fine with my theory about the mother. Her secret was safe.'

Arianna nodded. 'Then, the list of boys she slept with. One of them was even going to be a father. A seventeen-year-old carries much rage, especially one that was dumped by her after revealing his family's secrets. And then, seeing her move on to the next guy? That would be enough to push anyone off the edge. Pun intended.'

Adrian did not reply. He had his head stuck in the report. 'You noticed the time of death? Bit wide is it not?'

'Six to twelve hours before she was discovered? It is harder to tell when it is under a day. Body still relatively warm and all. Fits with what her friends said. The last saw her around eleven at night after leaving a beach party they were at together.'

'Means she was killed nearly straight away after leaving the beach if we found her at the crack of dawn. Someone was watching her, maybe?'

'Could be. Fits my theory of it maybe being one the boys in her class. Though none admitted leaving the party. Most slept down at the beach.'

Chapter Twenty-Two

Timothy fell back on his bed. He grunted in displeasure, throwing his Playstation controller to the side and picking up his phone. He read the messages again. His friends informed him of their plans, inviting him, urging him to join them. Yet, he was grounded. Not punished but protected. At least, that is how his mother plainly put it. 'Stay in my love, until I sort things out.' Her words replayed in his mind. 'How dangerous can it be, mum? Come on, I can't stay locked up in here. It's summer!' he had retaliated.

'Going to the park... going for a kebab... meeting up at Dora's house... going swimming at Valtos beach,' he mumbled as he re-read his friends' various messages.

His phone beeped again as he held it. Antony, his best mate, the mayor's son had texted once again. 'Hey, bro. Mary wants to go hiking up to that pond near the caves you like. Thought it was going to be just the two of us (little Antony needs a blow lol), but she is bringing Margarita along as well! Please, please, please, come along and keep her friend busy! You like Margarita. She's into the same lame videogames you are, hahahaha! Come on, man! You owe me! You love me! Did I say please? Pleaseeeeeeeee!'

Timothy could not help but chuckle. He stood up, approached the window, pushed his blue curtain to the side and starred out. 'Fuck it, I'm going! Mum will never see me out in the forest.'

His pyjama bottoms fell to the floor and he ran toward his wardrobe. In a matter of minutes -all a teenage boy needs to dress- Timothy left his house. He texted his friend that he was on his way, placed his cell in the right pocket of his blue shorts and dashed out of their neighbohood. With his heart still pounding, he reached the outskirts of the forest, opposite the fire station. His three friends were already there. All in much-needed trainers, yet all with a backpack with everything needed for a swim in the shallow pond. Not much water flowing into it during the summer months. The waters in June were those remaining from spring's melted snow. The two boys hugged and exchanged wide smiles. 'Dude, I've missed you!'

'If only he was as romantic with me, too,' Mary joked.

Antony laughed out loud, and his skinny figure shook. 'You're my girlfriend, I care for you. But he is my best bro. I love him. Don't be jealous,' Antony teased her back as he wrapped his arm around her waist and led her into the forest.

'Maybe he can jerk you off then and save me the trouble!'

All laughed, though Timothy turned a slight shade of red. His first thought was that he would not mind. He had always been attracted to Antony. Drawn to his kind eyes and deep dimples. Having seen him naked, did not help matters. The image of his friend in the camp's shower room was a constant in his fantasies.

'Hot, isn't it?' he changed the subject.

'As always,' Margarita replied, grabbing his hand and walking ahead along the dirt path that snake lined through the majestic forest trees.

The pond was said to be a twenty-minute hike away from the main road. The strong athletic group of youths did it in under a quarter.

The light fell strong onto the waters as no trees managed to grow upon the rocks that surrounded the tarn nor upon the nearby caves. The girls stripped to their bright and colorful bikinis as the boys lay down the towels to place the girls' bags on. Both girls dipped their feet into the waters with care. 'Freezing as always!'

Soon, the boys, having thrown off their T-shirts and dropped their shorts, ran past them, splashing around and diving headfirst into the centre of the pond.

Their laughter and screams echoed through the vast lands covering the forest sounds of birds chipping happily and silencing crickets in fear.

The swim did not last long. Antony and Mary drew closer and began to kiss. Mary could feel the young man's erection upon her wet body. 'Calm down,' she whispered. 'Margarita will see you.'

'Then, let's head over to the cave for a bit of... privacy,' he answered, and his mischievous smile made Mary giggle. As the two hot-flashed lovers made their way to the cave, Timothy and Margarita sat upon one of the pond's many rocks and began to chat about how it was their last truly carefree summer. Studies and university lurked ahead.

The cave was dark. Faint light reached its depths. The air was cool compared to outside. Antony went ahead clearing the way by kicking twigs and piles of dried leaves to the side.

'I hope I don't see any spiders, mister! Or I will be screaming myself out of this shit hole!'

'Hey, it can hear you! You will hurt its feelings. The cave is not a shit hole, okay?'

'Yeah? It surely smells like one.'

She was right. Antony sniffed the air. A putrid smell journeyed towards them, growing stronger with their every step. Antony never smelt such an awful scent in any of his previous entries to his beloved cave, AKA his love nest.

Soon, Mary would be screaming herself out of the cave. But it was no spider that spooked her. Antony froze at the sight. A blond girl lay on the grounds before him. Blood had dried upon her face attracting the wildlife to her. Flies buzzed around her, ants and cave insects crawled upon her body, while rodents had surely taken bites out of her. A chunk was missing from her ear. Antony had never seen a dead body before. He took another step forward and even knelt to get a better look. With a twig he raised the girl's hair from her face. Her eyes were closed. He did not recognize the girl. She looked around his age. In spite of all the macabre, she looked serene. He did not expect her to be so.

'Antony?' Timothy's voice echoed through the tunnel-like cave. The boy stood up at once as if woken up from a bad dream. The nightmare lay before him. He ran out to the daylight. 'Call the cops. Call your mum, dude. There's a dead chick in there!'

The forest suddenly seemed darker to them. As if the sinister act that had taken place in the cave managed to venture out into the open and spread its darkness around them.

The two boys sat upon a large, flat, greyish rock under a tall cypress with their heads firmly looking down. Their angry Greek mothers would be arriving soon. Antony watched the parade of ants taking place just inches from his bare feet. Leaf after leaf, they worked tirelessly. Timothy's eyes were open but focused nowhere in particular. He rubbed his thumbs and breathed heavily. '*Why didn't I just listen to her and stay the hell home?*'

Meters away, under dark green leaves provided by an oak, Mary wept in Margarita's arms, still trembling from the shock. She had also never seen a dead body before. Margarita had. Just days ago. She closed her eyes and thought of their classmate, naked, thrown upon the anchor. '*We have a serial killer! In Parga!*' The thought jerked her spine.

'You said the girl in there was young?'

Mary's silence made her repeat her question. 'Huh? Yeah. Probably our age.' She sobbed, wiped her mouth and continued. 'Young and blonde just like you.'

Another shiver. '*Just like Pandora.*' Margarita felt unsafe. Her eyes travelled around. So much darkness amongst the trees. Many shadows. '*Could the killer be watching? Oh, God, who is calming who here?*'

The siren from the police car approaching startled them momentarily yet brought peace to their worried minds.

The boys stood up at once and remained at attention as Arianna and Adrian came down the path towards them. Officer Leventi followed them, yet before reaching the opening of the pond, he paused and turned around. A black Mercedes had parked behind them. 'Keep the Mayor and any other parents back,' Arianna shouted. Leventi nodded which Antony found hilarious for two reasons. One, because he nodded to someone with whom he had no eye contact with. Two, because he wanted to see if the officer would manage to stop his 'force of nature' mother.

Arianna tripped on a root that did not know that its rightful place was in the ground. She lost her balance yet did not fall. She spread her arms and governed her body. 'Oh, for fuck's sake!'

'*Great! She is in a mood as well.*' Timothy could not stand her gaze. A look that carried her vexation and disappointment toward him.

Adrian stood by the cave's entrance, wore his white gloves, placed plastic bags on his feet, turned on his flashlight and entered. He had to duck slightly but as he went the cave gained height allowing him to walk with a straight back.

'So, who was it that found the body?' Her professional tone caught Timothy by surprise. He was expecting the mother tone yelling at him.

'That would be me, ma'am. With Mary.' The girls had approached and stood by the two tall boys.

'Did anyone else go into the cave?'

'No, Mrs. Kontou.'

Arianna took out her little notebook and her silver Parker pen out of her pocket. 'All right, then. Timothy escort Margarita home and go straight to home, too. Both keep your mouths shut. I need no press or worried parents up here. We have had every reporter possible outside of the station this morning asking about Pandora. I hope this is a simple task that you will manage to follow, mister Timothy.' She stood to the side and pointed to the path. Timothy and Margarita dashed forward without saying a word. 'Now, you two. Sit.'

Arianna knelt by the two clearly shocked teens. She placed her hand on Mary's knee. 'Relax, my dear. I understand that the sight you saw in there was not the prettiest. It was probably the worst thing your young eyes have ever witnessed. But it is crucial that you focus and give me the facts. Every detail. Everything you did and what exactly you saw, okay?'

Both nodded. Antony spoke first.

As the two teenagers retold their passage in the cave, Adrian had reached the dead body. He looked down at the fully clothed woman. She was most likely around twenty years old, give or take a year or two. Hiking boots and rough brown shorts. She was prepared for the forest. She looked foreign. Something about her sharp eyes and small nose did not sit well with Adrian's instincts. No blood on the walls. Adrian's light journeyed around. *'She wasn't killed in here.'* He turned his attention to the grounds leading up to the spot. A drop. Another crimson drop. And another. A lock of golden hair tangled on a lone bush. He looked at the small scratches on her legs and marks on her clothes. *'She was dragged in here.'* He began to photograph everything.

Yelling from outside echoed into the cave.

'I am the Mayor! Let me through!'

He could not make out what officer Leventi was replying. He did not care. *'Not my monkeys, not my circus.'* He was busy collecting evidence. The lock of hair was carefully placed into a see-through nylon bag.

'Arianna! Captain! You can't interrogate my son without an adult present!'

'His eighteenth birthday party was months ago. Please, cool down and stay put. This is a crime scene. Antony will be with you shortly! Now, let us do our jobs.'

Phoebe reluctantly stopped trying to pass Leventi and took a couple of small steps backwards. 'Five minutes! You have five.'

Arianna finished with the statements and looked at them. 'Who did you call besides your mum?'

'No one, ma'am.'

'I... I haven't even touched my phone yet. It's over there in my bag,' Mary said in a sulky, tired voice.

'Good. Keep this on the hush. Get your things and go home.'

Arianna walked up to the mayor.

'Take the kids home and please, please don't let this get out. The last thing we need at the moment is panic. Parents searching frantically for their daughters.'

The mayor nodded in agreement. 'Yes, yes. Of course. You're right. Oh, Lord. This is the last thing our town needs! A second dead body during tourist season!' Phoebe felt how insensitive her words may have come across and quickly asked, 'Who is the poor girl?'

Arianna shrugged. 'The kids did not know her.'

'Was her face... like... Pandora's? Unrecognisable?'

'No.'

Arianna turned and walked toward the cave as the two teens ran to the luxury car. The mayor kissed her son and asked him repeatedly if he was okay.

Adrian stood by the pond. 'Time to call the medical examiner and his team?'

Arianna frowned. 'We can collect the evidence. I trust you took photographs. The coroner only needs the body and samples. Call for the local ambulance. We will get the body to him. Let me have a look inside and I will call doctor Jacob and let him know to prepare for another body. God, what is happening here?'

'Seems like we have a serial killer on our hands,' Leventi commented as his boss walked into the darkness.

Adrian ended his call with Parga's lone hospital and

turned toward Leventi. 'I was waiting for you to come in today. I have a job for you.'

'Yeah, I was running late today...' he started to excuse himself.

'No problem. We were going over the autopsy report of Pandora's with the Captain. A woman's hair was found in one of her fingernails. It could be nothing, but we need you to collect a sample from each of her close friends, most importantly Iris and Nefeli, and then from all the girls that we have listed as having been with Pandora the twenty-four hours before her death. It must be done today. The lab needs to compare the samples ASAP.'

Leventi nodded and looked ready to walk off. 'What about her mother and the old lady?'

Adrian smiled. 'Great thinking, officer. But not needed. Arianna was there when the coroner called her. She took samples without them even knowing.'

'I doubt I can go round cutting hair unnoticed.'

'Say it's for their own good. Say it is standard procedure as to keep them off the suspect list. Lie if you must, if they refuse. Say we have a warrant. People love that word, movies and all.'

Adrian cracked his knuckles and stretched out his arms. 'Bloody back pain.' His thought went to the man waiting in his bed. *'Fuck if I will be home in a few hours now.'* He watched Leventi walk down the path back to town, leaving them the one patrol car they all came in. 'What about the mother and the old lady?' He repeated Leventi's question and scratched his jaw.

As Arianna came out of the cave, the ambulance came quietly and parked behind them. 'No sirens,' Adrian had told them.

Arianna placed her hand on his shoulder. 'Isn't it today you wanted to get off early? Got a thing, you said?'

'This is more important, boss.'

'I agree. But I've got this. I will stay here and search around to see where the body came from.'

Adrian nodded sternly. 'I've sent Leventi for the hair samples.'

'Great. That will take him all day. The post office will be closed to send out the samples late evening. You deserve the day off as you requested. Come in first thing in the morning and send out the samples to the lab. The coroner will not be in touch with us today. Go. Be human.'

'After I investigate the abortion, Captain. Remember? This morning when we were going over the report, we said Leventi will go for the hair and I will pay a visit to the two gynaecologists in town.'

'Of course. Get that done and clock out. Call me if she had the abortion at one of them and if they said anything to help us out.'

Chapter Twenty-Three

Arianna stood alone. The quiet offered by the forest was interrupted by a gust of wind that flew by, unsettling dried leaves and forcing the yellow police tape blocking entry to the long cave, to dance to its beat. The thin ribbon snapped as it went back and forth. The police captain knelt by the cool pond and splashed her face with a small amount of water.

She tried to put her thoughts into order.

'A second body? Another girl?'

She repeated the two questions and just could not accept the facts.

The body had not been dead long. Just a few days at most. She was probably murdered around the same time. *'One blow to the head...'*

Her thoughts reminded her that she had to call the coroner. As Parga and most villages nearby had either a small police department or none at all, the top medical examiner of the region was in charge of forensic services.

Arianna took out her phone but looked around the forest before dialling the number. The vast green relaxed her tired eyes.

'Hello?'

The medical examiner's voice sounded far away. She could hear metal objects clanging together. 'Yes, Doctor Petsa, this is Captain Arianna Kontou.'

'Hmm, yes, yes.' His voice came closer. It sounded as if he was chewing. The image of the cold morgue and sharp medical knifes faded in her mind and a homey kitchen with a knife and fork replaced it. 'Caught your killer yet?'

'Unfortunately, not yet, sir. And we have had another body. Another girl, most likely around the same age.'

'It will be a few hours before I can get up there...'

'No need, sir. My forensic team dealt with the scene. The body is coming to you by ambulance...'

'You should have called me. The position the body is found in is crucial to...'

'I will email you all the photographs taken. It was in a hard-to-get-in cave, sir.'

'Fine, fine,' he grunted. 'I will head to the morgue and wait. Get them pics to me.'

By the time, Arianna could utter a thank you and wish him a good day, the coroner had ended the call.

———————

Leventi drove with his window open. He had walked back to the station in a hurry as to take his personal vehicle. He pushed the station's front door open and stood still for a second as to let the inside's cold air settle on his red face and sweaty palms.

'There he is. Look. Cream pies. Adrian brought them in this morning. Not celebrating anything apparently,' Pauline said, pointing to the box on her desk.

'No time,' he replied and walked straight past the front desk. Out of the secretary's sight, he ran the distance to the cupboards by Adrian's office. He picked up a box of gloves, a roll of plastic bags, swabs, a sharp pair of scissors and a small forensic kit.

Soon, he was driving out of the parking in his blue saloon with his car windows down. He felt important and he smiled at the thought.

A short-for-a-Greek guy, Leventi was also quiet and shy for a Mediterranean man. The youngest of five boys, he never enjoyed the spotlight growing up, neither at home nor at school. His father passed away at the age of sixty-four when the youngest Leventi brother was only thirteen. His mother shrivelled up, hit hard by the loss of the love of her life a mere year before retirement. All her hopes and dreams for Greek island cruises and gardening together, vanished as they lowered her husband six feet under. It did not help that she did not yet have grandkids, though her two oldest boys had married. The following year the first grandchild came into the picture. The first of seven that followed in the years to come. All her attention fell to helping with their upbringing. All her sons, but her youngest, married, stayed close to home and produced offspring. She felt blessed and kept herself well busy. Leventi though felt that he had lost both his parents that year. Years of loneliness were mistaken and excused by 'He keeps to himself. He is a quiet boy. He likes it this way.' Leventi studied hard for his university exams... and failed. He needed purpose. He needed something that his mother would mention in her coffees with friends and family. He enrolled in the police academy the following year after studying again for a year with that goal in mind. Now, as he drove along, his mind travelled to his town of Ioannina and his family. *'When this case is solved and becomes nation-wide news, I will call her and let her know I was a part of it. Her son helped solve a serial killer case.'*

He parked his vehicle in the only municipality parking in Parga, happy to have found shade under the branches of a row of tall fir trees. He stepped outside, with his back up straight and paraded down the road with his forensic kit in hand. He had memorized the list of people he had to visit and had his planned route outlined in his mind. He nodded to fellow villagers as he went and acted relaxed and casual but inside, he was practicing his lines on repeat. *'Good day... standard procedure... warrant... thank you for your co-operation... have a great day...'*

Many hours later, Leventi returned to his car feeling proud of himself. He had taken every single sample requested of him. He placed his case on the back seat and switched on the vehicle's A/C. Before returning to the station, he called his mother. The phone call was a success. 'I am proud of you, son,' she had said after hearing the retelling of his day.

He was about to put the gear in reverse when a tap on the window made him jump. He looked outside at the young woman with the short red dress. It was Katie, the eldest sister of Iris. Theirs were the last home he visited as it was nearest to the car park. Iris was her usual moody teenage self and reluctantly agreed to her DNA sampling. Her sister had sat behind their mother and fixed her eyes on Leventi. He smiled at her once and quickly turned his attention back to his mission under the disapproving gaze of their mother's.

Leventi rolled down his window and greeted the girl.

'Well, hello again mister officer,' she said cheerily and leaned on the car. 'Finished for the day?'

'Finished with the samples, yes. But got to get these back to the station ASAP so they can be shipped off to the lab.'

'You're cute when you're serious, Gregory.'

The compliment caught him off guard. Out of the many adjectives he had heard in his twenty-eight years on the planet, cute was not one of them.

'I wonder if I will get a chance to see you... not so serious,' she continued.

Leventi placed his hand upon hers. 'That could be arranged. I get off work at six. How about a coffee around seven? Give me a chance to change and I will pick you up... from here?' He fought hard to keep his voice as relaxed as possible. He had not been on a date in years. The last time he felt a naked woman by his side, he had paid for it and the twenty minutes of bliss were not enough compared to the weeks of self-loathing that followed the incident.

'You don't have to change for me.'

'Guys in a uniform, huh?'

Katie laughed out loud. It was a contagious laughter. A sweet melodic laugh.

'Something like that. No problem. Change and yes, we can meet here at seven. I'm sure I will have more chances to enjoy you in your uniform.'

Leventi watched the twenty-five-year-old brunette walk down the path towards her house. *'Jesus Christ! What a body! Well done, Gregory. Real smooth! Don't you dare fucking screw this up! Wow, what a day. What an amazing day!'*

The sun hit the golden plate hard. Adrian squinted his round eyes as to read the sign. 'Dr. Eugene Karafoti, obstetrician and gynaecologist.' The coolness residing on his skin began to fade quickly as he stepped out onto the street. He dashed up the five steps before the entrance and entered the four-storey building. No lift available meant he had to take the stairs. With relief he entered the reception of the small clinic and let his body welcome the cold A/C air. A woman with high cheeks, red nails and dyed platinum hair smiled as he walked in. A warm red lipstick smile. The genuine smiles from the over-thirties raised in small villages. 'Good morning, officer Adrian. How are you today?'

'I'm fine, Eleonora. Is the doctor free?'

As he asked, the heavy wooden doors to his right opened and a woman with dark hair and high heels came out, smiled to them both and approached the secretary as to pay for her visit.

'He is now, officer,' Eleonora said with her bubbly tone and turned her attention to her client.

Adrian walked into the office, closing the door behind him. The bald doctor with the white moustache came towards him with his hand extended. He had a firm grip. 'Sit down, officer. I believe you called about some questions you may have about poor Pandora.'

Adrian sat down opposite the large desk and faced the tall man. 'Yes, doctor. I believe the girl was your client?'

The doctor nodded in reply. 'Her and her mother first came here a couple of years ago. They brought their files with them from their previous doctor. I only saw them a few times. I am not sure what it is you are looking for and if I am in a position to reveal such details about my clients.'

'I understand. But it is vital to our case and the girl is

dead. All I want to know is if you performed an abortion on her?'

The doctor was slightly taken back. 'An abortion?' He scratched his thick moustache. 'On Pandora?'

'Yes.'

'No, sir. The girl always came with her mother and her mother insisted as her daughter was underage that she was present in every check up. She believed her daughter a virgin. I knew that Pandora was sexually active, but I never saw any signs of any pregnancy. One day, as I was talking with her mother, I got Eleonora to talk to the young girl about contraception and diseases and such. The mother is really religious and strict, you see.'

Adrian wrote down on his phone. 'And was the mother sexually active?'

The doctor shook his head.

'Is there any chance the other gynaecologist in town performed the abortion? Or could the abortion have been done years ago, before they came to Parga? Would you be able to tell?'

Again, the man shook his head. 'No way. I would have noticed and the last time I saw them was only a week ago. She was not pregnant and never was.'

Adrian stood up and thanked the doctor for his help. He starred at the doctor as they shook hands. He did not like the worried look on his face. 'Is something the matter, doc?'

The doctor exhaled loudly with a sigh and turned towards his window. 'It isn't right of me to say something but am old and retiring soon and this is a murder case. Every detail matters.'

Adrian walked toward the doctor and stood by his side. The office had a massive window overseeing the bay, providing a stunning beauty of a view colored by all shades of Greek blue. 'I'm intrigued, doctor. You have my full attention.'

'You cannot mention my name, obviously, but there is something on my mind ever since those two came to town.' He paused and tapped the window gently. 'They presented themselves to us as mother and daughter, yet Melpomene has no signs of ever giving birth!'

Chapter Twenty-Four

THE PAST IV

Demetra was fourteen when she walked down her church's aisle as a flower girl for her stepmother. Just a year had passed since the barbeque meal in honour of Helka. Demetra could not lie to herself. She disliked the Finnish woman with the cold face and the love for wine. Yet, Demetra felt that she was God-sent. Her father never came to her room again since he had met the pretty woman with the cheekbones of a professional model. Demetra accepted her as her father's lover but would never accept her as a mother. Mothers were not rude. Mothers did not boss their children nor order them about. Mothers did not curse. Mothers were not lazy and took care of their homes. At least her own mother did when she was alive. All Helka seem to enjoy was alcohol and Demetra's father.

They married on a hot day in the beginning of July. Helka wished to set off for her honeymoon straight after the wedding.

'Then we will marry when schools close so we can send Demetra to an aunt of mine in the village.'

'Maybe she can stay there a bit longer than just the ten days that we will be in Italy? Maybe for the summer? I want my husband to myself.'

'We will see, my dear.'

'No.' Helka shook her head. 'Make it happen.'

The conversation replayed inside Demetra's mind as she threw rose petals along the carpet that run along the center of Saint George's Church. Her aunt had agreed to keep her for three weeks only, much to Hell-ka's disappointment.

By the end of the night, most guests had departed after hours of dancing, eating and drinking. The couple of the night was still on the dance floor, drunk in each other's arms hours after midnight. Demetra's young eyes ventured further downwards with every yarn. She saw a quiet dark corner in the back of the tavern. A table that had no guests left around it and had been cleaned by the waiters that rushed up and down trying to please the partying crowd. Demetra connected three chairs and lay down behind the table. Soon, she had drifted away in Morpheus's arms. The same recurring dream visited her. Demetra sat on the back of a tall majestic unicorn with bright white wings like mythology's Pegasus and was flying above Greece. Away from it all. Up to Heaven and her angel of a mother. Paradise was so bright. Demetra opened her eyes, and the light made her tired eyes burn. She sat up and cracked her back. It was daytime and she awoke in the back of the tavern. The place was deserted and closed. She looked at the clock on the wall. It was thirteen minutes past nine. She had slept through the night. The tavern was spotless. The dancefloor had been swept and mopped. No one had noticed the teenage girl asleep behind the table in the back. Anger brought color to the pale cheeks. Her father left without her. Demetra stood up and rushed straight to the bathroom. Thankfully, the doors were unlocked. The exit doors though were not. A green phone sat on the bar's glass counter. Demetra picked up the receiver and dialled her house number. It rang and it rang. No answer. 'Bloody idiots are drunk and asleep!' She slammed down the phone and contemplated her options. 'Call the police?' She shook her head. 'Dad will hit the shit out of me. Call the tavern's owner to open up? What for? I can open any window...'

Demetra jumped out of the window and closed it behind her. She was miles away from home. It was the longest walk of her life. She walked with her head down avoiding looks by everyone that lay eyes on the young girl with the long turquoise dress, the messed-up hair with glitter shining in it under the sizzling sun, the too-much make-up for a kid and the blue high heels. Her feet were killing her, cutting into her flesh. When she reached the high street, she took them off and continued her route for home barefoot. Two hours later, she stood exhausted and breathless outside her apartment's door. She placed her ear on the brown door. Silence. They were both still in bed. She lifted the fake cactus out of the white pot to her right and pick up the spare emergency key. Soon, she was in her room and fell back on her bed. She remained still for half an hour until she felt her feet strong enough to welcome back her weight. She stood up, undressed and headed to the shower. It was early evening when her father and his new wife emerged from their den. They found Demetra eating cereal on the living room sofa in front of the television. 'Good morning,' her father said and stroked her hair. 'Fun night, huh?'

Both were clueless of her ordeal. Neither remembered retuning home without her. Demetra never told them anything about that night. She just turned cold with them. Both thought it must be because of the wedding and put it down to jealousy and fear of losing her father's time. The only time she smiled at them was a year later when they announced Helka's pregnancy. The idea of having a baby in the house excited Demetra. She knew Helka would be an awful and unfit mother and she looked forward to having a baby brother or sister to care for.

Helka was three months into her pregnancy when she lost the baby.

Demetra remembered the night well. It was a chilly night for mid-October. Charcoal clouds have gathered yet seemed undecided as to release rain. Demetra had enjoyed a nice hot bath, compared to her hasty showers of week-nights. She wore only her beige bathrobe and had dried her wet hair. She stood by the window staring out. Two cats were arguing over a piece of trash. The strong wind had turned over many black trash bins, providing the strays with many valuable meals.

'And yet, they fight over the same piece of chicken...'

Demetra looked up at the starless sky. She hoped for rain. She loved to watch the droplets land on her window and form rivulets as they descended. She also loved being home alone. Her father and Helka had left in a hurry hours ago. They did not even bother to say goodbye or inform her of where they were headed. She just heard their voices in the living room and the slamming of the front door.

Disappointed at the lack of rain, she turned on the radio to LOVE FM and settled on her bed with her new book. 'Miss DoReMi,' she read the title. She was enjoying, with slight envy, the vivid description of Parisian life when she heard the front door opening. Helka was crying and Demetra heard her run into her bedroom and lock the door. Demetra placed the book on her bedside table, switch off the radio and stood up as to get dressed. As she opened her bathrobe, her father entered her room without knocking. His eyes fell upon her. She quickly covered her body.

'Father, what's wrong?' His eyes were red. Swollen. Restless.

He approached her and took her in his arms. 'There is no easy way to say this, my dear Demetra. We lost the baby.'

Demetra liked the expression, *my knees turned into jelly*. She found the saying hilarious as a child. Now, nothing was funny about her not being able to maintain her balance. She fell into her father's embrace and wept. He stroked her hair. 'There, there. Calm down. Shit like this, unfortunately, happens way too often than it should. Go get some sleep.'

He said no more. He turned and walked out of her room.

Demetra wore her pyjamas, switched off her ceiling light, leaving only her nightstand lamp to provide her with enough light as to continue reading her novel.

An hour past and her eyes began to fail her. Her book rested back in its rightful place and as Demetra was about to switch off her colorful lamp, her door opened and closed. Her father came close. He was wearing only a pair of black boxers. His erection was visible, and his breath smelled of cheap whiskey.

'Dad, I think you should go to your bedroom,' she said in a trembling whisper. 'Helka, is waiting for you,' she raised her voice.

'Sssshhh, relax, my dear. I need a hug. Your hug.'

He came close and lay on the bed beside her. 'Dad, go to your wife.'

'She won't have me. She locked herself in. The couch is so uncomfortable. Don't turn your father away.'

He turned her to her side and spooned her from behind.

He held her close. He held her tight. He kissed her neck, and his fingers ran along her leg.

'I'm not a child anymore. I will scream,' she threatened.

'And where will that get you? Have me arrested, will you? Helka will kick you out. You're going to live on the streets. An orphan rat? You will be raped and sold as a whore out there. Here, you have only me. Your father's warm loving embrace. I treat you as a lady.' His right hand squeezed her throat hard. 'Don't you dare threaten me again, child. I brought you into this word, I will take you out of it.' He slowly entered her. Demetra shivered and fought back tears. Her eyes fell on her alarm clock. She followed the thin clock hand round and round. She counted the seconds. All one hundred and fifty-two of them. She remained still as he pulled out and rolled to the other side. He was asleep within minutes. Demetra, on the other hand, could not sleep. She was already in a nightmare. A nightmare that repeated itself for four nights straight. He would show up drunk after Helka had fallen asleep. Always in his underwear. Always ready. Always with a sickening line of his perverted sense love.

'Dad, you have Helka now...'

'She is just a mere star, my dear. A man's sky can have many stars, but none shine as bright as the sun. And when I'm with my sun, all the other stars vanish.'

Demetra journeyed further into herself during that week. Her prayers were the only thing in her life offering her strength and courage.

She prayed for salvation. She prayed for a second pregnancy. She prayed for a short life, for her or him.

Looking back, one might say, God answered her prayers.

Chapter Twenty-Five

Adrian stepped out of the shade provided by a tall twisted centenarian olive tree outside of Parga's second gynaecologist's office and beeped his car open. The small clinic was housed in a renovated stone building. Mere decades ago, it was a warehouse for grapes.

The doctor had provided him with no new info. Pandora had never been a patient of hers. Neither had Melpomene. Adrian picked up the water bottle he had left in his vehicle. It was near boiling point. He took a needed sip as to water his dry lips and threw the plastic bottle on the passenger's chair. His eyes were set on the kiosk across the street. Its row of fridges was inviting. The ice-cold Mythos beer was alluring. Adrian switched off the engine and dashed the twenty meters needed to refresh his throat. The Greek midday sun showed no mercy, especially during July and August.

'Morning, Master Adrian,' the old man with the deep wrinkles said in a croaky voice.

'Good morning, mister Yianni,' Adrian replied to the

owner sitting comfortably on his high stool with the blue cushion.

'Drinking on the job?' he jokingly asked. 'Don't blame you, laddie. Dead girl on the anchor, the mayor having an affair, rotten meat sold and that teacher caging up her own flesh and blood. Tsk, tsk, tsk. I would be buying two bottles if I were you.'

'Add in another dead girl, an abortion and a fake mother and give me three!'

Adrian chuckled. 'I'm off the clock, sir Yianni. Half day today.' It was the truth. Adrian's mind flew to the man waiting for him in his cabin. Yet, he sensed that he would not be heading home just yet. Baked beans and German sausages were floating around in his mind. He drank his beer in just two slurps.

He texted Mario that he was sorry, but he would be just a bit late and that he would be bringing lunch with him. 'Do you have any allergies or preferences?' Adrian read as he typed the words. 'And... send.'

Just seven minutes later, he was parking his vehicle outside of lady Ophelia's house. He looked down at his phone. 'Surprise me, big boy. I pretty much eat everything. Smiley emoji,' he read the text message. He read it twice, smiling both times. Adrian placed his sweaty from the steering wheel palms on the A/C's exits. He gazed out the window to his right and whistled. 'What a sea view.' The turquoise waters running and meeting the clear deep blue sky. 'A sure delight, but I wouldn't change my green forest and mountains for the world.' He rubbed his face with his large hands. 'Now, stop talking to yourself and get to business.' He turned his gaze to his right. He could see Ophelia through her kitchen window. The woman was chopping up something. 'Strange that she did not hear me park.'

As he stepped out of the vehicle, he realized why. Loud music came from the house. A sweet melody that reminded Adrian of his childhood and his mother. Ophelia sang along to Haris Alexiou as she cut her carrots to the beat. As she added the vegetables to her roast, she saw the officer with the broad shoulders standing by her fence. She shook her head and rolled her eyes. Adrian smiled widely and invited her out with his fingers. 'Lord, holy Mary and sweet baby Jesus give me strength!' she mumbled as she wiped her wet hands on her red apron.

She trudged out of her house towards Adrian still grousing about the interruption of her cooking. 'How many of you work at the police station?'

Adrian was taken aback by the peculiar question.

'Huh, sonny? Cat got your tongue?' Ophelia continued.

'Why?'

'I want to see how many more visits I am going to get as it seems that you are all going to show up here one by one!'

Adrian controlled his laughter and transformed it to a sincere, tooth-flashing smile. 'I'm really sorry, ma'am but when I get a thought stuck in this thick head of mine, it sticks well and doesn't let go. I know it is nearly lunch time...'

'It *is* lunch time.'

'...and a strong woman like yourself has cooking and chores to attain to, so I will be quick.'

'You want Melpomene? Poor thing is absolutely exhausted from crying. Devastating losing a child! And like that!'

'It is you I wish to speak with, lady Ophelia. And about your cooking in fact.'

'Boy, are you pulling my leg?'

'I would dare no such thing, ma'am. Tell me, do you always cook for your two tenants?'

Ophelia nodded. 'Yes, I did. Melpomene did not really *have it* with cooking, if you know what I mean. She could handle a few simple dishes and soups but nothing complicated and Greek cuisine is ninety percent complicated, is it not? But I'm not complaining. No, sir. I enjoy cooking and baking. And the poor woman did help me out every time. She is a good student and followed directions well.'

Adrian placed his hands on the wooden fence. The sun had not been kind on the white paint. 'I see. And do you remember what you prepared the day before we discovered Pandora's body?'

The old lady closed her eyes. 'We had pastitsio left over from the previous day, so I fried some chicken and chopped up a nice leafy salad to go with it.'

'For lunch, right? And then, in the evening?'

'Yeah, yeah. For lunch. The girl then went out for the day. She... never returned. You know this. The captain made out a time... what-did-she-call-it? Schedule or whatever of Pandora's day.'

'She took no food with her?'

Ophelia stood up straight. 'You're a weird one, aren't you?'

Another smile swallowed a chuckle. 'I guess not, then?'

Ophelia shook her head. 'The skinny thing never ate much anyway. Always worrying about her weight. I always told her that a woman needs some meat on her. Some curves, right? Only dogs like bones. You're a man. You know what I am saying.'

Adrian whistled and replied, 'sure do.'

There was a moment of pause between the two and both could hear the happy crickets chipping away.

'I have to get back to my cooking, officer. Unless, you have more culinary questions or need to borrow a recipe of something?'

'Just one last question. What did Pandora call Melpomene?'

Ophelia raised her hands. 'Lord, help me with this one. You sure made him special. Son, what the heck are you talking about?'

'If Pandora needed Melpomene and she had to call out to her, what word did she use?'

'Mum!'

'So, she called her *mum*?'

'Son, I am beginning to believe your mama dropped you on that pretty head of yours when you were a boy!'

Adrian finally released his deep-bass chuckle. 'You've been a delight and a great help, Mrs. Ophelia. You have my thanks!'

Ophelia rolled her eyes. 'May God be with you,' she replied and ambled off back to her kitchen.

Adrian drove up his dirt track of a driveway and smiled at the sight of the Maserati still outside of his cabin. 'Good. He is still here.'

His front door was unlocked. It felt weird entering his home after work and not using a key. Adrian had lived alone since he was eighteen. Returning to an empty home had become a default in his life. Music travelled to his ears.

'Honey, I'm home,' he shouted jokingly. Mario appeared from his bedroom door. He wore just a pair of shorts and held a hard cover book in his right hand. A paper bookmark was placed in the middle of Life of Pi.

'Wow, you're a fast reader,' Adrian commented. 'You read with music on?'

'Two things more that you know about me now.'

Adrian walked over to the wooden kitchen table and placed the bag he was carrying on it. 'Pork and lamb shanks marinated in Koumandaria sauce, salad with dried figs and pomegranate, mashed sweet potatoes and Bougatsa for dessert.'

Mario chuckled. 'Now, that's a meal. I was expecting a kebab or KFC to be honest. No need to go all out for me.'

'In general, I like to eat well.' Adrian pointed to the fridge as Mario approached. 'There's orange juice that I squeezed yesterday, cold water and a couple of iced beers. Take your liking and bring me the same as I set up the table.' Adrian opened the cupboards and asked, 'so, how are you finding life of Pi so far? Have you read it before?'

Mario brought two beers and a bottle of water to the table. 'To be honest, I have seen the movie, so I pretty much know where it is going. But books always bring so much more to the table, right?'

'That's for sure. I did the same with Lord of the Rings. Saw the first at the cinema and then bought the books. So much more material.'

'It is an interesting read. It has always fascinated me how people can create elaborate stories in their minds just to cope with details and facts that they cannot deal with.'

The meal was devoured by the two hungry men as they went over their day jobs, towns of origins, ex lovers and hobbies. Adrian was amazed at himself and how relaxed he felt around the man with the short black hair and kind honey-colored eyes.

'Bougatsa and icy beer. Now, there's a match made in heaven.'

As the last drop of beer travelled down Adrian's throat, Mario stood up, pulled down his shorts and let them drop to the ground. He wore no underwear. 'You coming?' he asked and walked off to the bedroom. Adrian kept his eyes on the man's bare bottom all the way to the door. He leapt out from his chair and was half naked by the time he joined Mario on his soft bed.

The man's lips tasted of creamy pies. His neck smelt divine. Adrian did not want to stop the momentum, so he took a mental note to inquire about Mario's choice of cologne. Twenty minutes later, two pleased men lay naked side by side again, both breathing heavily.

Adrian waited for his blood to return to its normal flow and stood up. 'I'm going to take a shower.'

'I'll be here reading,' Mario replied and sat up on the bed. 'So, when am I going to get to see Parga?' he asked as he fixed the pillow behind his head. 'An exotic paradise just five minutes away.'

'You have never seen Parga before?'

'Nope. Thousands of tourists come from all over and I am just a few hours drive away and yet, it never happened. But now, I have a guide!'

Adrian closed the bathroom door behind him and closed his eyes. '*Shit! What should I say to him?*' The notion of walking with a man through town never crossed his mind. Adrian did not consider himself a closeted gay, but he kept his sex life to himself. Besides Arianna and a few close friends, no one in town knew his sexual orientation. '*And why should they?*'

Adrian took one of the longest showers in his life.

Mario had not moved from his comfortable reading position.

Adrian stood by the door with his blue towel wrapped

around him. 'Err... Mario?' The man lowered his book and looked up. 'As soon as it cools down a bit, we can venture out. You have to see the promenade and walk up to the castle.'

'Why are you sounding all weird?'

Adrian scratched the back of his neck. 'I am a police Lieutenant in a small town. I do not hide from who I am, yet I do not... err... flaunt my sexuality...'

Mario smiled widely and raised his hand. 'Adrian, it's okay. I get it. We can go for a walk together. You don't have to hold my hand or kiss me in public.'

'You sure it does not annoy you?' Adrian sat on the bed. Mario came closer and stroked his cheek. 'You mean if I will feel lesser for you or be angry at you for hiding who you are?' He shook his head. 'You do as you feel. I totally understand. Yes, in an ideal world, we would not be having this conversation, but we live where we live...'

'And we are who we are!'

'Exactly. So, let's just go out for a nice evening and just see how things go. Do as you feel. I will not pressure you or do anything to cause village gossip.'

Adrian replied with a kiss. Enough was said about the topic.

Chapter Twenty-Six

Arianna stood above a drop of blood. It lay atop a small greyish rock, mocking her. '*I'm the last one. The trail goes cold. You've failed.*' Arianna rubbed her forehead. '*She was definitely carried into the cave, but from where?*' Sixteen drops of blood she had spotted in total. A crimson trail from the body up to the oak tree she now stood beside. Arianna looked down at the ground. 'Was she carried or dragged across the dirt? Inside the cave she was dragged. But I can't see signs out here. Did the killer lift the girl on his shoulders?' The police captain began to whisper her thoughts as if talking to her own brain, hoping for things to register better and make sense.

She looked at her phone. She had taken photographs of the four teenagers' shoe prints. Their footprints were visible up to the point where they took them off. Arianna could not find any other prints. 'The soil was swept...'

Arianna returned to the last drop of blood. Trees and shrubs neighboured the bloody rock. 'The killer must have come from that direction...'

Arianna took careful steps. Her eyes scanned every-where. She had walked for ten minutes before hearing waters falling at a distance. The waterfalls of Parga were miniatures compared to the waterfalls of the world. For the next ten minutes, she walked around the area. Not a single drop of blood. Not a single string of hair. Not a single piece of ripped clothes. Nothing.

'Back to the station, it is then, Mister Forest.'

Across town, Koula, the priest's wife, held her wedding photograph in her hands. She held it throughout her last prayers. She tapped her fingers on it and wished she could scream at the top of her lungs. She was done with tears. She had shed enough of them ever since her husband revealed his evil sin. She closed her eyes and remembered the moment. Thankfully, all her children were out. Looking back, she realised that is why he chose that exact moment to tear down her life. She shivered as she thought of the nights she slept by his side, the sickening event unknown to her.

'There is no easy way of telling you this, and Lord knows how ashamed I am. I dare not ask for your forgive-ness as I do not deserve it. But I must come clean before you as I have come clean before God. I let a boy sexually please me,' he had said as he stood before her.

She had yelled and attacked him. She had hit him with her bare hands more times than she could remember. He slept at the chapel ever since.

'Oh, Hector, you have made a fool out of me. Out of our life. Our poor children...' Koula mumbled as she looked at how happy the two twenty-year-olds were in the photo.

'He swore it was a moment of weakness. The devil sure loves to play tricks. Oh, shut up, Koula. You're making excuses for him! That was a fifteen-year-old boy! What if your Hector is a paedophile? No, no. He can't be. He loves me. The gay boy came onto him. He's a man. He has never had a... oh, Lord, give me strength... a blowjob before. I need him. He is all I have ever known. And what will become of our kids if we... divorce? No, no. We need to get away from here. We need a new start. I need to forgive. It is the Christian thing to do.'

Koula stood up and crossed herself. She looked over to the Holy Mary icon that hang on her wall and bowed her head. 'Give me strength, my Panagia.'

Looking at Koula, you would never have guessed the month of the year correctly. The high temperatures outside meant nothing to her; changed nothing for her. A woman's body should be covered. A dark purple dress past her ankles and met her strict black shoes and a scarf covered most of her head. The dress had long sleeves and was buttoned at the neck. Koula looked up and down the street. Ever since Pandora's murder, she avoided all interactions. She spoke to no one. The shame she felt was unimaginable to her. She could not discuss it. The street was deserted. Its occupants had taken one of two options. Day at the beach swimming in the cool waters of the Ionian and devouring homemade fresh ice-cream or day inside with the air-conditioning units working overtime, enjoying the best cable TV had to offer.

Koula dashed down the street and headed over to her husband's aunt. 'I hope he is there and not at the chapel.'

Her hopes were lost as Angelica answered the door.

'Now you come to support your man? He is not here.'

Koula lowered her eyes. 'Would *you* support your man if he told you such a horrific act? You would have stabbed him on the spot.'

Angelica's facial muscles relaxed and Koula could even make out a faint smile. 'He was beaten up badly...'

'I heard...'

'And yet it was me by his side at the hospital and at the police station and on the ground as he bled. Not you, not his children.'

'The kids are embarrassed. Do you blame them? Everyone they know saw their father with his underwear around his ankles and that boy pleasuring him!'

'He is still their father.'

'I called at the hospital. They said he was released.'

Angelica placed her hands upon her hips. 'What do you want him for? He is broken enough.'

'I want to forgive him.'

Angelica took a step back and shook her head. 'My, my. That was the last thing I was expecting to hear come out of your mouth.'

'It is the right thing to do. And I have a plan. We are going to leave this place.'

Angelica sighed. 'Are you on foot?' Koula nodded in reply. 'Let me get you my car keys.'

'Where is he?' Koula asked under the sounds of Angelica's bracelets rattling and her red heels clicking as the baker rushed to fetch her keys.

'That little church behind the mountains. The one no one visits. He said he needed space.'

Memories flashed by as Koula turned off the main road and the vehicle's wheels touched down on the bumpy road leading up to the mountain top. It was hers and Hector's favourite picnic spot. During her many pregnancies, they avoided the rutted lumpy road, but as soon as their new family member arrived, off to their patch in the trees it was (God and weather willing).

Hector's old banger of a car, the one he refused to sell and spent too much money fixing it rather than giving up on it and changing it, was parked outside the small stone-built church. Renovated and painted white, Koula never felt close to the church again. Saint Helen was always one of her favourites, so the decor did not keep her away from praying inside on their every trip there.

She brought the borrowed car to a halt and stepped outside. She took in a deep breath and walked slowly up to the church. She stood outside the wooden door. She could hear her husband singing hymns. She did not open the unlocked door. She rested her head on the wall and listened to his melodic voice. Minutes went past and she still could not muster the courage. The words she wished to say were scrambled in her mind. Suddenly, Hector stopped. Complete silence. Then she heard it. The chair falling to the ground and Hector struggling to breathe. She rushed inside. She let out a wild scream. Hector hung from a thick rope from the church's thick wooden beam. She ran to him, raising him by his tangling legs. He looked down at her. His eyes were wide open from the choking, from the excruciating pain. 'Leave me,' he mouthed. Koula brought the chair near her with her leg and pushed it under his feet. She stood on the chair, facing him eye to eye, and removed the rope gently from his neck. It had cut into him, bruising him severely. Multiple blood lines ran around him. Hector gasped for air. Both settled on the ground under the watchful eye of Christ on the cross above them.

'Hector, no! What are you doing? What were you thinking?'

Hector shook his head and began to cry. He leaned his head toward her. Koula took him into her arms. 'I feel so dirty, so ashamed...'

'We have kids, Hector...'

'They are better off without me. Without the shame that I have brought upon them. To carry my sin on their shoulders for the rest of their lives!'

Koula stroked his face. 'I came here to tell you that I have thought things through and have a plan for us. I was not sure if it was the right choice, but now I am. This is a sign. The Lord brought me here just in time. He does not wish you dead, my dear.'

'*I* wish me dead.'

Koula let him have a good cry in her arms. Catharsis was invented by the Greeks after all. Her eyes fell upon the piece of paper held by tape on the icon of the Holy Mary.

'The church committee called me in today. To tell me that I am no longer a priest. I did not go to their meeting. I came here... to think.'

Koula did not comment.

'You said you have a plan for us? Have you forgiven me?'

'Not yet, but I feel that I will. That I must. We have to think of our family. We are going to put our house up for sale and move to a small island. One with a primary and high school, of course. We move there and leave our past behind. We do not mention that you were ever a priest. We do not even say we moved from here. We will say we are city folk from Athens or Thessaloniki.'

'And what will we do for a living? We have kids to raise, to study, to marry...'

'We will choose a touristy island. You are an excellent cook, and everyone loves my dishes. I have always dreamt of owning my own place. A little fish tavern of our own. And on top, our little nest of a home.'

After a long period in his life, Hector smiled. He turned

around and looked at his wife. 'What have I done to deserve you? My angel!' He kissed her on the lips. They stood up together. Koula walked over to the letter on the icon.

'No, don't. No need now.' But Koula did not listen. She read the letter and sobbed. His farewells were touching. He wrote a paragraph for each of his children. He explained how much he regretted that one mistake. How the boy came on to him and he succumbed to temptation. Then she read the last note.

Twenty minutes after leaving the serene woodlands, Arianna slammed her office door behind her. It moaned and groaned as always, yet it had grown used to her abuse over the years. She headed for the top desk drawer. Her cigarettes and her shiny lighter were on top. With them in hand, she headed outside to her little smoking oasis. With her heart beating funny once more, she lit the first of two cigarettes. One before her phone call to the Timothy and one after. The boy was fine. Home alone with his head glued to one screen or another.

'Who the fuck is this second body? Shit! Two bodies... this is going to bring attention... I hate dealing with the press. Always twisting words, snooping...' she mumbled to herself as she paraded up and down in the narrow space with the many clay pots, home to Greek wild shrubs and blossoming summer flowers.

Her office phone was ringing inside. She rushed in to answer it. The flashing light informed her that it was from the front desk. 'Yes?'

'Captain, Mrs. Koula, the priest's wife, is here. She wishes to speak with you.'

'Send her in.'

Koula walked into the Captain's office flushed with her heart beating fast. She held her husband's final note in her hands. The two women exchanged pleasantries and the petite woman sat down in the chair on the right. Arianna sat upon her desk, facing the woman, with her hands crossed on her chest.

'My husband did not kill Pandora.'

'The police never said...'

'I just want to get it out there. He tried to commit suicide today. I managed to stop him just in time.'

Arianna stood up and pulled a chair near to the woman. She sat down and looked into Koula's eyes. 'What happened?'

Koula retold her day and handed Arianna the note. 'I brought it in not so much because he admits having nothing to do with the girl's death but for you to read the last paragraph.'

Arianna kept her eyes from watering up as she read the former priest's goodbyes to his loved ones. She then read about Pandora and how he had nothing to do with it. She then read the final words out loud. 'Before I die, I wish to help out with the investigation. For something good to come out of my cowardly death. As a priest, it was forbidden for me to reveal what was said to me in confession. Now, minutes away from going to eternal hell (where I belong), and no longer a servant of the Lord, I feel like I must confess three facts that I think will interested the police. Atlas, the town hall lawyer, slept with Pandora. He confessed that he flirted with Pandora when she was dating his son and one night when his wife was out of town, he came on to the girl. How forced the intercourse was, I do not know. Butcher Eva also had an encounter with the girl when she was dating her son. She caught Pandora sneaking out of her house and slapped her out of rage. Called her a whore and threatened to kill her if she saw her around her son again. Her mother, Melpomene, once asked me in confession if God could ever forgive us if we murdered our own flesh and blood if the cause was just. Happy investigating, Mrs. Kontou. I truly do hope you catch your killer.'

Chapter Twenty-Seven

Parga's promenade had nothing to envy from similar stone paved esplanades along the Adriatic. For years it was considered a secret seaside gem, enjoyed only by local visitors. Then, the Italians cruising the Ionian Islands discovered its beauty, its hospitality and its great food. Nowadays, it welcomed tourists from all over the globe.

Among the tourist, Adrian and Mario walked, talking the small talk accustomed on get-to-know-you first dates. Adrian enjoyed watching Mario looking around him, taking in the place. 'That castle on the hilltop really adds a note to the whole place, huh?'

'We can walk up there if you please. They have tables along the edge. Coffee and a view?'

'Sounds divine. We are eating up there, too?'

Adrian shook his head. 'We are eating here,' he said, pointed to the restaurant that occupied the corner where the two seafront streets collided. 'Zorbas does the best meat meze. And the moussaka is to die for.'

Mario looked at the small place with the wooden tables

covered by checkered tablecloths. His eye fell upon the olive tree painting that ran along most of the wall. He breathed in loudly through his nostrils. 'My nose agrees with you.'

Adrian tried to control his guilty thoughts that kept spawning inside his mind. Everyone around him was relaxed and enjoying their holidays. And there he was, with new knowledge about Melpomene, strolling with a new hot man as if without a care in the world. *'Tomorrow, I must ask him to leave. I need to get to the bottom of this without distractions.'*

'You've gone quiet,' his distraction said as they sat upon the brick wall opposite the notorious anchor. The mayor had made sure nothing remained of the horrific scene they all faced just days ago. After the forensic team gave the clear, she gave the order to remove all police tapes and washed the place down. 'No tourist is to see a single blood drop, you hear me?' she had said in a strict tone to the council's sanitation workers.

'Just enjoying how serene this all is.'

'I was hoping for romantic being the adjective used, but oh well, glad you're relaxing. I could never do what you do. I'm an office type of guy.'

Adrian stroked Mario's fingers for a quick second. 'Serene, relaxing, *and* romantic!'

Officer Leventi was also getting his hand caressed, just meters away. He sat with Katie in the cafe by the dock.

'Funny how life goes on so quickly. Look at them,' Leventi said as he watched tourists taking selfies in front of the landmark. He took another sip from his ice-cold Alpha beer.

'Because it does not affect them. Humans are a selfish species. We look at our own lives and if we are content, we are happy, if not, we are sad. Simples. I mean, Pandora died, right? To those tourists over there, she's just another death. To most Greeks, she is just a headline. To us here, she was a shock. To her mother, it was devastating, but here we are enjoying beers.'

'I get your drift.'

Katie giggled. 'You don't talk much, do you Mister Cop Man?'

'You on the other hand, do though,' he said and laughed. Katie had an amazing smile, and he was mesmerized by it. 'Good point, though. Each death is dealt with differently. I read about children dying from famine and wars and it really saddens me, but I do nothing, I go on with my day.'

'I wish my sister would go on with hers. All day locked up in her room. It isn't healthy.'

'Iris is taking it hard, huh?'

Katie played with the label on the bottle of beer in front of her. 'She was in love with Pandora, you know?'

'Close friends...' he nodded.

Katie shook her head. He watched as streaks of her hair danced around, falling on her youthful face. 'Proper in love, love. My sister plays for the other team. She has never had a girlfriend and Pandora is to blame. She knew well that Iris wanted her. Iris is obsessed... was obsessed with Pandora. How beautiful she was, how funny she was, how smart she was. Her death must have been a major blow to her. I feel bad for her, but we were never really close, to be honest. We never bonded as sisters. We both had our friends to hang out with and reveal all our secrets.' She took a long sip. 'There I go talking, talking, talking again.' She laughed out loud. 'Go on, Mister Officer. Interrupt me. Say something. Anything.'

'What's your favorite movie?'

'Clueless. Yours?'

'Hmmm. A toss between Jurassic Park and Infinity War. Oh, and Lord of the Rings. And Terminator, the second one. Yeah, you can't beat that can you? Then again, I love horror, but none of these are horror, right? Hmm, err, The Exorcist, The Conjuring and It Follows. Oh, and Aliens, of course!'

Katie could not control her laughter. The couple from the table next to theirs turned to look. 'Oh, it talks! It really talks! I have found your button!'

Leventi sulked for a split second, then shook his head as if forcing his mind to snap out of it. Out of memories of his older brothers and cousins constantly making fun of him. To his luck, Katie laughed with her eyes closed. He looked at her and smiled. She was having fun. She was having fun *with him*. Leventi was amazed by how much he wanted the date to be a success. He was ready for a relationship. A meaningful relationship.

More drinks followed. 'If food takes any longer, I will be one drunk lady.'

'Should be here in a minute. That family being served over there came just before us. We're next.'

'Ohh, the observing detective.'

'I wish. I'd love to be...' He paused. Adrian came to mind and there he was standing by the wall talking to a man.

'A detective?'

'Yeah, yeah. Listen, give me a minute. Just saw a friend. Got something to tell him and I will be right back.'

'You'd better,' Katie said and picked up her third drink of the evening.

The waves crashed upon the rocks below the short wall and splashed Mario. He laughed and with a hop, landed by Adrian. 'I think there is a man coming straight for you.'

Adrian turned around and nodded to an approaching Leventi.

'Good evening, sir.'

'Adrian is fine, Leventi.'

'Sir,' Mario whispered and flashed a cheeky smile towards Adrian.

'Sorry to bother you at the moment, but can I have a word?'

Adrian took two steps forward. Mario took the hint and walked over to the stone wall and gazed the horizon.

'I am on a date, right now. I'm with Katie, Iris's sister? It's just something she said and the way she said it and it got me thinking.' Leventi came closer to Adrian and lowered his voice. 'She said that Iris is a lesbian and had a major crush on Pandora. The way she described how obsessed her sister was just did not sit well with me. I was just wondering if we knew about this angle and thought to let you know. It could be nothing, really, I just... probably just me being silly... stupid of me to tell you now. It could have waited for tomorrow...'

'No, no. You did right. We are always on a case. Thanks for telling me. This info is new to me. I will see if the Captain has anything to say about it in the morning.'

The two officers said their goodbyes and each returned to their respective dates.

Ten minutes later, slightly out of breath, Mario stood before the most impressive view. 'The walk up to here was worth it. Boy, now that's a beauty!' The entire town of Parga spread across the hills and Mario had a clear view of all of its bays.

'Come round this side of the castle,' Adrian said. 'My favourite beach. Valtos.'

The long sandy beach ran for over two miles. Multiple

sun beds filled the golden sand and green trees provided a tranquil background.

'You must bring me here in the morning. After I buy some swimming trunks, that is.'

Adrian did not reply. He slightly bit his bottom lip. 'Let's go to our table. I need a strong coffee.'

'I'm sorry. I forgot. You're working in the morning.'

Adrian turned around and walked up to Mario. 'The thing is...' Adrian paused and exhaled. 'I must work. All day tomorrow. I need to clear things out with this case. I can't be distracted by your good looks and fine body and be eager to return home. I need to put in one of my notorious sixteen-hour shifts. And I feel shit for wanting to do such a thing because this is going perfect. You're perfect...'

'Sssshhh!' Mario said and stepped in, kissing him on the lips. 'Relax. I totally get it. If you want, I will leave first thing in the morning when you get up for work.'

Adrian shook his head. 'I want you to stay...'

'Don't worry, handsome. I own my business. It's easy for me to give myself breaks. Finish with your murder mystery and I will be back up here for a long weekend. Hell, I'm off work for most of August.'

Adrian stroked his hair. 'Thank you.'

Chapter Twenty-Eight

'Melancholy.'

Adrian whispered the word as he turned on the radio and drove down his driveway. In his rear-view mirror, he watched the Maserati follow him. He remembered his high school language teacher explaining the word and as in most cases -at least according to Mr. Kyriakou, it had a Greek etymology. The word stuck with young Adrian. 'Melas and khole. Black and bile,' his teacher had explained. 'An abyss of bitterness.'

Adrian turned onto the main road and looked once again behind him. 'And then you turn left, and I turn right.'

Adrian shook his body as he drove into town as if shaking off unwanted feelings. His mind had to be in top game mode. He had many thoughts and he needed to get things straight on the inside before releasing them out towards his captain. 'Grow up, man. Stop acting silly. You can't be in love with your Grinder hook up. Shake it off. Get to work. Focus on one thing. The case.' His face went cold, and his gaze settled on the newly paved road ahead. 'Anyway, August is just around the corner,' he added as comfort to his heart.

Adrian parked in his reserved spot and stepped outside, for the first time not caring about the weather. The scorching heat had woken up early, but the sunrays and the high-for-the-time-of-year temperatures held not enough strength as to penetrate his abyss of bitterness. Arianna's vehicle occupied her spot. She was always the first one there, clocking in a good hour before her shift began.

Adrian walked straight to her office. His characteristic knock followed, and he opened the door as soon as Arianna's '*enter*' reached his ears.

'Good morning, Adrian.'

He nodded. 'Good morning, boss. I have much to tell you.'

Arianna sat up straight and chuckled. 'Me, too. Shoot.'

Adrian pulled out a desk chair from the corner, swung it around and sat down, leaning on the chair's back. 'I think I know what secret Pandora was going to write about Melpomene.'

'Robbery?'

Adrian frowned. 'What? No. Worse. Much worse than that. She is not the girl's real mother.'

Arianna remained still. She then slightly shook her head. Her eyes widened as the words registered. 'What? How can that be? You sure? How did you...'

'Neither gynaecologist in town performed an abortion on Pandora. Her doctor thought the idea absurd as he examined Pandora just weeks ago and she was definitely not pregnant. Did the coroner mention how long ago the abortion took place? Can he tell? Can he be wrong?'

Arianna raised her hand. 'Wait. I'm still in shock about the whole mother, not mother business.' Arianna puffed her cheeks and blew out air. 'I will call the coroner and ask him. Now, please tell me, how you came about Melpomene not being Pandora's mum?'

'The same doctor took me aside and even though he knew he was breaking the confidentiality between doctor-patient, he said he wanted to help with the case as he is retiring soon. He examines Melpomene, too and he said that Melpomene has never given birth in her life.'

Arianna fell back into her chair. She rubbed her temples and closed her eyes. 'An adoption, then?'

'It's an angle we have to look into. You know that my gut has always pointed toward that woman. I don't know why. I don't believe her to be innocent.'

Arianna tapped her hands on her desk. 'You just made everything am about to mention seem small. Before I retell you my yesterday meeting with Koula, Hector's wife, is there anything else I should be shocked by?'

'Nothing as shocking as that, but Leventi found out that Iris, her best friend, had a crush on Pandora.'

'A crush?'

'It could be nothing. An innocent teenager falling in love with her friend, but Leventi seems to believe there is some-thing more to it.'

'Where did he get this from?'

'Her sister, Katie.'

'Hmm.' Arianna seemed lost in thought.

'Your encounter with the papadia*?' (*The wife of an Orthodox priest)

Arianna snickered. 'Not a papadia anymore. Hector got the boot and tried to kill himself.'

'Did he now?' Adrian shook his head. 'What is this place coming to?'

'Koula stopped him and brought me in the letter he left

behind.' Arianna picked up the folded piece of paper and extended her arm. Adrian stood up, took the paper, opened it and began to read it as he walked around the office.

'It seems with have a shitload of work on our hands.'

'Sure does. So, here's the plan.'

Minutes later, Adrian walked out of the police station and headed to his car. As he sat and turned the ignition key, he swore. 'You forgot to mention the baked beans.' He reversed out of his spot. The spot he fought hard for. The shady spot below the trees. 'And you forgot to ask her about her investigation in the forest.' He turned onto the highway. '*Why didn't she say something?*' He stopped at the red light. '*I shocked her with the whole not being her mother thing. That's probably it.*'

Chapter Twenty-Nine

Leventi felt important again.

He replayed the scene inside his mind again. He wandered into the station feeling like Saki Rouva. His date had been a success. They made out in his car and he scored a second date. He offered to cook at his place and Katie did not say no. As soon as he entered the police station, he was informed that the captain needed him. Needed him. She told him about the latest outcomes and sent him on his way to Butcher Eva.

He was officially an investigator.

A minor shiver made the hair on the back of his neck stand at attention. It was not the sea breeze coming through his window, it was his gut. His soul's abyss was sending out a warning. He repeated his late grandfather's line. 'Never expect happiness. It will never satisfy you. Expect shit, son and then whatever comes your way will offer you bliss.' Leventi feared being happy because he knew the downside when that happiness vanished. He had not drunk anything stronger than a light beer for the last four years, but he remembered well the blackouts from his whiskey days. Depression did not suit his addictive character. His inner beast always wished for more. More alcohol, more chocolate spread, more women, more money. He turned and drove downhill towards the town's largest butchery. He parked opposite in amazement. The shop was dark. The blinds were down. The sign left no doubt. Closed. Leventi chuckled. 'That girl really got ya, huh, Eva?'

Leventi picked up the receiver. 'This is officer Leventi, front desk come in, please.'

The crackling robotic voice that always came to his eighties-born radio reminded nothing of the secretary's sweet voice. 'How may I be of assistance, officer 302?'

'The butchery is closed. Can you please forward me the address to my suspect? The butchery is closed. Over.'

The mansion that belonged to the crooked butcher was a ten-minute drive away. It was a part of a gated community that calved into the hill on the outskirts of town. 'Serene Hills,' Leventi read the sign as he drove up to the front gate. No guard was on duty and the rail rose automatically as his car approached. Leventi read the house numbers as he went along the row of Mediterranean four-bedroom villas. He parked in the driveway of number twelve. He stepped outside and felt the eyes fixed on him. He looked around. Among the well taken care of olive trees and tall oaks, many senior citizens stopped their gardening and turned their eyes toward the young man in a police uniform. Most were Europeans that had retired to the seaside village, living their golden years under the golden sun.

Leventi fixed his shirt and gave his belt a jolt. He walked steadily up to the front door and prepared to knock. As he raised his hand, the wide wooden door opened. Eva stood before him, fixing her hair. She closed her salmon-colored robe and waved him in. 'Get in here, before everyone sees you. Noisy Italians, gossiping Brits and snobbish Germans.'

'*And yet, you choose to live here,*' he thought. 'I need a quick word with you, Ma'am. Are you alone in the house?'

'My son is grounded upstairs. Eighteen, my ass. He is staying in his room until he learns that he doesn't talk shit about his mother to every little skank that opens her legs to him,' she raised her voice. 'Come join me in the kitchen, officer?'

'Leventi.'

Eva ran her eyes from his head to his toes. 'Hmm. If you say so.'

He followed her into the vast kitchen that featured the biggest fireplace Leventi had ever laid eyes upon. A white corner sofa occupied the corner by the glass window, offering both a mountain view and a sea view.

A bottle of white wine was on the counter. Not much of its contents remained. Eva picked up her wine glass and sat down on the sofa. 'I hope those boots of yours are clean, young man.'

'Spotless.'

'So, what's new? Catch the girl's killer yet?'

'We're getting there.'

She drank the remaining wine floating around in the tall champagne glass and leaned back into the couch. 'What do you need me for? I gave my testament...'

'A piece of new info to run by you.'

'Like?'

'Was Pandora ever in your house?'

Eva's face remained still. She placed her hands upon her legs. 'Why?'

'It's a simple question, ma'am. A simple yes or no will do.'

'Probably. Matthew has friends from class over often.'

'Even at night? For let's say a sleepover?'

Eva straightened her back. 'New info, huh? What is it you have heard, officer? What do you really want to ask?'

'What was the nature of the relationship between your son and the victim?'

'They were shagging for a while. I did not know. I only saw her once in my house, sneaking out before morning.'

'And how did that encounter go?'

'Just fine.'

'Just fine? You did not get annoyed? You did not threaten her?'

Eva frowned. 'Did she write about it?'

'Could have.'

'For you to be asking about something only her and I know, it means she has. I hope not public again.'

'No, ma'am. Only the police know.'

'I did hit her. I regret it of course. I was...' She rolled her eyes. 'I was a bit tipsy. Had a few too many and did not control my anger well. You see, my son is a good boy and was dating a good girl. Nefeli.'

'Nefeli?'

'Yeah, nice, sensible girl. They had not yet slept together and along comes Pandora and starts secretly coming over at nights? Fucking her best friend's boyfriend? Who does that? I gave her a piece of my mind and when she talked back, I slapped her. I slapped her hard.'

'And you said something, right?'

'I said if I ever caught her in my house or around my son again, I would kill her. But that was just talk. Alcohol talk. Greek mother talk. I just wanted her away from him before Nefeli found out.'

'Did she ever find out?'

Eva shrugged her shoulders and stood up. She walked over to the bottle of expensive Chardonnay and poured the rest into her sparkling glass. 'A drink, officer?'

'No, thank you. Err, is it possible that I may talk to your son and ask him if Nefeli knew?'

'Why? To make that sweet girl a suspect? The notion is ludicrous, but oh, well.' She downed her wine and threw the glass into the sink. 'Matthew?' she screamed. 'Damn videogames. He can't hear a thing.' She repeated his name again, even louder.

A faint reply came from the stairs.

'Get your skinny ass down here, boy. The police are here for you.' She chuckled and whispered, 'that should scare the little shit a bit. Wanna take him into custody and ask him?'

Leventi shook his head. 'That won't be necessary, ma'am.'

'Well, it should be. My business is ruined because of his big mouth!'

The kid with the bad case of acne appeared in the doorway. He was slightly shivering and awkwardly scratching his arm. 'Yes?'

'Relax, Matthew. I was just having a talk with your mother. I know we have spoken before about your adventures with Pandora. Just a couple of quick questions. 'Are you still Nefeli's boyfriend?'

'Err, yes, sir.'

'So, she never found out about you and Pandora?'

'She asked me about it after the website went live. I lied. I told her that I got drunk after a party of a classmates and got talking with Pandora and my mother's secrets just came out. I swore to her that I did not sleep with her like the other boys that spilled the beans.'

'I should fucking spill your little brain out, you dumb shit. Go back to your room and stay there.'

The boy obeyed without uttering a word.

'Are we done now, officer? I have a second bottle waiting for me in the fridge and my talk show is about to begin!'

Arianna drove in silence. With the radio off and the windows shut, Adrian sat shotgun, lost in his thoughts. At least the hush in the car did not go on for long. Small town, small distances. In a matter of minutes, Arianna parked outside a renovated two-storey house. It had belonged to Atlas's mother-in-law and she gave it to her only daughter upon marriage. His in-laws preferred living on their farm, than in town. 'Nowhere to keep the chickens and I highly doubt the neighbours would appreciate the pigs!' his father-in-law had joked.

Arianna went up the four steps leading to the front door first and took the knocker into her right hand. After a quick hit, she noticed the doorbell to her right. She was contemplating ringing it when she heard footsteps from inside. The door opened. Aliki, the cheating lawyer's wife, seemed to have grown a decade since the last time Arianna had seen her. Her white roots were visible in her dark hair, blackness surrounded her sore eyes, and her fingernails were chipped from all the biting.

'Good day, Aliki.'

Aliki just nodded.

'We were wondering if we could have a quick word with Atlas?'

Aliki sniggered. 'Wrong house, honey.'

'Excuse me?'

'Atlas doesn't eat, shit or fuck here anymore. He has moved in with his whore. Now their affair is out in the open, he has no need to put up with me. He can be with the one he says he loves.'

Arianna sighed. 'Aliki, I am so sorry...'

'What for? His loss. Worthless piece of shit. Let me see the Mayor put up with his crap. He is high maintenance that one, but then again, so is our Mayor. A perfect match, aren't they?'

Arianna walked back to the vehicle with sorrow painted across her face. She recognized the bitterness well. Her Timothy was only a kid when she discovered that her husband was sleeping around. For a long time, she hated him, and then she hated herself for falling in-love with a bad boy. A player as her mother warned her. At least he was good with Timothy and gave him good genes.

'Off to the mayor's house then?' Adrian asked as they re-entered the car.

'I can't stand that woman. Let's hope Atlas is alone.' Arianna turned the ignition key. 'She has a good kid though,' she added as she stepped on the gas. 'Antony is a good friend to my Timmy. Not like some of the other bad influences in their class.'

The Mayor had recently moved to a new house. After her election, her small bungalow did not seem significant enough. 'Better salary, better house,' she had thought and the next day she put down a deposit for the corner house of a complex being built on the hill overseeing the bay of Lichnos, just a twelve-minute drive away from the town's center. 'A home that says I am doing well, but nothing too flashy as to put off my lower income voters,' she had requested from the agent. 'It's just me and my boy anyway.' At the time, the last thing on her mind was a man. Now, her handsome lawyer lay on the sunbed beside her, holding her hand as she drank her sangria, enjoying her son showing off his diving skills in their private pool.

The doorbell startled her. She was not expecting company. 'I'm not opening the door in my bikini. Do you mind, love?'

She watched as the tall man with the broad back that she loved to scratch, walked round the house to see who was at the door. '*Hmm, having a man around can be helpful.*'

Adrian tapped on his Captain's shoulder and when she turned around, he nodded to his left. Atlas was approaching wearing blue swimming drunks with dolphins printed on them and a pair of white sandals. 'Good day, officers,' he said and flashed a smile. His teeth were like a row of pearls. '*Well done to the Turkish dentist,*' Arianna thought.

'Good day, sir. We need to have a quick talk with you.'

The lawyer's face darkened. He thought they were there to talk with the Mayor. It was her house after all. 'Err, sure, sure. Sit down,' he offered as he pointed to the garden furniture on the patio. 'Do you mind if I just pop inside and grab a T-shirt?'

Both nodded. 'We will wait,' Adrian said as he sat down on the rattan-weaved sofa with the soft brown cushions.

Atlas rushed inside.

'Who is it, dear?'

'The police! Phoebe, they are here for me.'

The once-secret couple appeared together. Phoebe came out clothed and holding a jug of lemonade. Atlas followed with a tray with four classes and a plate of chocolate-chip cookies.

'No need for fuss,' Arianna said as they both sat down, placing their offerings on the glass table with the cherry wood legs. 'We only need *Atlas* for a few minutes.' Phoebe did not seem to catch her drift. 'We only need Atlas,' Arianna made it clear.

'We have no secrets, do we, dear?' Phoebe asked, giving her lover a look of puppy eyes.

Arianna could not resist rolling her eyes.

'Fine, if you wish to hear it, that's your problem, ma'am,' Adrian said. 'Was Pandora ever at your house, Atlas?'

'A few times, yeah. The kids hung around with my boy often. He is quite popular.'

'Any times that she visited alone?'

Atlas smiled. 'I know that you have discovered that she had slept with my son on multiple occasions as she had with Phoebe's son as well. That is how she knew all these secrets. Our boys told us everything you asked.'

'And did she ever visit you rather than your son, Mr. Atlas?' Arianna asked, her eyes fixed on the mayor. The mayor's jaw dropped.

'That's ludicrous,' Atlas answered. 'Why would she visit me?'

'Was the sex consensual?'

Atlas stood up. Sweat appeared on his forehead as his cheeks began to rose up. 'How dare you?' he said and started to walk off.

'Where are you going? To call your lawyer? Please, get back here, sir,' Adrian raised his voice.

'This is absurd, Arianna,' Phoebe said. 'Who told you such a lie?'

'Our sources are credible and have been checked out.

Now, Atlas, you either spill the beans or should we get a warrant for your arrest?'

'On what grounds?'

'Sex with a minor and refusal to co-operate with the police in a murder investigation. Withholding of evidence if you want me to speak your language.'

'Is it live?'

'Excuse me?'

'Was it posted online?'

'That is what you care about?' Phoebe said, standing up. 'So, it's true?'

Atlas nodded. Phoebe slapped him in his face and head and stomped off.

'Let me explain. She was nearly eighteen and it was consensual, of course...'

Phoebe screamed at the top of her lungs. 'Shut the fuck up, Atlas! I'm going upstairs. I can't even look at you right now!' As she ran into the house, she yelled, 'Oh, I am so done with men!'

Atlas sighed and with his eyes fixed on his feet, he spoke softly. 'Listen, the girl was a month away from eighteen. I found that out later. Most in my son's year turned eighteen before school closed. I am not trying to make excuses, but I am not some freaking pedo. Pandora was... a highly sexual being as you have probably discovered. She was a right flirt. She knew I was in the living room alone watching TV and she would come out of my son's room wearing only her undies. She walked straight past me to head to the kitchen for a glass of water. My wife often goes out of town for business. When my son slept, she would come down and sit with me in front of the TV. One night, one thing led to the other. Of course, I regret it. I'm just an old fool proving to myself that I am still young and wantable.'

'And did you keep seeing each other after she broke it off with your son?'

'No. I never saw her again after that.'

Back in the police vehicle, the two officers looked at each other.

'What a cunt! Pardon my French,' Arianna said. 'He had his wife, his affair and slept with his son's girlfriend. Sleazebag!'

'And now he has lost all three.'

Arianna took on her Mona Lisa face. Adrian used that phrase to describe his boss whenever her face went still but a faint smile twitched around. He never uttered the words though. 'You really believe that?'

Adrian turned his body toward her. 'I'm intrigued.'

'The Mayor is not going to kick him out. She is madly in love with him.'

'She slapped him.'

'Did you hear a slapping noise? Did she call him names? Did she ask him to leave? When I found out my ex-dead-beat of husband was cheating, I broke his nose, called him every profanity in the book and told him that when I came back home in an hour, I wanted him and all his shit out of my house. No, no. The Mayor is keeping her playboy. She probably knew. That was some cheap acting right there. No real shock.'

Adrian took her words in. He put the puzzle pieces in place in his mind before commenting. 'Do you suspect them?'

Arianna sighed. 'They are smug scum, and everything is possible, but their secret is not that severe as to want a teenage girl dead.'

'Then who?'

Arianna tilted her head. She read his eyes well. 'You are still fixed on Melpomene, right?'

'That one is a bit off,' he said as the car's engine roared to life.

Chapter Thirty

Adrian sat on the station's toilet playing games on his phone. He chuckled as his virtual monkey had to dig a tunnel underground to pass to the next level. He had also been metaphorically digging all day.

He had *ran* Melpomene through the system.

It was as though she had come into existence when Pandora was born. Everything about Pandora checked out. Her previous schools, her previous addresses, everything. Melpomene on the other hand had everything in place from eighteen onwards. Nothing from before.

'System protection?' Adrian whispered to himself as he lowered his cell phone.

He left the lavatory and headed back to his computer. *'Maybe she was escaping a violent husband or relationship? I found no wedding certificate. She was young. If so, how did she adopt a child?'* Adrian scratched his nails upon his desk. His inner passionate investigator longed for answers.

'Should I go face her? And get what? The truth? Just like that? Without evidence? Something to go by?'

The fax machine behind him roared and shrieked as it came to life. White paper slid in and gradually began to reappear on top. Adrian recognized the stamp on top. Excitement accelerated his heart beats. His veins twitched as his blood ran around faster than usual. 'The coroner's report! That was quick.'

Adrian did not wait for the six-page document to come though. He picked up each page as it came out and speed read through it.

'Fucking baked beans and sausages again.' He looked around. He was alone. 'Severe blow to the right temple. Most likely from a heavy rock... Minor hit to the left temple... Post-mortem cuts from woods and rocks...' He read out loud the parts he wished to register better in his mind. 'The time of death is placed during the same gap as the first body. Maybe even earlier...' Photos came through as well. 'She doesn't look Greek...'

'The victim's DNA matches the hair found under the nail of the Jane Doe on the anchor!'

Adrian lowered the paper. He shook his head. 'What a case.' Adrian heard voices coming his way. He took out his cell phone and quickly took pictures of the report. He then placed all papers back in order and slid them on the fax machine's black tray. As the door opened, he dashed out the back. Arianna was talking to Leventi. Adrian tiptoed out of the station and took out his car keys. 'Into the woods.'

As he drove up to the woodland opening with the serene waters of the pond, Adrian lowered his windows. All of them. In the summertime, he drove with his air-con on but now he needed air. Strong air gushing on his face.

He did not wish to leave his car by the side of the narrow road. He drove further up and parked in an opening under a row of tall trees.

Twigs crunched and broke under his boots as he made his way down to the cave. Adrian stood by the entrance to the cave and looked out to the forest. It was darker than usual. A few lone clouds had been roaming the summer sky from the morning, annoying sunbathing tourists by blocking the sun every now and then. Now, they provided darkness to the woods. 'Was she carried? She was a thin girl... the cuts by branches and bushes would indicate being dragged at some point out here. Not just inside.' Adrian gazed around. *'If you look long enough into the abyss, the abyss will look back at you,'* he remembered a professor's line at the academy. *'Or something like that. Sorry, Nietzsche.'*

Adrian rubbed his lower back and set off for a hike. A hike through all possible routes that the murderer might have used. Walking around estimating the way, Adrian felt like he was stuck in a maze like the ones his nephew loved to draw. 'Take the dog to the bone,' he would say and pass the piece of paper to his uncle. 'Remember, you can't go through walls.'

Half an hour later, the first clue came. A tiny piece of cloth caught on a root that spawned out of the ground and had grown a wicked pointy end. Adrian recognized the color and the material. 'The girl's shorts.' He took a photograph of the evidence, then carefully bagged it, picking it up with his tweezers. Adrian looked down at the ground. The rainless previous months had dried the land. 'Still, there should be some sort of marks if the body was hauled through here. Unless...' He looked around at the unsteady, uneven grounds around him and the large even rock by the piece of torn clothes. 'Unless she was carried, and this was a spot for the killer to relax. Yes, that's it. She was carried and then placed here for the murderer to catch his breath.' Adrian mumbled to himself. His mother warned him that only crazy people talked to themselves. 'We are all crazy, mama. Some just show it more,' he had replied as he stole one of her freshly baked cookies with cinnamon and rushed out of the kitchen.

'Where else would he have rested?' Adrian climbed up the small rocky hill before him to get a better look of the area. Amongst the chirping of woodland birds, he could hear water. 'The waterfalls. I doubt the killer would have passed through there. Such a large open space. Someone would have seen him... or her... or them.'

As he went along the top of short hills, he stopped to look down. 'Could Pandora have been killed out here, too? A great fall...' He shook off the idea with a movement of his head. 'No steep mountains. Where could she have fallen? Been pushed from?'

He turned his attention to the waterfalls. They fell from the highest point in the area. He made his way done to the small valley. *But they fall into water...mostly,'* he thought looking at all the rocks behind and around the thunderous falling waters.

As Adrian exited the thick bushy area, he had found himself tangled up with, he saw a familiar figure standing by with a fishing rod.

He approached and called out the boy's name. 'Timothy?'

Timothy turned around and stood still. 'Err...hi, Mr. Adrian.'

'Fishing, huh? Didn't know you fished?'

'Me neither,' the boy said and chuckled. 'Thought to give it a go but I suck at it.' Timothy tipped his large white bucket to reveal his zero catch.

'Shit. Now Arianna will be asking me why I came out here alone,

without telling her. Especially after she already went through the woods. Why did I talk to him?'

'Alone? Or are your friends off in some cave or what?'

'I doubt any of us will ever go into a cave again,' he said, looking at the river. 'Yeah, alone.' He scratched the back of his neck and turned toward Adrian. 'You know, with everything going on, my mum wants me at home, inside all the time. Erm, if you don't mind not telling her that you saw me out here? Especially by myself.'

'*Suits me just fine, kid.*'

Adrian nodded and went to walk off.

'Can I ask...' He heard Timothy's voice but then only silence followed.

'What's that?'

'Nothing.'

'Are you okay, Timothy?'

'With all this going on, not really. I know it is in your line of work, but seeing a dead girl is an image I can get out of my head.'

Adrian returned to the boy's side. 'Do you want to talk about it? Is that what you wanted to ask? I know your mother is one tough cookie and maybe you...'

'No, no. I wanted to ask you about... homosexuality.'

'Come again?'

'Did my mum say anything?'

'About what?'

'I came out to her.'

'Ooh.' Adrian nodded and placed his hand on the boy's shoulder. 'Your mum and I don't really talk about personal stuff. She did not say something, but knowing her, I bet she took it better than you were expecting.'

Timothy's eyes opened wide. 'Yeah, exactly. I feared the worst.'

'No crying like my mother, huh?'

'Your mother cried?'

'Oh, yeah. First about her damaged son, then about all the grandchildren I was not going to offer.'

The two spoke for the next twenty minutes about gay life in a small town, about university, bullying, dreams, hopes and expectations.

'She has raised you well,' Adrian commented.

Timothy had no time to reply. His rod began to shake. 'Oh, shit.' He took the blue rod into his hands and started to reel the line in. Soon, a small trout splashed upon the river's surface. Adrian clapped. 'Well done, Timmy.'

Timothy brought the fish near him and held it down in his bucket. He removed the hook from the fish's mouth and gagged at the blood that sprang out and colored his hands. 'I can't stand the sight of blood.'

'Here,' Adrian said and passed him a tissue.

'Thanks.' Timothy wiped his hands and threw the tissue into the bucket. The fish was still rattling about. 'I doubt lighting will strike twice. I better be heading back. I'll get Antony to come round and eat this baby before mum returns. Thanks for the talk.'

'Anytime, kid. Be proud. Be you.'

'*You sound like a cheesy cologne advert*,' Adrian thought as he watched Timothy take the path back to town. 'Now, let's have a snoop around.'

Chapter Thirty-One

THE PAST V

Greece might be famous for its summers, but it is in springtime that true beauty spreads across its lands. God used his palette generously when coloring the scenery during the blossoming month of March. Demetra walked the meadows of Sparta for the last time. The sixteen-year-old girl took off her shoes and dipped her toes in the shallow waters of Eurotas, the main river of the region. She cut flowers as she went by humming Byzantine hymns. She never cut lone blossoms. She only stole from the ones that had many. She did her best to find one of each color. Her father and Helka sat on their picnic cloth drinking and listening to old tunes from a new portable radio. Demetra remembered learning about the river in geography. It began its journey where so many journeys ended in ancient times. On Mt. Taygetus. The ancient warriors that once inhabited Sparta used the mountain to punish criminals, traitors and captives. The fierce fighters threw their unwanted in a chasm known as Ceadas. A myth even stated that they disposed of any newborns that were born with what they considered flaws, though no baby bones were ever found on the mountain's slopes. Only adolescent and adult bones were discovered.

'I wish I had been thrown...'

Demetra knelt and splashed water upon her face. Swallows flew above her head, dancing in the clear sky.

'Demetra? Honey? Come here, darling. We need to talk to you about something.'

She resented her father's voice when it uttered sweet adjectives.

She did not reply. She simply stood up and with her aromatic bouquet in hand she walked slowly over to the pair of drunks.

'Sit, Demetra. Have a glass of wine. You are old enough, now,' Helka proposed. The way she said her name, brought her lunch up back her throat. That heavy Scandinavian accent was a part of Demetra's nightmares.

'No, thank you,' the girl answered as she sat down at the edge of the tablecloth, resting on newborn grass.

'We have a surprise for you,' her father said. 'We are moving!'

'What? Where to?'

Demetra was not one to acquire many friends, but she loved their neighbohood and her school. The familiar roads, the familiar faces of teachers and pupils, the familiar places.

'To the island of Elafonisos!' His excitement was obvious. 'We have found better jobs at a new hotel built there. Better pay, less hours. And we will be offered accommodation, too! A beach house! Can you imagine?'

Both raised their glasses. Demetra could not help but smile. Living by the ocean did not sound that bad and the island was not far away from Sparta where she could always come and stay in a couple of years and study.

Just a week later, Demetra stood outside their apartment block staring up at their empty balcony. She sighed and entered her father's running vehicle. The previous day she had said her farewells to her few friends at school, her fewer friends in the neighbohood and her local priest who stood by her through thick and thin.

'*Maybe a new start is what I really need.*'

She took out a small photograph from her pocket. She looked down at her smiling mother. '*You are all that I need to take with me from my old life, my guardian angel.*'

The short drive to the port gave her comfort. She was leaving, yet not going far. Her father drove slowly in general, but today he went even slower as the mover's truck tailed them. Soon, the two vehicles boarded the large ferry that was to transfer them to their new Greek island life.

Elafonisos was a beauty. A gem offered by nature. An arrow-shaped isle dropped into the turquoise waters just below the Peloponnese Peninsula.

They drove into town with their heads turning from left to right as they made their way through the quiet streets.

'Our house is on the outskirts of town. Near the beach,' her father commented. 'The sea just a few steps from our front door. Imagine that!'

Demetra leaned forward. 'And the hotel you will be working at?'

'Just a ten-minute drive away. The Simos Mare Resort. Named after the island's best-known beach. You must have seen it on postcards before. The golden sand beach with the sandy corridor that connects Elafonisos with a smaller islet.'

Demetra nodded. She had seen it before in geography class.

'Well, it isn't really an island if it is connected to this island, is it?' Helka said.

'Hmm, you have a point dear. We'll have to look that one up,' he replied and placed his hand upon hers. They exchanged a sweet look. Demetra fell back and controlled a sigh from gaining too much noise. He used to look at her mother like that during their happiest of times.

Island life suited the odd pair. Both with a lazy mentality and yearning for a chilled daily life, they had the summer of their lives. Their small bungalow by the beach did not require much maintenance and their jobs at the resort were easy and enjoyable. Demetra fit in well at the small local school, turned seventeen and became more independent. They hardly ever noticed her anymore. They seemed madly in love and her father never even entered her bedroom since their arrival.

Demetra enjoyed the last carefree summer of her life.

She went to the beach with her newly found classmates and lingered under the sizzling sun for hours. The group of teens drank, listened to music and ate cheap gyro kebabs until nightfall.

September though arrived and changes came to Demetra's life.

Schools reopened and Demetra prepared for her final year in high school. She avoided socializing much as her goal was to improve her good grades and succeed in her university entry exams. Her dream. Her only dream. She visualized being eighteen years old with a scholarship and she would be free. Free to leave. Free to live. That was her only goal.

The next change came when once again her father and Helka sat her down to announce their pregnancy.

'You remember how we lost the first. Helka will take it easy from now on. Spend as much time as she can in bed or on the sofa. You, Demetra, must help out more around the house. Cooking, cleaning and so on.'

'Of course, father.' She forced a smile. '*I already do more than your lazy cow.*'

Helka's first of many scares came end of the month. 'Blood in the toilet!' she had screamed and off to the hospital they went.

Helka had to remain laying down. No activity what-so-ever.

End of October, her father's visits began.

Demetra had never escaped Hell. It had only been dormant.

She resisted more this time. And that is when the beating started. Her father would choke her half to death if she pushed him away. He threatened to kill her if she ever went to the police as she threatened.

'And what future will you have, my sweet child?' He laughed and mocked her as he left her room. 'Who would believe you?'

Demetra drifted into herself. Darkness roamed her mind.

In desperation, she decided to talk to her mother-in-law.

It was a rainy evening in February when her father was at work and she had returned home from school. She dropped her No-Fear bag by the door and went straight to Helka's bedroom. Soap operas boomed from the TV's speakers. Demetra waited for a commercial break and then knocked on the door.

Helka sat upon the bed with her back leaned into four soft pillows. Her baby bump was visible under the sheets. Vinegar flavored crisps had taken over the bedside table and their odor filled the air of the small room.

'What's up, little one?'

'Can I talk to you about something?'

'Speak up, child!'

'I need to have a word with you. Turn off the TV, please,' Demetra said, raising her voice.

Helka tried to read her expression. She then rolled her eyes, sighed and reluctantly switched off the blurring television.

Demetra approached and sat down on the edge of the bottom of the bed.

She had rehearsed her lines many times before and now found herself lost for words. She struggled at first, but as soon as she began retelling her ordeal since her mother's death, the words came flooding out like a mighty river that broke down its dam.

'…I wished, hoped, our move here would change things, but he is still the same. As soon as you can't be with him in that way, he turns to me!'

Tears fell freely. She shook all over as she spoke.

'Poor, poor little Demetra,' Helka said and Demetra picked up her patronizing tone.

'You must believe me!'

'Oh, I believe you, child. You think I am a fool? That Helka is an idiot? Of course, I know about your father's escapades in your room!'

The revelation shocked Demetra who could not believe what she was hearing. She shivered as she tried to stand up. She stumbled a couple of steps back. Her anger rose as she stared at Helka's apathetic face. 'You know? And did nothing? You monster! You fucking heartless bitch!'

'Ooohh, who's a big girl, now, hey? Cursing and all?'

Demetra clenched her hands into fists. 'You let your own husband rape a child? Cheat on you?'

Helka waved her hand and chuckled. 'Oh, please. He is

a man. He only goes to you when I can't serve him. I'd rather have him be here with you than out with another woman that could steal him.'

Demetra shook her head. 'No, no. This can't be. This is unthinkable. It is twisted and insane…'

'Relax, girl. Men will be men. It will do you good. You are experienced now and know what to expect.'

Demetra found it difficult to breath. The walls were closing in. The stale air was chocking her. 'I will report you both. This is not normal. It must end!' The words came from the depths of her courage. She yelled each word. She had reached her limit. She turned to run out of the bedroom. Helka's words followed her.

'Don't you dare, or I will ruin you! I will support my man. I will testify that you are a liar. A little whore that sleeps around. No wonder your vagina is so wide! I will say you always want more money and asked for a car and because we refused you made up this lie. No one will believe you! They will ask, why didn't you say something all these years? Why now? They will believe me. Your father and I are respectable adults with a perfect record. You stand no chance against us, child! None! You will be left homeless and alone!'

Demetra screamed and rushed out of the house. She ran all the way down to Kontogoni Bay, sat down by the large gray rocks that were splashed by the restless sea and wept. Wild thoughts roamed out of the darkness of her mind. *'Go away, demons!'*

She brought her mother to her mind. Her angelic face with the shinning halo. Her smile calmed her. She wiped away her tears and accepted her fate. With her shoulders lowered, she walked the peaceful beach until nightfall. She returned home and headed straight to the shower. She could hear them enjoying their dinner in the living room in front of the TV. She returned to her bedroom without speaking to them. Hungry and tired, she studied her homework and fell asleep within minutes of slipping under the covers.

The next few months passed without any late-night visits. Helka must have spoken to him. The thought gave her hope. She avoided them as must as she could, and the uneventful months swam by.

Helka's belly grew large during her last trimester. She wobbled about the bungalow with a happy glow. She had managed to carry her embryo into a safe enough to be born stage. She was going to be a mother.

One June night with a clear sky and a hot breeze, they called Demetra into the living room.

'Come sit down, sweetie,' her father said, patting the sofa.

'What's up?' she casually asked and sat down in the armchair away from them.

'Well, as you know, Helka's days are nearly up. The baby could arrive any day, now.'

'Yes, I have noticed your preparations.'

Her father had taken days off work and had fixed up the nursery. The walls welcomed a stroke of fresh paint and her father set up a DIY cot for the newborn. His stay at home worried her, but her nights remained without nightly visits.

'Well, we need to discuss a name,' Helka declared. 'We all get one vote. Even you.'

Her father read her puzzled look. 'We can't settle on a name, so we decided to leave up to Lady Luck. We will all write down a name and put in my hat. I will give it a swirl and the first paper to fall out will be our baby girl's name.'

Demetra smiled and nodded. 'Sounds like a great idea, dad.'

Helka picked up the blue pen from the coffee table and ripped a small piece of paper. She spoke as she wrote. 'I looked for a name that is the same in Greek and Finnish. I settled on Elli which means pledge to God, who I thank for this blessing. Elli is used here and can be the short version of Elina or even Elizabeth. That way she will have a Finnish name but not sound like a foreigner.' She folded the piece of paper and threw it in the hat.

Her father spoke next as Helka passed him the pen. The wind blew in hot, and he wiped his forehead. 'I vote for Melpomene. It is a hard and long name, but it was my grandmother's, and no one took on her name. She was a strong intelligent woman and I admired her greatly. I looked it up as you, my baby, love names with a meaning. Melpomene was the Greek muse of tragedy...'

'You want to name our baby after tragedy?'

Her husband laughed out loud.

'*I should be named after that,*' Demetra thought.

'No, no. Her name means to celebrate with dance and song. You always wanted to be a dancer and you sing so well, so I thought it would be a fitting name for a girl that will come from you.' Helka leaned forward and with one hand on her belly, she gave him a kiss on the lips. He rolled up the piece of paper and tossed into the hat. Both turned to face Demetra.

'Err, you kind of caught me by surprise, but I have something in mind.' She took the pen from her father's hand by its edge, avoiding touching his skin.

'I like the name Pandora.'

'Pandora?' they both repeated.

'Yes, Pandora. Because whenever something bad is

released or happening, there is always hope. Hope is always there. Nothing horrific can go on forever. Better days will come. Always!' Her piece of paper landed by the other two.

Her father stood up and theatrically picked up his sports cap. 'Well, he we go. Name time!' He began to shake his cap and spin it around. A piece of paper fell out and landed on the floor. 'The moment of truth!' He picked it up and looked at his wife. 'I think I recognize this folding! Oh, yes! It's Helka's! The baby will be named Elli!'

Helka stood up and clapped. The joy on her face was obvious. She sang an old traditional Finnish song and swayed to its rhythm. A song that she never finished as water wet her sweatpants and ran down her leg, darkening the light blue fabric.

Elli came into the world hours later.

Returning home days later, Helka transformed into a control freak with a bossy attitude. At least, that is what her husband complained about to his friends at work. Elli was a restless baby. A restless baby with a love for the nighttime. She cried all day to be fed and with her tiny tummy full, she would take long naps. Naps long enough to give her strength to cry through the night. Demetra could see that Helka was not coping well, and her inner mean spirit multiplied. Her arrows were shot though toward her father, something Demetra was happy about.

As always, her happiness never lasted.

It was a warm night as most were during the first days of August. Demetra turned her air-conditioning on and headed to her en suite shower. Upon her return, she found her father sitting on the edge of her bed. Demetra froze on the spot.

'Get out.'

Her father replied with a smile and a pat on the mattress.

'Get out, please. I want to dress.'

'Nothing I haven't seen before. I made you. Now, come here. Sit down.'

Demetra remained firmly still. She could feel the strength in her legs. She was going to stand her ground. 'No! Get out, now!'

Her father stood up and walked up to her. He brought his face inches away from hers. She could smell the cheap whiskey on his breath. He leaned forward and licked her neck. 'Sleep tight, sweetie,' he said and wobbled out of her room. Demetra closed the door behind him and slid down the door, holding her mouth. She did not want to give him the satisfaction of hearing her cry. She wished she had a key for her door, but the monster would never allow such a thing.

It took her hours to relax and to finally fall asleep.

Her door though was going to be reopened. Her father twisted and turned on the living room sofa all night. He could not bear her rejection. Cold sweat formed on the back of his neck and on his wide forehead. He looked across at the clock on the wall. Its hands were illuminated by the moonlight creeping in. It was half past three. He pulled down his green boxer shorts and grabbed his erection. He began to masturbate violently. No release came. He picked up the bottle of whiskey on the coffee table and drank the rest of its remains. Naked as he was, he walked over to his daughter's room.

Demetra was awoken by his hand covering her mouth. She could feel him trying to pull down her pajama bottoms. She bit down with force on his suffocating hand. Her father yelled out in pain. He punched her on the back of her head.

Demetra fell out of the bed and ran for the door. Her father stood up and pulled her by the hair, throwing her on the floor. He fell down upon her.

'Get off me!' Demetra struggled to break free. She scratched him on his face with her nails. She dug deep into his skin and stopped only at the sight of blood.

'You little bitch,' he yelled and began hitting her across the face. Demetra kicked him with force and pushed him back. She ran to the kitchen. She could hear his footsteps following her. Demetra opened the kitchen drawer as he grabbed her from behind. His fingers intertwined with her hair and he hit her head down on the counter with force. Demetra felt drowsy. She found it difficult to keep her eyes open. She felt her pajamas and underwear being pulled down. Her father entered her with might. Demetra cried out in pain. Her hands searching through the open kitchen drawer. She picked up the large kitchen knife firmly. The first stab was to the side of his chest. He shook from the pain and stepped back in shock. Demetra turned and without hesitation stabbed him in the neck. She watched as blood splashed out high in the air. Her father fell back and landed on a small glass table, smashing it to pieces. Demetra stood above him and with delight shining in her eyes, she witnessed the light go out in his. He panted and exhaled one last loud breath.

She was finally free from him.

Suddenly, Helka's animal-like scream broke the silence. She ran straight for Demetra, leaping upon her, bringing her to the ground. 'You killed my man. My husband! How could you?' she howled. She shrieked as she slapped Demetra all over. 'Then go join him,' Demetra said calmly as Helka tried to strangle the girl. She stabbed her mother-in-law in the same spot. Straight through the neck.

In a matter of minutes, Demetra viewed a second person leaving their last breath behind. She stumbled over to the sofa and collapsed back into its soft back. She threw the bloody knife away from her and sat hollow and serene in the silence.

A silence broken much later by the baby's cries. Demetra stood up and walked into her bedroom. She quickly emptied her school bag from her books and threw in a change of clothes. She then rushed into the master bedroom. The baby continued crying. Demetra headed to her father's closet and took out a large cupboard box. She opened it, threw out the old clothes and took out his hidden cash from the bottom. Crunched-up notes prisoned together by a rubber band. He was saving for a new car yet did not want Helka to know that he had his eyes fixed on an expensive car. She would not have approved. Demetra placed the thirteen thousand in her bag and stood up. She looked across at the blond baby with the two blue eyes set upon her.

'I'm sorry. The police will come, soon. You will be fine. You are better off without them.'

Just then, the doorbell echoed through the bungalow. Banging on the door followed. It was the neighbors. 'Hello? You alright in there?'

Demetra picked up the crying baby and rocked her to be quiet. It felt good to hold her in her arms. Looking into her sister's eyes, she changed her mind. 'Come on then, sis. It's just us, now.' Demetra placed the baby in the box and closed it, hoping the darkness would soothe the infant back to sleep. With her bag on her back and with the heavy box in her arms, Demetra climbed out the window and vanished into the night.

Chapter Thirty-Two

Adrian watched as his front porch light flicked to life. It was still evening, but nightfall came earlier to his cabin due to the tall trees and the towering mountain range that embraced the forest. His mind was in overdrive but a victim of his empty stomach. He turned the key and entered inside. He headed straight to his freezer. A see-through blue container held a large chunk of Mousakka. His mother had sent an entire tray via his uncle who visited the area a month ago. Adrian had cut up the delicious dish into equal portions, eating one, saving two in the fridge and storing the rest in the freezer. 'Such a Greek boy,' he sniggered as he placed the last piece into his rather unused microwave oven.

It went down nicely with a leafy green salad and a cold beer.

After placing the lone plate into the sink, he ventured to his back warehouse. 'It has to be here somewhere,' he mumbled as he went through gathered belongings. His search was a success as he found his pin board. He blew away the dust that had settled on the brown wood and smiled at the sight of multiple-colored pins all lined-up in the down right corner. He had formed lines out of them, grouping them by color. 'A touch of your mother's OCD showing big boy.'

The bulletin board left the dark damp storage room and entered the bright and clean living room. Adrian was not a fan of souvenirs nor photographs. The mantelpiece was nearly bare. Saved only by his trophy in basketball from his academy days. He pushed the prize to the edge and placed the board on it. He brought his coffee table up to the seasonally empty fireplace and spread out his police notes. He took out a new blue pen and placed it on a pile of A4 papers. His phone was placed next, opened to his gallery. He read the coroner's reports again and went through all his photographs taken over the previous days.

'Everything is here. This must make sense.'

He went over his notes and then read through Leventi's and Arianna's contributions. He began to scribble down every vital detail and pinned it up on the board. He cut pieces of paper and wrote down his suspects. The names of everyone interviewed followed. String by string he connected the pins. He used different colors for different patterns. He mumbled to himself as he looked for connections. 'The two bodies are connected. A hair from the first body was found on the second body, both died on the same day and they both ate the same food.'

And the killer remained unknown.

'Something is missing from the equation. What am I missing here?'

Adrian tapped his fingers on Melpomene's photograph from the case file. 'Who are you? And more importantly, if it's not you, then who?'

Adrian took a deep breath. 'Maybe I don't need to add

to the equation, but to remove. Not everything here can be correct.'

A weird thought crept forward from the back of his mind. A thought he knew had been born days ago, yet he feared to analyze it.

'Let's take *you* out of the equation, then.'

Ten minutes later, Adrian ran out of his house for what he called a power-run. A head-clearing run. He pushed himself to his limits. *'Could it be so?'* The last light of the day allowed him to trek the perimeter of the woods. The path below his feet was narrow and overgrown weeds had invaded, but the lack of rocks made it a sensible running route.

As darkness engulfed the valley, Adrian returned home sweating all over and out of breath. He headed straight to the shower. The cold water washed away sweat and dirt. It could not, though, wash away the peculiar emotion of guilt.

With his body dried and clothed, he picked up his phone. He was finally ready for confirmation. He looked down at his notes and punched in the number.

'Hello?'

'Yes, this is Police Lieutenant Adrian Metsovitis with the Parga police...'

'Yes?'

'... I am sorry to bother you, sir, at such an hour but I truly believe this might be a conversation of the upmost importance.'

Leventi was not expecting a call. Surely, he was not expecting the call that came on that hot night. He muted the television and answered to his colleague. In clear disbelief, he sat in his boxers on his two-seater and listened to what Adrian had to say.

'Is there no one else? I… I am dating Katie now and…'

'For fuck's sake, Leventi. Put on your uniform, get a patrol car and do as I say!'

Leventi had never heard the Lieutenant curse before. Never had Adrian's voice crack or brake before. He was always steady, sure in what he was saying. Leventi stood up and threw punches in the air. 'Shit!' He rushed to his room and took out his uniform from the washing basket. He was not about to dirty another pair. He wore the same one, he had on that day. He splashed some cologne on his unshaved neck and sprayed some deodorant upon his upper body. In a matter of minutes, he was out the door and took the elevator to the underground parking. With his head drowsy from the new information, he drove to the station.

'What are you doing back here?' the front-desk secretary asked.

'Extra hours, apparently,' he joked as he headed to the key locker. 'I'm taking vehicle KRZ.'

With the key in his hand, he exited back out to the parking. He still could not wrap his head around who he was about to arrest. He drove slower than usual as if his mind knowingly was delaying him from his task ahead. He parked outside of the house. Most lights were on. He could see heads from inside turning to see who had parked outside of their home. '*You are a professional. You've got this!*'

Leventi straightened his shirt and walked up to the house.

The front door opened before he reached it. Katie stepped outside and closed the door behind her. She wore a casual flowery dress that ran to her knees. Leventi hated that he noticed that she was not wearing a bra. '*Concentrate!*'

'What are you doing here? My father is home. He…'

'Katie, I'm sorry. I truly am. I am not here for you. I am here on police business.'

'Police business? Ten at night?'

The front door reopened. Iris stood between her parents. She resembled her father. Same cheeks and eyes. Yet they wore differently expressions. One of curiosity, one of fear.

'What's up, officer?'

'Sir, I am sorry to bother you all, but I am here to escort your daughter to the station.'

'What?' his mother screamed. 'Are you mad? Your questions can surely wait for the morning.' Her anger grew as she noticed curtains moving around on many neighbohood windows. 'This is ludicrous. Babe, do something.'

'For what reason?' her calm father asked.

'In connections to the Pandora case, sir.'

'Well,' he said, scratching his short grayish beard, 'we refuse.'

Leventi looked straight at the man. 'You don't understand, sir. I am here to arrest Iris. There is no need to make this any more difficult than it already is.' He starred across at Katie who had sat down on a garden chair and placed her head in her hands.

Both her parents had turned their attention to Iris. She was trembling all over.

'I did not kill anyone! You have to believe me!'

'Of course, we do, sweetie,' her mother said and hugged her.

'Leventi, is my daughter being accused…'

'Sir, I cannot reveal anything. She is being arrested for questioning in connection to the murder. If she cooperates with the authorities, I am sure everything will work out. Iris, put some shoes on and please come with me to the vehicle.'

'I am coming with you.'

'Ma'am, she is over eighteen…'

'Just! It has only been a few months.'

'She is an adult.'

'She doesn't require a chaperone. But you are free to come to the station in your own vehicle.'

Her mother wept in her husband's arms as they watched their youngest daughter walk out of the house and into the backseat of the police car. Katie, unlike most of the neighbors, could not bear to witness the scene.

Iris looked out of the window as Leventi drove off down the street. She closed her eyes and told herself to be strong.

'*What a fucking brilliant night,*' Leventi thought as he headed back to the station.

Adrian felt the same way about his night. After he had finished his phone call to the coroner, he had sat down on the floor, trying to control his raging pulse. He knew where he had to go. He had one stop though before that. The local park.

Chapter Thirty-Three

'Popcorn's ready, mama!'

'Yeah, I can hear it,' Arianna shouted as she nested comfortably in the corner of her sofa. 'You better not have made a mess in there!'

'Do I ever?' Timothy replied as he entered the living room with a large orange bowl in hand. 'Butter *and* salt. Just like you love them.'

'My perfect boy.' Arianna kissed her son on his cheek as he sat down beside her. 'Only you forgot to turn off the light. I can't enjoy a movie with the lights on.' The 65-inch television was on pause. The latest James Bond movie had been prepared.

Timothy jumped up again and headed toward the switch. 'Did you find subtitles for it?' he asked before turning into a statue. His eyes were fixed at the window.

'What's wrong, Timmy?'

He did not reply. The doorbell echoed around the house. Arianna stood up. 'Who can that be?'

'It's Adrian,' Timothy said, and his eyes trembled as he turned toward his mother.

'Be quiet and sit down.'

Adrian rang the bell one more time. He could hear their voices coming from inside. He was getting ready to knock when the door retreated to reveal Arianna standing in a pair of tracksuit bottoms and a black tank top.

'Hey. What's going on, Adrian?' She looked down at her phone as if asking, why didn't you call?

'Can I come in, boss?'

Arianna tilted her head. 'The house is a bit of a mess. Can we talk out here? Timothy is inside…'

'I want him to hear what I have to say, too.'

Arianna placed her hand upon her heart. 'Adrian, what's up?'

The tall man did not reply as he walked past her. He dragged the armchair nearest to him next to the television. He switched off the TV before sitting down opposite Timothy. 'Captain, please sit down by your son. Hands where I can see them.'

'Now, you watch your tone there. I am your superior and you dare waltz in here telling me what to do or not, in my own house. Get the hell out of it. Are you drunk?'

'Please, sit down. This is hard enough for me, already. We need to talk,' Adrian said and placed his hand upon his firearm. Arianna noticed the clip of the black holder was unbuttoned.

Arianna sat down and crossed her arms. 'Talk, then, Lieutenant. Thought I doubt that will be your rank by noon tomorrow. I am filing this in. You are way out of line.'

'More out of line than withholding evidence and lying throughout an entire murder case?'

Arianna opened her arms and leaned forward. 'Those

are some serious accusations, Lieutenant. You sure about this crap you are uttering?'

'Jane Doe?'

'What about it? We have had this conversation before. The coroner...'

'Yes, we have. That was the problem. Every time I went over the case, things just did not add up. Things that should have, did not make sense. But, when I finally dared to remove *you* from the equation and look at the case with what I knew, not with what I knew from you, I came to very different conclusions.'

'And what conclusions are these?'

'Pandora is still alive.'

'You're insane!'

Adrian bit his bottom lip and sighed. 'I have already told myself that. I admire you greatly and always paid attention to your professionalism, and maybe that's why I noticed all the gaps that you were creating in the case.'

Arianna patted her legs and sniggered. 'Such as, mister investigator?'

'The waterfalls.' Adrian looked straight at Timothy. He glimpsed the terror on the boy's face before he turned away. 'You searched the woods alone. You did not mention anything or put any input into the case file. I went up to the cave. It is obvious the body was dragged in the cave but carried there through the woods. From somewhere near the waterfalls. The waterfalls are the only place in Parga where you can die from a fall, as it is rocky as hell before landing in water. Did you search there? I did. The rocks had been wiped clean. All other rocks had gathered dirt and mould. Not all though. A line of them had been cleaned spotless. No so much as to not react with luminol. Blood had been there. I'm betting blood from the first body.'

'Pandora's.'

'You're still sticking to that line? I spoke to the doctor, Jacob. The coroner confirmed that the DNA did not match that of Pandora's. He told you so when he called you. But you told Melpomene lies about the body being her daughter or whoever she is to her. I drove myself mad seeking for a reason why you would lie. The only possible answer was to cover up for the killer.'

Arianna stood up. She was flushed and breathing heavily. 'You are so getting fired for this bullshit. I have had enough of your accusations. I am the captain of the police and you believe I am covering for a murderer?'

Adrian took out his gun. 'Sit down,' he said with a strange serenity in his voice. 'You would do anything for your son. You always have.'

'I...' Timothy opened his mouth.

Arianna fell back and placed her hand upon her heart. 'Shut up, Timmy. Shut the fuck up. Don't you dare utter a single word.' She turned toward Adrian. 'You have zero evidence.'

'I have enough to get you off the case, out of office and investigated for tampering with a murder case. I also went to the park before coming here. Spoke to your classmates, Timothy. Antony said the waterfalls was your favorite spot. On the day of the murder, you lot were supposed to meet there. You went first, they said. You always went first. Then you texted them all saying the camping out day was cancelled and quickly sorted out a party down at the beach. You changed the plans pretty quick. What happened at the waterfalls, Timmy?'

'I... I didn't mean to hurt anyone...'

A loud gasp escaped from Arianna as a heavy sigh departed from her trembling lips. She placed both her hands upon her chest and fell forward. 'Mum? Mum?' Timothy cried out as he knelt by her side. Arianna's eyes were opened wide, but no words left her mouth. She shook all over. 'I think she is having a heart attack. She has been having these weird feelings lately.'

Adrian stood up and took out his phone. 'This is officer Metsovitis; I am requesting an ambulance immediately at Captain Kontou's house. Hurry! I think she is having a heart attack.'

Arianna reached out her hand toward Adrian. She struggled with the words. 'Don't... Don't...'

'Sssh, Arianna. It is going to be okay.'

'Mum, relax.'

'Don't ruin my boy's life. Please. It was an accident. Blame me.'

She seemed to want to say more, but had no power left in her. She felt as if an elephant was stomping upon her aching heart. She closed her eyes and fell back, losing her senses.

The ambulance lights invaded through the thin curtains and danced around upon the walls. The paramedics rushed in and ordered the two men to stand back.

Adrian placed his arm around the boy's shoulders as he cried watching his mother not responding. The paramedics carried her out. 'We need to get her to the hospital ASAP,' the short woman with the thin-framed glasses said.

Timothy looked at the tall officer holding him. 'Can I go or am I under arrest?'

'Go. Be with your mother. You are her reason to live. Go!'

Chapter Thirty-Four

Maria watched as her husband got up and walked around their living room with his phone glued to his ear. She paused their movie and sat up straight. The late hour and the fact that her husband stood up and walked for the call worried her. *'Another dead body ruining our date night. I can't wait for his retirement!'*

The coroner finally lowered his phone and formed the sign of the cross on his body. 'Well, I'll be damned.'

'Let me guess. Got to go?' Disappointment colored her voice.

'No. It was from an officer in Parga. Remember the body on the anchor? His Captain lied that it was Pandora when it wasn't. I told her it wasn't. And I fucking wondered when I saw the news talking about the dead girl in Parga but shook it off. I thought it was just a ploy to get the girl to lower her guard and make a mistake as to find her. I assumed that the missing girl was probably their main suspect.' He sat down and smacked the wooden coffee table.

'I am a fool. I should have checked! It was only a phone call to ask why.'

Maria pushed up against him. 'And you would have called the captain and she would have lied to you and mention all the excuses you thought of. You have no blame in this. My question is why in hell did the captain lie about the body's true identity?'

'The officer has a theory that she was protecting her son.'

Maria bit her lip and sighed. 'The things Greek mothers do for their offspring will never seize to amaze me!'

Chapter Thirty-Five

Iris taped her fingers on the white table and observed the circles that formed in her glass of water. It reminded her of the T-Rex attack in that *old-nineties* movie she once saw. She wished the ferocious dinosaur would show up and devour the police officers and wreck the station. She wanted to flee. She dreamt of running out of the bright room and screaming like a mad woman, only to vanish forever in the woods.

Her thoughts were interrupted by the door opening behind her. She had seen the tall handsome man before. She could not remember his name.

'Hi, Iris. Remember me? I am Lieutenant Adrian Metsovitis,' he said as he pulled back the chair and sat down comfortably in it. His smile seemed genuine but the sorrow in his eyes scared Iris. He was controlling his emotions. He was keeping his nerves in place. '*Why is he so upset? His facial muscles are twitching…*'

'Iris?' The girl was lost in thought.

'Yes?' Her voice trembled. She scratched the shaved side of her head.

'You can relax. Take a deep breath. All I want is a few honest answers. This charade has gone on long enough.'

Iris nodded.

'And no need for lies. I imagine carrying the burden of the truth is eating you up inside, right?'

'I... I don't know what it is you want me to say.'

'Where is Pandora?'

Behind the mirrored glass, her parents exchanged a shocked look. Both turned to face officer Leventi who was with them. He looked more surprised than them.

Inside the room, though, Iris did not flicker. She remained still for a second, before sniggering. 'Dead. You were there. You saw her. Murdered and thrown on...' She paused and closed her eyes. She wiped her eyes, though Adrian noticed that neither had produced any tears.

'I saw *a* body. And I also saw you come forward and say it was Pandora. You even explained the slight difference in the hair color, claiming that it was you that dyed it for her. It was also you that provided us with a timeline of Pandora's whereabouts of the previous day.'

'Nefeli was with us, too.'

'True. But Nefeli was with you for only a couple of hours that day as it turns out, right? She did not mention being at any hair dying. She, and others, too, did mention though that you were acting weird that night. You said Pandora left early. Nefeli did not see her leave. According to your statement, she left at eleven and you were the last person to be with her before she disappeared.'

'Before she died!'

'DNA results, my dear child. Zip it with the fairy tales and get talking before I charge you with obstruction of justice, for starters. I know that was not Pandora on that anchor. So, where the hell is she?'

Iris played with her fingers and kept her eyes closed.

'Don't risk your future, Iris, for a foolish high-school crush. You have your entire life before you!'

Iris opened her eyes. 'Thanks for outing me in front of my parents, dickhead!'

Adrian crossed his arms upon his chest. 'Put your phone on the table.'

'What?'

'Put your phone on the table and you are free to go.'

Iris remained still and silent.

The door flung open, and her father rushed in. Officer Leventi trailed him, ordering him to get out.

'Just give him your damn phone, Iris, before I rip it off you. Now!'

The veins on his neck ganged up for a party. He breathed heavily.

'Fine! For fuck's sake, here! Have it! Can I go now?' she asked as she threw her cell on the table.

Adrian took the phone, pressed on the contact's list and scrolled through it.

'Pandora's phone is off by the way!'

Adrian could not control a chuckle. 'You think no one has thought of calling her number? Of course, it is off. And probably smashed to be untraceable.' He continued scrolling. Only one contact had been created within the last week. 'Who is Sexy Smart One, huh?'

Iris's face went pale.

Adrian dialed the number with the speaker on loud.

'Hey, bitch! What's up? Thank God, you called. I am dying of boredom in this...'

'Pandora, shut up! I have been arrested! They know!

Not from me!' Iris yelled as her father pulled her out of the room.

'Pandora, your game is over. Please…' Adrian did not manage to finish his sentence. Pandora ended the call. Adrian punched the table and looked at Leventi. 'Put out a signal to Athens's headquarters. I want Pandora's photo up everywhere. She is now officially a missing person and most likely a suspect in a double murder case. She can't leave the country.'

'Yes, sir.' Leventi took a step back but did not leave the room. 'Err, sir? Shouldn't we inform her mother that her daughter isn't dead? Imagine hearing it from elsewhere.'

'I will head over there right away. I need to speak to Melpomene anyway.'

Adrian watched as Leventi rushed out. He then picked up his phone and called police tech support.

'Yes? Hi there. I am Lieutenant Adrianos Metsovitis, 5692 with the Parga police. I need a pinpoint on the phone number, 6927461095. As soon as possible, please.'

Chapter Thirty-Six

'Fuck!'

Pandora threw her newly bought cell phone to the wall of her rented studio apartment. The pieces fell to the ground on an old worn-in carpet. The old lady that owned the place had not bothered to renovate it since 1995. Pandora picked up the sim card and folded it in half. She took it to the kitchen counter and with a rusty pair of scissors she cut it into four equal slices.

'Why? Why? Why the hell, why?'

She paced up and down the small room, waving her hands in the air. She picked up the laptop she had stolen from school without anyone noticing and sat down on the screechy bed. Her mother's photo appeared. Pandora read the passage she had written underneath.

'No reason to delay revealing your sins, dear *mother*!' She mocked the word and rolled her eyes. She looked down and pressed UPLOAD. As soon as it reached one hundred percent, Pandora took the battery out of the computer. She quickly began to pack her few belongings. Mostly clothes bought from a local store around the corner.

'Goodbye, charming little shit hole,' she said and out into the night she went.

Adrian had just parked outside Pandora's former residence when he received the call from the Electronic Crime Division.

'Lieutenant Metsovitis?'

'This is he.'

'Calling to inform you, sir that the Pandora's Box webpage has just had some activity. Someone logged in from somewhere on the outskirts of Ioannina. The text from the final photo was uploaded. I have emailed you the text as we have locked access to the site from the public.'

'Thanks a freaking billion! Have police units been sent to the spot?'

'Already on their way, sir.'

Adrian thanked the officer again and ended the call. His fingers trembled as he opened his emails.

'Melpomene Whatever! Fake ass murdering bitch!' he read the title. 'Born Demetra Agriou. Does the name ring a bell, crime fans? Yes, Melpomene is the young girl who seventeen years ago butchered and slaughtered her own father and mother-in-law! Covered in their innocent blood, the lunatic teen kidnapped their baby, her half-sister! ME! She murdered my mother and raised me as her own. If the police have one chore to do tonight that is to arrest that psycho killer! I bet she is the one dumping bodies all over Parga, as well!' Adrian read it out loud. He read it twice and still could not believe it. He gazed across at the house. The conversation ahead had just transformed into an arrest. He Googled the nearly two-decade-old case. The picture of a school photo of the wanted girl appeared. He could see the similarities now. The spark in her eyes, the sharp nose, and her thin lips. She had obviously dyed her hair and aged since then, but Melpomene was definitely Demetra Agriou. Adrian was a teen at the time yet remembered the case well. It was all over the news and his parents discussed it over dinner. His father was sure that the girl killed her parents -as the evidence pointed to, but his kind-hearted mother supported the notion that the two girls were taken by the murderers. 'Or worse, the killer murdered the girl and the baby and buried them as to escape getting life,' his mother had said.

Adrian walked up to the house as the slice of a moon above shone down on the sealed-for-the-night blossoms of Ophelia, wondering if there was a possibility of Melpomene's innocence. Or how likely it was that she was connected somehow to the body found in the cave. He pictured the face of the old woman as he knocked on her door at such a late hour.

Lights came to life inside the dark house. Melpomene opened the door. She opened and closed her eyes in disbelief. She quickly stepped outside and closed the door behind her. 'Grandma Ophelia is asleep. Let's try not to wake her. What's up, officer? Did you find my daughter's killer?'

Adrian looked at the woman in her white night gown that fell to her ankles. 'There is no easy way to say this, ma'am, but I have to ask you to follow me to the station. I will come inside with you and wait outside your door as you dress.'

Melpomene ran the tip of her tongue through her sealed lips. Her eyes gave away the turmoil in her soul. She struggled to speak clearly and without pause. 'Why is that officer? Haven't I been through enough? Can't this wait until morning?'

'It is not a request, ma'am.'

'Am I under arrest? What for?'

Adrian placed his hands upon his head and walked up and down the porch. 'My grandfather loved asking, do you want the good news first or the bad news? He had an entire theory about judging people based on their answer.'

'May I ask his theory before answering then?'

Adrian sat down on a wooden chair. Melpomene noticed his firearm hung low as it was unclipped. 'Well, roughly, he said the brave and daring opted for the bad news first, the scared and weak for the good news as they wanted to lift their spirits before embracing for the impact of the bad. His favorites were those who replied that they didn't mind. He said those were the ones that enjoyed life the most and would live to one hundred!'

'I was gonna ask for the bad news first. I'm guessing it will be the reason for my arrest.'

'We know you are Demetra Agriou.'

Melpomene took a step back. Her knees shook. 'It has been forever since I have heard that name. I have almost forgotten that that is who I truly am.'

'Now, you know why you are coming with me.'

Her fingers played around with the golden cross hanging from her neck. The thin chain it lived on was hardly visible. 'I kind of knew that this day would come. It is rather peculiar. I did not expect to feel so calm. I guess I do not care anymore. My baby is dead. I am tired of hiding and living in constant fear.' She exhaled loudly and looked up at the cloudless summer sky. 'Lord, do as you must.' She turned her attention toward Adrian. 'And the good news?'

'Pandora is alive.'

Melpomene placed her right hand upon her heart and knelt to the ground. Her trembling eyes watered up. 'Don't mock me. How can this be true?'

'The body is not hers. The coroner confirmed it. DNA was not a match.'

'But Arianna said…'

'She was wrong.'

Melpomene raised her hands. 'Praise you, Jesus. Praise you Mother Mary!' Tears of joy ran down her pale cheeks. 'How can I be sure that you are not the one that is wrong?'

'I spoke to her over the phone. She panicked. She is the one that uploaded who you really are on that webpage of hers.'

Melpomene stood up quickly. She was shaking her head. 'No, no! How did she find out? She must think I am a monster. Is this why she ran away? You must take me to her. Please, I have to explain it to her. She can't believe that I am such a brutal murderer! Oh, Lord, she must hate me so much right now. Take me to her!'

'Explain what?'

Melpomene chuckled. 'You know what? I was about to say it is a long story, but now that you've asked, I have realized it is not that hard to explain. My dear mother died from cancer when I was a child and my father abused me ever since. He abused me for years. Sexually. He raped me again on that night. The beast he married knew all about it and approved. I had had enough. I was simply defending myself.'

'I am so sorry to hear that, Melpomene. I truly mean it. You do not come off a bad person to me, but you do understand that I have to take you in.'

'Of course.' Melpomene breathed in through her nostrils. She loved the night air of the summer from that

217

exact spot. The garden's aromas danced around in an endless waltz with the fresh and salty sea breeze. She doubted that she would ever be at that very spot ever again. 'I'll go get ready. I won't take long but I have to write a message to Ophelia, too.'

Chapter Thirty-Seven

The last zero on the black digital clock collecting dust on his desk switched to a one. The day had changed, and Adrian was still busy with filling in forms and making phone calls to police headquarters in Athens. He had arrested his Captain for obstruction causing her heart-attack, announced that Pandora was still alive and solved a seventeen-year-old case by arresting Melpomene.

As the one clicked and vanished, giving way to the two, his phone rang. He did not recognize the number.

'Hello?'

'This is Helen, the head nurse from the hospital. I am calling about Arianna Kontou? I am sorry to inform you that she passed away during surgery.' The nurse paused to give the recipient of her call time to process the news and let the grief sink in. 'Her son is here alone. His father is driving up from Athens and will not be here for another couple of hours, for sure. Timothy requested we call you.'

'I'm on my way,' was all he managed to say. He quickly

ended the call and placed his hands on his eyes. 'Damn it. No, Arianna, no!'

Grief and quilt are an awful cocktail.

Adrian drove over the speed limit for the first time in his life. He wept as he drove. He yelled profanities and punched the steering wheel.

It took him a while to gather his mind and walk up to the hospital's entrance after he parked. The nurse working the front desk was fixing her Rasta hair into a knot. Two paramedics sat on the hard uncomfortable gray chairs of the waiting room and were laughing over a meme one was showing the other on her cell phone.

'Hi, I'm officer Adrian Metsovitis…'

'Yes. They are expecting you. The kid is on the first floor in room twelve. We gave him an empty room to be alone in. He said he doesn't want to speak to us. Only you.'

Adrian thanked her and rushed up the stairs to his right. He pushed open the heavy fire door and looked straight at the numbers on the white doors with the blue frame. Room twelve was on his left. He stood outside the door and he could hear Timothy crying. He knocked and without waiting for an answer, he opened the door. Timothy was sitting on the floor, curled up and weeping with his head against his knees. He looked up at Adrian and pushed himself up. He did not bother wiping away his tears. 'She's dead.'

'I am so sorry. I…'

'It's my fault, not yours. I do not blame you, Adrian. I worried her to death.'

Adrian walked over to the boy and opened his arms. Murder suspect or not, he knew the boy for years. He owed it to Arianna. He hugged the boy and Timothy cried harder upon his chest.

'My mum made me record a message for you,' Timothy said, taking a step back. He took his phone out from his pocket and press play. Arianna's voice echoed out of the tiny speaker. Her voice was frail, and she spoke slowly.

'Adrian. My good partner, Adrian. I have really failed you, huh? Your high moral standards? I can sense myself falling from the pedestal you have placed me on. They are taking me into surgery any minute now.' She coughed and a minute went by before she spoke again. 'Allow me a dying wish. Do not arrest Timothy. He will tell you exactly what happened. This is all on me. I am to be blamed for panicking. An accident needs no suspect. Please! He has his entire life ahead of him. Do not taint his name just as he is about to go off to uni. He is eighteen! An adult in the eyes of the law. Even if he goes to jail for just a short period of time, can you imagine? A sweet gay virgin in there? I beg you, Adrian. On my dying bed, I plead to your sincere heart. I love you and respect you. It was an honor to call you my partner.'

The phone went quiet.

'Fuck, Arianna. Putting this on me!'

Timothy placed his hand on Adrian's shoulder. 'I don't mind if you choose to arrest me. I have had enough of guilt and lies and hiding these days. I don't want you to carry around something on your soul for the rest of your life. Do what you think is right. I'm tired. I'm exhausted from all this.'

Adrian sat down on the armchair behind him. 'Timmy, tell me exactly what happened that day.'

Timothy walked up to the window and gazed outside. 'The waterfalls are my favorite spot. We, the senior class that is, decided that we would spend the entire night of the last day of exams together partying. I proposed we camp there. Bathing suits, barbeques, speakers, the works. I could not relax and set off to the waterfalls an hour before the rest. I was swimming when I spotted the girl standing by my bag. I waved and she smiled. I swam up to her to found out who she was. My initial thought was that someone from class had invited her. She did not speak Greek. Her English was not good, either. We got talking anyhow. She was a German tourist camping out in the woods. She was interested in the waterfalls and asked if people jumped off the cliff into the waters. She wanted to try but feared the rocks below. I told her there were several safe spots and we walked up there. She took off her shorts and T-shirt. I dived first and shouted to her to jump in the exact spot. She was a perfect diver. She came out from the waters with a huge smile on her face. Again, she said, thrilled by adrenaline. As we went up, she placed her hands on me. She complimented my body. She leaned in and kissed me. Her hands...' Timothy paused. He looked down. 'She groped me there. Between the legs. I pushed her hand away. I tried to turn her down nicely, but she was vulgar. Talking about how she wanted to suck some Greek dick while on holiday and about how skillful she was. She tried to pull down my trunks. I panicked and stepped back while pushing her arms off me. She lost her balance and fell backward, rolling off the cliff on the rocky side.' Timothy turned around and looked straight at Adrian. 'I can still hear the awful sound of her body hitting against the rocks. Again, and again, she hit on the side of the hill until landing with a thud on the sharp rocks below. I rushed down. I went to her. I did not leave her. She was bleeding all over. Her face had...'

Adrian stood up and walked over to him. 'You are doing great. Please, continue. Get it off your chest.'

'Her face had smashed into the rocks. It looked like

collapsed into itself. I knew she was dead, but I still checked for a pulse. Nothing. She was dead.'

'And that's when you called your mum?'

'Of course. You call the police, right? That's the right thing to do. I should have called the station, not her cell. She was nearby, driving along the main road. She was there in minutes. I was expecting her to start calling, you know, ambulances and police and coroners and such. Yet, all she did was kneel by the body and check that the poor girl was dead. She then asked me when my friends were coming. Then she ordered me to go home. Let the next person find the body, she said. It was an accident. A clumsy foolish tourist fell to her death. No need to get into trouble. I could see the worry in her eyes when I told her that I pushed her off me. I never would have imagined that she would cover it all up.'

'So, what happened next?'

'I obeyed and went home. She stayed in her car further down the road and waited. Her plan was that the first kids to the party would discover the body and call it in. She would then arrive at the scene and declare it a tragic accident. A tourist that dived to her death. That way, the events would have nothing to do with me. My mate, Antony texted me twenty minutes later. He also went up there early. He video-called me from the waterfalls. You can picture my shock when Antony's smiling face appeared on my phone. No dead body in the background. The dead body was gone. I called my mother. She told me to text everyone that the party will not take place at the waterfalls but down at the beach. I was class president and team captain. Everyone just presumed it was a group decision and that I texted the decision out. The party took place down at Krioneri bay and mum searched the woods. Nothing. She found no sign of the missing body. It drove her mad. She was sure the girl was dead. I believed that maybe she was okay and got up and left. I wanted so badly to believe that that was the case. Mum wiped the rocks with some special detergent and told me to forget all about the incident. You can imagine our shock when the body turned up on the anchor. I was sure someone was going to out me or blackmail me or something. But then, Iris said it was Pandora. And she held Pandora's box, too. And her ripped bikini! How was that even possible? Mum was about to go insane. She freaked out and told me to stay home until she knew what the hell was going on. And now, she is dead. Fucking stupid heart attack!' Timothy controlled his tears. 'I swear to everything sacred, Adrian. I did not push her hard. She lost her step. She might have tripped on the rocks anyway. She was too busy trying to undress me and wasn't paying attention. I never meant for her to fall.'

'I know, I know,' Adrian said, embracing the trembling youth.

Adrian stayed with Timothy until his father arrived. Just before exiting the room to go be with his dad, Timothy heard Adrian's voice.

'If no one comes forward to say that they saw you, I won't be arresting you. I will go by the evidence that I have. Blood and DNA of the body on the anchor found at the waterfalls. I will write that it was most likely to have been an accident.'

Timothy thanked him and rushed out to greet his father.

'*Now, the real mystery is how did the body get to the anchor?*'

Chapter Thirty-Eight

The first rays of sun crept out from the horizon. The small country bus stop looked deserted from a distance. At such an hour, only the lady behind the counter and a cleaner were there.

Four buses slept in a row as their drivers were not expected to arrive yet.

The street was quiet. A small street in a small town.

The short-haired redhead walked alone with just one piece of luggage. She seemed agitated. Nervous and jumpy, she was looking over her shoulder every other second. She crossed the road and rushed into the station. She avoided eye contact with the thin lady with the round head, beady eyes and thick-framed glasses who was observing her every move. The young girl went straight for the toilet. Her clothes were dirty and wrinkly as if she slept in them on the ground. The girl sat down on the toilet for her morning needs, then went up to the sink and splashed water on her tired face. She looked at herself in the mirror for over a minute, before exiting and walking up to the ticket booth.

'Good morning,' she said quietly. 'I need a ticket for the first bus to Bulgaria.'

'Return?'

'One way.'

'You got your student card, honey?'

'No. I'll pay normal price, thank you.'

The lady typed in a few words and the printer beside her came to life. 'Here you go, dear. Forty-five euro. The bus leaves in two hours, though. You're here early.'

The girl nodded, paid in cash and took her ticket.

Soon, more people showed up as the sun began ascending in the clear sky. The first bus of the day always headed to Athens. After its departure, the station quieted down again. The bus to Bulgaria showed up on time. It was already half full when she entered it. She sat alone in the back and with relief she slept the entire route to the border. A border the bus never crossed with her upon it. Two tall muscular police officers with serious faces and black moustaches boarded to inspect the passengers. Fifty-two sat on the bus, fifty-one journeyed to Bulgaria.

The thin eighteen-year-old was escorted off the bus. 'Pandora Papaioannou, you are under arrest…'

The arrest of the once-dead girl was the first news of the day for Adrian. The restless night had taken its toll. Adrian felt his head heavy as he brushed his teeth and rubbed his black eye bags with his moisturizing cream. He chopped up his morning fruits and threw them in the blender. His smoothie was ready, but he was not. He dressed quickly and with his heart reaching triple beats per minute, he rushed out to his car. Not even the fresh mountain air of the forest could relax him. He had a long drive ahead. Pandora was taken to the metropolitan police station in Thessaloniki, Greece's second largest city. First, he had to go by the local station and pick up Melpomene to deliver her to the main authorities.

Melpomene was a woman of few words. She replied to him that she had rested well and that her breakfast had been sufficient.

'Sorry, but handcuffs stay on,' he said as he opened the back door of the police vehicle for her to enter.

'I understand,' she answered and that was the last thing she said to him. For the entire five-hour drive, she gazed outside. Vast countryside ran up to the horizon for hours before mountains conquered the lands around them. Adrian enjoyed skipping through stations in search for decent music. Anything was better than thinking. Thinking of Arianna, the case, the dead girls, Melpomene's past, and Pandora's secrets. His mind had been over things all night. It needed a rest and a long drive with radio-friendly hits were just that. Restful and relaxing. Thessaloniki's majestic bay welcomed them as the city spread before them. The seafront avenue running up to the glorious White Tower, the city's famous landmark was a sight for sore tired eyes.

'*No dead girls thrown on there.*'

Adrian checked his GPS screen and headed into town. He was not used to heavy traffic and tapped on his steering wheel on all the way to the station. Only after he parked, did Melpomene speak. 'Do you think they will let me see her?'

Adrian looked in his rear-view mirror. 'After I interrogate her, she will be placed in the same row of cells as you. If you ask the officers and if Pandora agrees, I am sure they would not mind letting you two meet in the visitor's room.'

'If she will see me. I have to explain the past to her.'

Adrian turned around. 'Even if she avoids you, your court cases will be months away. You're gonna be here for a while. You will see her during lunch and during outdoor hours.'

'Thank you. You are a kind young man. Your mother must be proud. Jesus definitely is.'

Adrian smiled. 'If it means anything, I believe you. And I hope the judges see that you did what you did in self-defense.'

Only after stepping out of the vehicle, did Adrian notice the many vans parked along the road. 'Wait a minute,' he said to Melpomene and left her inside the locked car. He walked up to the building slowly. He could hear the commotion going on at a distance. He crept to the corner and had a look around. Over a dozen TV stations and newspapers had sent their crews. All in hope for a picture or a word from the teen killer of the past. The new case sparked national interest, too. The headlines from the girl returning from the dead sold well. Adrian remembered how Arianna wanted to keep the second body a secret. She used her hatred for the press as an excuse. If Adrian held any sort of hatred was for himself for not listening to his gut sooner. He could tell Arianna was off on many occasions. He sensed the case was being screwed with and regretted not facing her sooner. He thought of her smoking and constantly worrying, and remembered her saying that a dead girl should be the worst thing, how she kept him away from Melpomene, Nefeli and Iris, how she sent him off and investigated the forest alone while sending off the second body as to keep the coroner and his team away, her passion to keep reporters away. So many details and he took days to connect the dots. Maybe he could have helped her. Maybe things did not have to have come to such a breaking point. He returned to the police car and explained the situation to his prisoner. 'We will use another entrance. I have called them. They are waiting for us around the back. A police officer will come out to talk to them as a distraction.'

Melpomene found herself thanking the kind man once again. Melpomene was not one to talk to men. She avoided them her entire life. A mixture of fear and disgust kept her from ever getting to know any man. Now, she starred at the young officer and his manners somewhat gave her hope that maybe there were a few good men out there. Not for her, of course. She had no such interest. All she ever cared about was Pandora.

———————

Pandora shriveled up as much as she could on the hard chair. Her game had come to an end. Her overanalytical mind had produced multiple scenarios over the last few days, and she figured out that she would have gotten away. Now, she sat and scorned herself.

'*Why didn't you leave the country on the very first day? Waiting for things to settle down, huh? Now, look where you are. Just play it cool and stay out of shit, Pandora!*'

She was not expecting to see a familiar face. A face from Parga. It was the tall handsome policeman that she saw on the streets of her former seaside town. He introduced himself never the less. '*Not for you, silly. For the camera.*' Her pupils moved slightly, and she saw the camera lenses focused on her. She wished she could focus as well. The officer was explaining her rights.

'Glad to see you alive, Pandora. You gave us all such a fright.'

'*Oh, you're going down the good cop routine, huh?*' Pandora fixed her hair, pushing it behind her ears. You could tell that she was used to having longer hair as she stroked her bare neck. 'Yes, I heard. What were the chances that the day after I ran away you would find a dead body in town?'

'Not any dead body. Your body.'

'That was your mistake, not mine. The police's, that is. Not yours personally.'

'A coincidence, then?'

Pandora shrugged.

'It was your friend that said it was you.'

'Iris panicked and thought it was me because I had mentioned that I was planning on running away. That is why I left the beach party early.'

'I never said which friend.'

Pandora's jaw clenched. Her eyes tried to remain still. 'She was my only friend.'

'Really? I heard you were quite popular. The most popular girl in school actually. Going around, digging up secrets. Nice webpage, by the way.'

'I always fancied myself as an investigating reporter.'

'It suits you. It is unbelievable what you managed to reveal.'

'Flattery, mister officer?'

'Just the truth. Something I am expecting to hear here today.'

'I ran away. You caught me.'

Adrian sat up straight and chuckled quietly. 'That's your story?'

'What do you want me to say?'

'Why did you kill that second girl?'

A small shiver ran through her body. Adrian could see her skin pores standing at attention.

'Second girl?'

Adrian placed his hands on the white table. He picked up his cup of water and took a sip. 'Pandora, do yourself a favor. I called you from Iris's phone. We arrested her last night. She broke. She revealed everything.' A lie hidden in truths.

Pandora shook her head. 'She would never.'

'As fast as we fall in love at eighteen, the faster we can fall out of it and move on, Pandora. You're a clever girl. You think Iris sat between her parents and gave up her university future to protect you? You are going to be arrested for murder. This isn't about your webpage anymore. This is serious. You're in deep trouble.' He could see her eyes following his lips, weakening with his every word. 'Do yourself a favor. Tell me what really happened that day. Let me help you. You know me. If you don't talk to me now, two strangers are going to come in here and grill you until you break. We have two bodies on our hands and you in the middle of it all. Tell me what went down that day.'

Pandora bowed and placed her head in her hands. She took a few deep breaths before raising up again. She looked straight into his eyes. 'What did Iris tell you?'

'She is calling my bluff.'

'I can't reveal details that...'

'You know shit.'

'She told us that she helped you carry the body.' Adrian was certain of this. Only strong muscly Iris could have helped the petite girl sitting before him. At least, one of the bodies. He hoped his words would work.

Tears ran down from her eyes as she looked up at the ceiling and the powerfully bright fluorescent lights.

'Who is going to believe me that I am not a killer?' Her question struggled to come up among sobs.

'Me. All I want is your side of things.'

Pandora wiped her eyes. 'I seriously have no clue of where to begin. This is just all so surreal. I feel like I am trapped in a movie and forced along the plot. I never thought something like this would ever happen. My life was great until a few months ago.'

'Start there, then. What happened a few months ago?'

'All this for a stupid jacket.' She could see his clearly puzzled face. 'It was November. No one was home. There was going to be a party at Nefeli's house, and I wanted one of my mother's jackets. Retro making a comeback and all. It was high in her upper closet. I stood on a chair and tried to reach it. I lost my balance and fell forward. Thankfully, I didn't break anything, but there, hidden behind clothes and a thin piece of wood was a box, like a small pirate's treasure chest. It was locked. My curiosity got the best of me. Melpomene with secrets? The good Christian mother hiding something? I looked through her drawers and found it. The key to unlock her past. She never spoke about her childhood and never mentioned any relatives. I was told that my father died, but to have no grandparents? A Greek without any family? Can you imagine? So, I opened the box, and all evil came out. Her old ID and her birth certificate. Photos of her as a child. Mostly with her mother. It was Melpomene's photo but who was this Demetra Agriou? You can imagine my shock when I googled the name. My world fell apart. She was not my real mother. She killed my birth mother and our father. I hated all these years of lying to me. Loathed her more than anything, but I decided not to confront her. I was still seventeen...' Pandora paused and looked down. 'I know how this is going to sound, but I had university coming up. I wanted to go study abroad. Melpomene was going to work and pay for my studies. I thought why should I give up on my dreams? I was going to move out anyway and let her pay my way through college and then, with my degree in hand, I would turn her in. Inform authorities of who she really was.'

'What changed your plan?'

'My mind. I went mad lost in thoughts. My entire life was a lie. Everyone I saw was like an enemy to me. I could not trust anyone. I became obsessed with secrets. I believed no one was who they truly said they were. I wanted to know everything about everyone. And the more I searched, the more I found out. Dirt and shame everywhere. People are scum. That is when I decided to set up the website. As a hobby at first, then I took it serious and thought to release it after I got my degree.'

Pandora looked at Adrian. 'I know what you are going to ask.'

'What's that?'

'What changed your plan? Well, the fucking closet again! One day, when Melpomene went to the market, I returned to the box. I wanted to take photos of the evidence. The key though, was not where I first found it. So, I kept on looking. I found another box in the back of her bedside table drawer. Just a small souvenir one. It was filled with cash. She had been saving it her whole life. It made sense. She was always working for old ladies paying her in cash. She had a fake ID, but I doubt she had a social security number or a bank account. She would not have risked such a move. It had more than twenty thousand Euros in it.' She picked up her glass and watered her lips. 'You have to understand, that as time went by, I despised her more and more. I hated myself. I could no longer stand the fact that I was living with my true mother's murderer. I spend most of my time out of the house, dreaming of the day that I would get away from Melpomene and turn her in. And that's when opportunity came.'

'The body at the waterfalls?'

Pandora's eyes opened wide. 'You truly know, huh? Yeah, the body at the waterfalls.'

'You found her there?'

Pandora nodded as she tapped her short nails on the table. 'I went up there early. We were planning a senior party up there. An all-nighter sort of thing.'

'Why did you go up there early?'

'I thought Timmy would be there. He loves it up there and he is like a super party planner. I was sure I would see him up there before the others. You see, I sort of had a crush on him. He was the only boy not drooling over me. And the only one that I fancied. For weeks, I tried to be alone with him. I thought this was going to be my chance. And then...' She exhaled a short sigh. 'I exited the woods and saw her. It was so unreal. A pile of a human. After my initial shock, I approached. I made sure she was dead and then as I was going to call for an ambulance, the thought dawned on me. Her face was bashed in. She was my height, my skin tone, same hair length. And the insane idea was born. I would place her somewhere in town and get Iris to say it was me. I would take Melpomene's money, head for the border and vanish, just like she did all those years ago. A new life. A real life. My life. Not this lie. Now, that I retell it, I know it sounds ludicrous but at the time, it seemed right. You have to understand the state of mind I was in. I was desperate to escape from her,' she said, looking at the mirrored glass wall. Adrian could picture her and her youthful puppy eyes staring at the judges the same way.

'What happened with her friend? The second body?'

'The body was heavy. Real heavy. It took all my strength

to drag her. The water helped. I was only going to hide her in some bushes nearby until Iris showed up who I called to come immediately before everyone showed up. As I was going through the trees, I heard a wild scream. A girl saw me and came running at me, screaming in a foreign language. I'm guessing German. She took out a knife! I tried to explain in English that I did not kill her friend, but she jumped on me.' Pandora raised her T-shirt to reveal a large bandage on her lower stomach. She pulled the edge up. A red wound was below. 'I managed to kick her off before she could push her knife further in or I would have truly been the dead girl of Parga. The girl fell back but continued screaming like crazy calling out her friend's name. Johanna, Johanna, Johanna. She got up and ran at me again. I picked up a broken off tree branch at my side and swung it at her. I was only defending myself. She was animal-like wild.'

'*Defending myself.*' Adrian's mind traveled to seventeen-year-old Demetra.

'I didn't mean to hurt her. I was trying to explain the whole time that I found her friend dead. So, I hit her, and she fell. She… err… and…'

'And what, Pandora?'

'The side of her head landed on a large pointy rock.' Pandora choked. She reached for her water. She was breathing heavily. 'The sound was awful. I still hear it in my nightmares. Her skull must have shattered. I heard the bone snap on that rock. And there I was, standing between two dead girls. Iris found me there. You can imagine her shock. She wanted to call the police. I couldn't let her do that. I was not going to prison when my true freedom was so close. I now had to go through with my crazy plan. I had just killed a person. So, I hugged Iris and gave her a kiss. Begged for her help. Told her that as soon as I made it out the country, she could come visit me. I told her that we could finally be together. Please, don't blame her for anything. All she did was help me carry the bodies into the cave and then at three in the morning, she returned to take the unrecognizable one and place it on the anchor. I took off the dead girl's bathing suit and gave her my bikini top. I then placed my box on the body, kissed Iris farewell and walked for miles away from Parga.'

Pandora leaned back in her chair and focused on her feet. 'I am not a horrible person. This is not how I pictured things to be. Please, Mister Adrian, you have to help me. Explain my position.'

'Just as you told things to me, you will repeat them in a court of law. The judge will decide your fate. Not me.'

Pandora placed her arms on the table and lay on them sobbing.

'Your mother wants to see you, by the way.'

'My mother's dead and you should have fucking arrested Melpomene by now.'

Adrian stood up and approached her. He placed his hand on her trembling shoulder. 'Just like you have a story, so does she. Does she look like a psycho killer to you? One that would butcher two people, her own father, for no reason at all? You like secrets being revealed and you refuse to hear the one that would explain your life?'

Two hours later, the two women met in the visitor's lounge. Adrian watched as Melpomene controlled her urge to run and take her daughter into her arms. The smile on her face was the widest and happiest Adrian had ever seen. Tears ran freely as she covered her mouth. 'Thank God, you're alive. You're alive, my sweet girl.'

Pandora remained still. She sat down in the blue chair

and said, 'talk. We haven't got long. Why did you murder my parents?'

Melpomene wiped her face and sat down opposite the young girl. Word after word, Melpomene told her the story of Demetra. Word after word, Pandora's stern look, softened. The two cried uncontrollably and ended up in each other's arms.

'Why didn't you ever tell me?'

'I couldn't. I had buried the past deep down in the abyss of my soul. I was not Demetra anymore. I was Melpomene. I was your mother. Raising you was the best thing I ever did in my life and I thanked the Lord daily for having you.'

Pandora fell to her knees and placed her head on her mother. 'I'm scared.'

'I am here with you. By your side always. We will get through this together.' She stroked her daughter's hair. 'I am your mother and always will be. I promise you I will do my best to get you out of here as soon as possible. I have already found a lawyer. A strong smart woman. The kind you like. She will take on both our cases.'

'I love you, mum!' Pandora stood up and embraced Melpomene tightly. Melpomene smiled and looked up at the Lord. He surely did work in mysterious ways. And there, in prison, both of them charged with murder, they bonded like never before.

Chapter Thirty-Nine

The next day found Parga different.

Less innocent. Its people less trusting.

More suspicious. More closed doors.

News spread like wildfire in a hay field. Arianna's heart attack, Pandora coming back from the dead, the two dead German campers, and Melpomene's hidden past were topics on the tip of everyone's tongue.

Arianna's funeral was set for noon. The entire town came out to honor their beloved police Captain and offer their condolences to her brave boy. Adrian stood in his official uniform in the shade of an oak tree, listening to the speeches given in her honor. Hearing all the good she had done in her life and all the love that people had for her, made him glad on his decision to not speak out against her. All everyone needed to know was how she died from a weak heart and that he solved the case. The first tourist fell from the cliff's edge at the waterfalls and Pandora killed the second one in apparent self-defence. Case closed. Or so he thought.

Timothy cursed and cried uncontrollably as they lowered his mother into the ground. His father held on to him, preventing him from falling into the hole after her. Both picked up a handful of dirt and threw it on the wooden casket. One by one, the citizens of Parga followed. 'Goodbye, boss,' Leventi said as he knelt and tossed his handful of dirt. Katie stood behind him, her hand on his shoulder. Arianna slowly descended to her final resting place. As the crowd thinned and walked down the hill toward their cars, Adrian noticed the parked Maserati. Adrian looked around. Mario was sitting on a bench further down. Adrian walked up to him picking up speed as he went. Mario stood up nervously.

'I heard the news. I had to come. I hope I am not intruding…'

Adrian embraced him and kissed his neck. 'Thank you. I just want to go home and cry.'

'Let's go then.'

At home, Mario listened in shock about how the case truly played out. 'That's one hell of a story. A maze of lies leading to dead ends. And your Captain tangled up in the middle of it all. Seriously, such a clever woman, did she really think she was going to get away with it?'

'At heart, all she was trying to do was protect her boy. It was an awful accident and to her, not one worth losing a bright future. Timothy wouldn't be able to fulfill any of his dreams with a criminal record. She thought that his friend would discover the body, she would investigate, rule it as an accident and case closed. All good. She never would have guessed that the body would go missing. You see the problem with stepping in shit, is that if you do not clean it off immediately, the stink will follow you around. She knew the body was from the waterfalls. I saw her reaction that dawn. She was deeply lost in thought. I remember being jealous of her calmness. She was thinking. Probably worried if the person that carried the body there saw what really happened. Then her friends said it was Pandora and her webpage became known. I believe Arianna freaked out then.'

'Why?'

'She knew Pandora was still alive. In her head, Pandora saw Timothy push the German girl. The thought of Pandora uploading the truth, ate away her heart. It would go down as murder as it would be Pandora's word against Timothy's, and Pandora had already stated many truths.'

Mario whistled and took a sip from his cold Frappe. 'Yeah, but how did she expect to clean the shit off, then?'

Adrian shrugged. 'No wonder she gave herself a heart attack. She was falling deeper and deeper in her web of lies. She tried hard to cover things up. To send me and Leventi on side actions while she interrogated Pandora's friends and mother. She was looking for the girl. Then the second body was found and that was a true shock. Arianna was smart. She must have realized the two bodies were connected but she could not figure out how. She tried to keep things on the hush. From the press, from the coroner... from me. It drove her mad.'

'All this for her son. She should have just come forward with the truth in the first place.'

Adrian chuckled. 'You know what? I do believe if we turned back time, she would have protected him all over again. She would have put that body in her trunk and disposed of it herself. Nothing was above Timothy. Not the law. Not her morals.' Adrian stroked Mario's cheek. 'I need a shower. Find us a movie. Something light. No police in it!'

'How about a series? I plan on staying a while.'

The following day, the morning rays found them asleep together when Adrian's phone began to ring.

'Hello?'

Mario watched as Adrian jumped up in shock.

'He did what?' Adrian yelled, then punched the door and exited the room.

Mario got up and went to the doorway.

'What happened?'

'Arianna's kid? Timothy? He left his father's house one hour ago and turned himself in for the murder of the first victim.'

Mario just nodded. 'Go.'

'He is not here. After the funeral, he returned to Athens with his father.'

It took Adrian a few phone calls to Headquarters before reaching Timothy on the phone.

'Why, Timothy? Why?'

'I heard Leventi talking after the funeral about the case. He said the first girl was pregnant. I killed her! I killed her baby. A baby, Adrian!'

After his phone call, Adrian put on his trainers and vanished into the woods. He ran for miles. He pushed himself to his limits. He reached the waterfalls and stopped on the edge. He was not a religious man, nor believed in the afterlife. But at the very moment, he gazed up to the sky and liked to believe Arianna was looking down, proud of her boy.

Epilogue

The year provided plenty of gossip to the small town.

Not a dull month went by.

Iris was sentenced to nine months of community service. Hers was the first of many rulings that the people of Parga were waiting for. Timothy's came next. Twenty-four months in prison. The least he could have been charged with. The German girl's family protested and filed a complaint against Greece's justice system in European courts. He was out after fourteen months and on parole for three years. The second family was more satisfied. Mila Schmidt's parents flew out to Thessaloniki to hear Pandora being sentenced to seven years in prison. Greek papers called the decision harsh but analyzed that the judges went hard on her as they were presented with evidence about how she hit the face of the first dead body to make it totally unrecognizable, her manipulative behavior, her website, her cover-ups and use of a dead body and even doubted her wound which Mila's attorney called superficial and most likely self-inflicted. The backlash from Timothy's short sentence also played a part. Melpomene appeared a broken woman to hear her sentence just a week later. She still had not accepted her daughter's long prison sentence. Melpomene also got seven years. The court accepted the self-defense plea for her father's death but not for Helka's. Melpomene thanked them with a smile. At least, she would be there with Pandora.

The bizarre case went down in history as the 'accidental-case' murders. Timothy stated that he did not mean to kill Johanna. Pandora said she did not mean to kill Mila. Melpomene stood by her statement. She did not plan to kill anyone. Her father attacked her. Helka attacked her.

Minor sentences followed for the rest of Pandora's list. After long investigations, hefty fines closed down a bakery, a butchery and a restaurant in the small town. The only ones that received prison sentences were the math teacher and the priest. Stephanie got eighteen months and was banned from teaching juveniles for life. Hector got four months in jail. In that time, his wife set up their new island life. They are now proud owners of one of the finest taverns in the Aegean.

Even after the case had no more to provide to the local folks that thrived for gossip, many topics kept their coffee meetings interesting.

Phoebe lost the next election by a landslide and left town for good just as most from Pandora's list had. The new mayor was the one that announced Adrian's promotion to local Police Captain at the end of the year. The following year she was the one that blessed the union of Adrian and Mario as new laws allowed them to marry.

Pandora's box may have unleashed terrible evils in the small community but hope always sticks around.

Hope for better days. Hope for better people.

vinci-books.com/AchillesHeel

Everyone has a weakness. Some are fatal.

Lieutenant Damien Levante is called to a Corfu mansion and finds four dead, one alive—and too many lies. As he unravels the survivor's story, buried secrets and personal demons collide, forcing him to face a killer who knows his deepest weakness.

Turn the page for a free preview…

Achilles' Heel: Chapter One

May, 2022

Out of all the ways a person could wish to be woken up, violent screaming is definitely not one of them. But that was the case for the residents of Saint John's village, just a twenty-minute drive from the town centre of Corfu. Well, at least it was the case for the ones living on the street that led up to Livos Mansion. One by one, they were shaken out of their trip to the abstract lands of Morpheus as the decidedly female shrieks grew louder. Some approached their open windows, pulling back thin curtains dancing upon the night's cool breeze, in search of the person in need. In danger. Some stared at the time in disbelief. A quarter to two. Darkness roamed their once tranquil road, and none dared to venture outside. They were all past their prime, in their late seventies and early eighties, and none desired an encounter with a dangerous robber. The only place with any sign of light was the house on the hill that overlooked

246

their homes. It was a single light, faint and weak, shining alone in the pitch black.

The police station in town received four calls on that spring night concerning the incident, each merely seconds apart.

Lieutenant Damien Levante was at his favorite place when on night call. The infamous Italian-built cabaret on the outskirts of town. 'Cheap drinks, cheap women, close to everywhere in ten minutes,' he would excuse his choice to his disapproving partner. Sergeant Anneta Georgiou would just shake her head and bite her lower lip with her rather large front teeth. 'Whatever you say, boss. I'll be at home in front of my TV, enjoying the miracle of our modern era. Streaming!'

Damien had just ordered his fourth whiskey. 'Just two cubes of ice, this time, Mike. It's the alcohol I'm paying you for, not water.' He spoke without facing the bartender. His eyes were fixated on the dance floor. Bodies wearing the least possible coverings moved around to the euphoric beats provided by the resident DJ. As he brought the cold glass to his parched lips, he felt the vibration in his pocket. Incoming call from the station. He quickly stood up and dashed outside. The cold night air swept off the droplets of sweat that had formed on his wide forehead. He hated the fact that his hairline receded year by year. He despised that next year he was going to hit the big four-zero. At least, he had fewer grey hairs than most of his same-age friends. But they had all married and produced offspring, so a majority of greys was unavoidable according to his theory.

'Hello? Lieutenant Levante here.'

'Sir, we have received multiple calls about screams coming from a house out in Saint John's village. The pinpoint of the location has been texted to you. A unit has just left the station and should be arriving there in fifteen minutes tops.'

'I'll be there in ten,' he replied.

He was inside his Mercedes SUV in a matter of seconds. On the main road within a minute. He drove with his windows down, letting the night air -with a bit of help from his energy drink to awaken his relaxed senses. He sped along the deserted highway checking the pinpoint location on his GPS screen. Final destination in six minutes' time. Damien gazed up at the crystalline night sky and exhaled. *'No more clouds. Summer is just around the corner'.* He loathed rainy days. Days when he was forced to remain indoors with his German Shepherd and his thoughts. The dog was good company; his mind was not. Memory lane was a horror road for Damien. He shook his head as he made a right turn into the silent village. Old stone houses mingled with a few newer ones revealing that the younger generation had fled to the main town of the island and even toward the city of Athens. One street on the village's outskirts had their lights on. No one stood outside but Damien noticed many eyes peering out from the safety of their homes. He was the first to arrive on the scene. For comfort he turned on his siren lights to let the residents know that help had arrived. He entered through the open gate and drove up the small hill. The enormous mansion now rose before him, blanketed in darkness. He parked away from the building and stepped out of his vehicle, leaving the lights on. Red and blue danced upon the dull grey rocks, illuminating the massive ivy that had conquered most of the wall. Damien fixed his belt and pulled out his gun. He took a few short steps forward. Only silence welcomed him.

'Hello? This is Lieutenant Damien Levante with Corfu Police...'

The sound of the front door being pushed open made ...m jump. A shadow was coming toward him. The limping figure came into the light provided by his running car's headlights. A young red-haired woman, dressed in only her underwear and covered in blood, came out of the mansion weeping and with her arms stretched out, begging for help.

'Miss, are you hurt? Where have you been hurt, ma'am?' Damien asked as the woman collapsed in front of him. He knelt by her side.

'I was stabbed in the leg,' she struggled to say.

'Who else is in the house?'

Her blue eyes looked straight into his. 'No one. They are all dead.' The woman replied with pain coloring her every word. She closed her eyes as she settled her head upon his leg.

'Miss, try to stay awake. Help is on its way. What's your name?'

She swallowed what felt like a slab blocking her throat. She could taste the blood in her mouth. 'Zoe. I'm the old lady's nurse.'

'Where is the old lady now?'

'Dead! I said, they are all dead! She's dead and she fucking killed my boyfriend! Leo...' Tears fell uncontrollably as Damien called in to check on the arrival of the police unit and to request an ambulance.

'Miss, I have to get my first aid kit from my car. You are bleeding out. We need to apply pressure immediately.'

The woman looked up at her savior, mesmerized by his rich, husky, authoritative voice. She felt drowsy and blamed her fragile state of mind for concentrating on the handsome man's chiselled features and row of symmetrically perfect white teeth. She felt secure near him and that is all that mattered to her at that moment. Anything to not think of all the death that took place inside the mansion.

Two cars arrived simultaneously as Damien was attending to her deep cut, shooting a spasm of pain through her weak body. Two young officers exited the police vehicle, while Damien's partner Anneta jumped out of her car and rushed up to him.

'Stay with her. Help is on the way,' he said looking at the two men in their twenties dressed in their police uniforms. One thing he missed, one he did not. To be young again was a thought of his that occurred often. But just the thought of wearing the navy-blue clothes with the uncomfortable black shoes, made his dinner float upward.

'Let's get inside. The girl said everyone is dead; but who knows?'

Anneta took out her firearm and followed him inside. 'Did she say who the attacker was?'

Damien shook his head. He was already by the door. 'Corfu Police! Anyone here?' He ran his hand against the wall inside and switched on the lights. The vast living room lit up as expensive chandeliers came alive revealing fine furniture, walls featuring art and an enormous fireplace dominating the room. Upon it were dozens of frames of various sizes. Most featured black and white photos, some were of colorful family moments and some sat empty. Damien's eyes looked at the blood stains on the dark brown parquet floor. He followed them to the corridor. The lights were on. A woman's body lay before him. She wore a pair of bloody jeans and a ripped black T-shirt. Her red hair was stuck to her bruised forehead and mingled with the blood oozing out. A massive wound through the chest was responsible for painting her clothes red.

'Dear Lord.' Anneta's voice came from behind him. 'Look.'

In the middle of the long corridor a man's hand lay alone on the carpet, while at the end of the corridor an old lady dressed in a pink nightgown sat apparently dead next to the wall. 'Go check on the old lady. I'll go find the owner of the arm.' Damien stood up and called out once again. Still no reply.

Damien reached a bedroom door. Faint light was provided by an antique lamp on a cherry wood bedside table. The owner of the hand was definitely dead. He lay in a pool of blood in the middle of the king-sized bed. A butcher's knife stuck out of his neck, having made it halfway nearly decapitating him. The man with the now permanent shocked expression was in his late forties and completely naked.

'The old woman is dead,' Anneta called out.

'Hand's owner, too. We have to secure the house. Make sure no one else is here.'

The ambulance siren broke the silence as the two investigators made their way around the mansion, checking it, room by room. Stuffy air welcomed them as much of the enormous house was no longer used. The upper floor had not been used in years. But nothing compared to the putrid smell emanating from the basement. Damien covered his mouth and nose as he kicked in the locked door and the nasty odor escaped. He waited a second before taking a deep breath and descending the cement steps. The decaying body of a headless young man lay on an old, worn-out green sofa. His skin had crawled into itself, and blood had pooled, a victim of gravity, as no beating heart existed to circulate it. Flies attracted by the foul smell buzzed around him and as Damien moved closer, he noticed maggots slithering near the neck wound. Based on the putrefaction, Damien knew the body was at least a month old. '*What the hell went down in this house?*'

Achilles' Heel: Chapter Two

Her eyes fought to open. The intense white light scarred her pupils. Her head felt as heavy as an elephant carrying a whale. She smiled at the thought of her grandma's silly saying. The constant beeping noises around her were growing in volume. Voices echoed around her, but she could not make out clear words.

'She's waking up.'

Yes, that is what the male voice said. She was sure. Her dry lips parted. Her breath came out with difficulty. She was not sure if she had spoken or not. She felt like smiling but resisting. A euphoric feeling spread inside of her.

'Can you hear me? I am Dr. Helena Petra. What is your name?'

'*What is it with everyone asking me my name tonight?*' She raised her hands and stroked her leg. The pain had gone. Her wound was dressed. She felt the need to touch her cross hanging from a thin chain around her neck. 'Zoe,' she managed to say, and the word scratched her throat as it escaped her trembling mouth.

'Zoe, you are going to be just fine, dear. You are a fighter. Very strong. But you need to rest and relax. Let your system take care of itself.'

'*God, she talks a lot for a doctor with such a strict face.*' She fixed her head on the soft pillow. 'Thank you.' She slurred the two words. It reminded her of that one time she felt anything remotely similar to a hangover. A night of gin and wine with old friends from school. She was never much of a drinker.

'Is there anyone we should call? A relative?'

She shook her head. 'No, no. I am not from around here. I came to work as a nurse for an elderly woman and...'

'Surely your parents would like to know that you are alright, even if they live far away.'

Zoe sat up uneasily. She could see the tips of nearby conifers from the lone window of the room. 'I'm an orphan.'

'Oh...' The doctor looked down at her notes. She was not reading. Just avoiding Zoe's gaze. 'If you need anything from us, do not hesitate to call. Just press this button and a nurse will be here for you.'

'Some water would be nice.'

A male nurse who was standing silently to her left came forward and poured her a glass of water from a small bottle on a plastic wheeled bedside table. It was cold. Just as she liked her water to be. Her lips welcomed it with joy.

Another nurse with blonde hair and pretty features popped her head through the door. 'Doctor, there is a detective here for you.'

Doctor Helena stood unimpressed by the man waiting for her by the fake bushes placed in big cheap Japanese-knockoff vases. Damien stood nearby the row of windows that provided precious light to the long hallway during the day. From behind her thin reading glasses, her beady-eyed look fled and headed straight to the scruffy-looking man that introduced himself as a police lieutenant. Helena had a strong sense of smell, and she could tell when smoke, strong deodorant and chewing gum blended to cover up a residual scent of alcohol. She thought of the hour and tried to bring a certain amount of logic to her inner judgement of the man. *'He was probably off duty and had been just called in.'*

'...so, as you can see, it is of the utmost importance that I speak to the witness as soon as possible. Every second and every detail matters...'

Hesitation sparks went off inside her mind but having heard the number of bodies found inside the mansion, she reluctantly agreed that the Lieutenant could visit her patient.

'But at the first sign of distress or agitation, you're out.'

Damien nodded in agreement. 'You've got it, doc. Sure thing.' He fixed his belt as he walked up to the door and ran his long fingers through his hair. He knocked twice and opened the white door. The woman that had run out to him surely looked better. Her cheeks had found their lost rosy color and her eyes seemed more alive. He hoped she had the strength to retell her ordeal. 'May I join you?' he asked, and headed toward the armchair by her bed. 'Feeling better, I presume?'

'They have doped me up pretty well because I am feeling no pain.'

She spoke without struggle. Damien felt confident about his following question. 'Miss Zoe, believe me, the last thing I wish is to bother you at such an hour and under such circumstances, but experience has taught me that our mind tends to lose details even of the strongest memories as the minutes fly by. Would you be brave enough to cope with some questions?'

Zoe swallowed the lump lingering inside her throat. 'What is it you want to know exactly?'

'Everything.'

Zoe closed her eyes. 'Where do I even start?'

He could see her eyes watering up. He could not afford to lose his witness to sentiment. *'Get her to start from happier moments.'* He forced a smile. 'How about you tell me where you are from and about the day you found the job as the old lady's nurse?'

Zoe scratched her forehead and exhaled. 'It was only a week ago and yet it seems so far away. So much has happened since I arrived on the island.'

Damien looked up at her. He had been preparing his notepad and his blue pen. 'Not from Corfu?'

'I came from Ioannina.'

Damien leaned forward. 'How did you find the job? Answered an ad?'

'No, no. I had just finished nursing school and I needed a job. I did not want to work in a hospital.' She paused and laughed. 'Tragic but I hate these places because of too much death. Oh, the irony. So, I signed up with an agency offering my services as a live-in nurse. You see, I was raised by nuns in the orphanage in Ioannina and I needed a place to live. The agency covered Epirus, West Greece and all the Ionian Islands. I told them I preferred an island. I needed to get away from the rain and the snow. I am an islander in my heart. I need the sun and the sea. And I have one lone passion in life, diving.'

'She's a talker. Good.'

'So, the agency set you up? What agency is this?'

'Nurses, SOS. They said they had a wealthy client that

needed a young girl to live with her. I spoke on the phone with her daughter in Athens and she made all the arrangements.'

'What's the daughter's name, and do you still have her number?'

Zoe looked out of the window and wiped her eyes. 'Her name was Alice. She is one of the bodies in the house.'

'Who killed them? We are on an island. If your attacker is on the run, we need to get the coast guard...'

Zoe raised her palm. 'No one to chase, detective. We are all killers. It was a fight till the death. I was the only one who managed to get out.'

'And what about the basement?' He left out the description. 'Anyone go down there last night?'

Zoe's eyes opened wide, and her entire body twitched. 'I have no idea, Lieutenant. It was always locked without a key in sight. What was in the...?' She exhaled as she shook her head. 'Detective, I am clueless about the basement. Never been down there. I have only been living there for the past few days before...' She swallowed another lump in her throat. She looked around for water. A small glass stood on her bedside cabinet. Damien brought it closer to her and as she drank, he said, 'I think you're going to have to tell me your whole story as to get to the bottom of this.'

Achilles' Heel: Chapter Three

3 days ago

Zoe sat close to the slightly opened car window. Near enough to avoid choking on the heavy cologne dominating the confined space of the vehicle. It rose off the sweaty taxi driver who wore a checkered shirt that was missing a button. Yet not near enough as to inhale any part of the cloud of dust that the speeding car had given birth to as it sped down these country roads. She held on to the grab handle as the driver attacked the road's speed-control bumps. She regretted entering the maniac's taxi, but it was too late now for regrets. After stepping off the boat from the mainland, her stomach was a swimming pool on a stormy windy night, she was too dizzy to be fussy. She had approached the first driver she laid eyes upon. She had wobbled across the street, dressed in her light-blue dress -a gift from the nuns for her degree ceremony, rolling her luggage behind her and had walked up to the tall man with the long black beard and the heavy gold cross semi-lost in the thickness of his chest hair. 'Saint John's village? Livos Mansion at the end of Anexartisias Street?' Her voice had been reserved and low.

'Huh? Speak up, girl.'

Zoe had repeated her desired destination and watched as the large man picked up her suitcase, threw it in the back, opened a door for her and squeezed into his car. He had then switched on the radio and stepped on the gas. Zoe found the music deafening but then again it meant there was no talking from the driver. Greek taxi drivers were notorious talkers and believed themselves experts on every topic, ranging from politics to sports.

The vehicle coming to a halt made her reopen her eyes. She had closed them and tried to get lost in prayer.

'Here, little missy. Gates are closed. You calling them or walking in?'

'Walk. Walking. Yes,' she replied, and her black shoes touched the gravelled road as she practically dove outside. It felt good to be safe on solid ground again.

There was a side door to the main gate, and it swung happily, creaking in the wind that reigned permanently on the hill. Zoe formed the sign of the cross on her chest. Then she took a deep breath and began her walk up to the hilltop villa. An aroma settled on the entrance of her nostrils. A blend of roses and citrus flowers. Zoe took a moment to look around. The gardens were perfectly kept, in full contrast to the walls of the house that stood defeated by time and the weather. Zoe was not sure for how long she remained outside the main door, contemplating knocking or ringing. She could not delay the inevitable any longer. She had to dive into the deep end. Her first job. Her new home. Her first home, really.

Her index finger pushed the white button and a ring

echoed around inside the house. 'The key is under the cactus pot,' an old lady's voice came from a window further down. 'Okay, ma'am.' Zoe looked down at the three cactus pots ganged up in the corner of the bricked wall. She found the key on her first go and smiled at the fact. '*Good luck all the way, I hope.*'

In and around went the key and the door to her new life opened. Zoe gawked at the wealth spread out before her. She had never witnessed such a living room before. Ample light journeyed in from the row of open windows, their draperies prancing upon the breeze.

'Hurry up, girl. Don't keep me waiting.' The harsh voice travelled toward her, giving haste to her tired feet. The corridor smelled of detergent. Wild berries. Everything was spotless. Zoe could not believe that she was going to be living in such extravagant surroundings. The first door revealed an empty bedroom, so she quickly dashed for the next. A large bed conquered much of the space. The curtains were thick and drawn shut. The only light came from an old lamp that was placed on the floor even though two empty bedside tables existed on either side of the antique bed. Zoe remained in the doorway looking at the shadowy figure sitting up on the bed, supported by a number of white pillows. 'Switch on the lights, girl, let me get a better look at you!'

'Shall I open the curtains, ma'am?' Zoe asked, thinking of the strong, beautiful sunlight that filled up the rest of the house.

'Did I say such a thing? Learn to listen. Lesson one. Do as I say.'

Zoe's shaking hand pulled the switch down and the chandelier brought light to the room. Both women gazed at each other. Zoe with her head still and a genuine smile on her flushed face, saw her new boss.

She was definitely not like the old ladies at the orphanage that Zoe was used to.

No benign expression was to be found.

A still face bordering on angry was hidden among messy gunmetal-grey hair. Her thin lips formed a straight line and small honey-colored eyes rested in the centre of deep crow's feet. A slightly crooked nose reminded Zoe of evil Disney witches and the time-ravaged yellowy skin did not help matters. A gold chain hung from her neck featuring a cross and a small key that fell into a gang of pea-sized moles. Zoe lowered her gaze. She did not wish to be seen shocked by the sickly appearance of her new boss/patient. The old lady's hands were inflamed, and her nails were begging for a good cut.

'Why are you just standing there like an idiot, child? Come closer. Hand me my glasses so I can also study you.'

'Yes, ma'am.'

'The name is Mirela. Cut the ma'am crap. Times have changed, you know.'

Mirela's hand trembled as she struggled to wear the black thick-framed glasses just handed to her. 'Hmmm, you sure is a pretty one, child. Clean face, slim figure, rich hair. I hope we don't have men knocking on my door at all hours.'

'Of course not, ma'...Mrs. Mirela. Definitely not. I am here for you and to help you get better.'

'No one gets better after a lifetime of illness. I'm too weak to fight any longer. You cannot turn back the hands of treacherous time. I doubt I have many years left in me.' Mirela's voice broke. Zoe wondered if her gravel voice was due to a dry throat. She poured the old lady a glass of water from the bottle on the bed stand. 'Here you go. Yes, we cannot beat time, but we can surely make our final years much more comfortable. And that is why I am here. I will truly work for your health and convenience.'

Mirela sniggered. 'Is that a poem you learnt at nursing school? Do you really believe that, child?'

'I wouldn't be here if I didn't!'

Mirela closed her eyes and shook her head. 'Your optimism is annoying. Go see your room.' She waved her hand. 'It's two doors down, to your right. Relax from your journey. Then go get familiarized with the kitchen. Lunch time is approaching.'

Zoe smiled and retreated without speaking. She picked up her luggage that she had left in the long corridor and headed to her allocated quarters. Her room was smaller than Mirela's but much brighter. Both windows were open and ample light and fresh air filled the room with the single bed and the empty bedside table. Zoe closed the door behind her, sat down on the soft mattress and exhaled loudly with a sigh. She took her phone into her hand. She felt the need to hear Leo's voice.

'No, Zoe. Resist.'

She left the cell on the bed and approached the window. 'Talk to yourself.' She gazed out and admired the unobstructed view of beautiful blossoming meadows that ran up to the first stone village houses. '*What have I gotten myself into? She is going to be difficult to work with. Strong-willed and bossy. Weird how her daughter described her as bedridden with Alzheimer's. Who takes care of the house? Who opened my windows? Who cooked yesterday? Probably a lady from the village.*' Zoe looked back into the room. 'A room of my own.' Zoe walked slowly around the bed, her hand running along its cherry wood. She let the thought sink in. She could not remember a time when she had her own room. There were always at least three girls sharing a room at the monastery's orphanage. During her studies she stayed with two other girls with limited funds on campus for the first two years and then with another orphan roommate at a nun-owned apartment for the rest of her nursing course. She smiled with the thought and opened the wardrobe doors. One side was completely vacant, obviously emptied for her. The other side was overrun by cupboard boxes of various sizes, all taped shut and squeezed into place. Whistling to her latest favorite tune, Zoe unpacked and neatly tidied her few belongings away. After one more look outside at the serene image painted by nature, and taking a deep breath, Zoe exited her room and as her lady commanded, she headed to the kitchen at the end of the hall. The neglected, dusty blinds were lowered all the way and the room was dark. Zoe did not switch on the light as she always opted for sunlight. More natural, more alive, warmer. Sunrays invaded as the worn blinds rose and Zoe gazed around her. It was a kitchen from an era long gone. A country kitchen from the fifties, yet the electrical appliances gave the correct century away. The fridge and cupboards were well stocked. '*I have to impress.*' Zoe looked at the clock hanging on the brick wall to her left. She had plenty of time. She placed the salmon on the wooden counter and left it to defrost while she gathered the rest of the ingredients that she had in mind.

Zoe contemplated turning on the radio but decided not to risk it. Music was her companion. Through thick and thin, music helped her escape. Escape her true life, her thoughts, her depression. The house was quiet, too quiet. '*Has she fallen asleep? What does she do all day? Both her kids are away…*' Zoe walked silently with light feet towards Mirela's door. She stood behind the closed door and brought her right ear to its cool surface.

'What is it, child? Why are you lingering outside my door?'

Zoe jumped back, quickly collected herself and opened the door.

'Did I say you could enter?'

'I'm sorry, ma'am... Mrs. Mirela.'

Mirela rolled her eyes in dramatic fashion making sure Zoe saw her. 'Well, you're here now. Pour me some water.'

Zoe approached. 'Time for your pink pills, too.'

'All I do is take pills. A rainbow of them from dawn to dusk. I'm fed up, child. This is not living.'

Zoe passed her the two pills and a glass of water. 'Don't talk like that,' she said with a genuine smile, sparkling eyes and an upbeat tone. 'Life is what we make of it. What is it that you enjoy doing most? Maybe its time for a new hobby.'

Mirela's notorious sniggering followed. 'You really are an optimistic fool.'

'Better than a pessimistic Einstein.'

Mirela's croaky laughter echoed around the room. A laughter that raised her chest and brought on a terrible cough. 'Your humor will kill me, girl. You are a funny one.'

Suddenly, Mirela's face went cold. She closed her eyes and pointed to her right. 'There's someone at the door.'

Zoe looked at her patient. Her mouth opened but she was unsure on what to say. She just stroked the old lady's wrinkly hand and got up to leave. Just then, the doorbell rang. With the sound of the bell, Mirela lowered her hand. Zoe licked her lips and rushed out of the room to answer the door. Another ring followed. 'I'm coming,' she called out. Her right hand grabbed the golden door handle, and she pulled the heavy door toward her. No one was there. Zoe stepped outside and gazed around. 'Hello?' The day breeze had lost its cool as the ferocious Greek sun made its ascent to the clear blue sky above. Zoe felt like a Lady from one of her medieval romance novels, exiting her castle upon the hill and laying her eyes on the village below as the commoners went about with their daily duties. The front garden was mostly empty. A twisty olive tree stood at her right while now she noticed a row of neglected rose bushes that ran along the side path leading up to the porch. All around was yellowy grass begging for salvation, for water, for its long-lost green days. 'Is there anyone there?' she asked as she walked around the mansion remembering that she was not there to inspect and judge the yard. 'Probably kids annoying the old lady. Pranksters!' She shook her head. 'She heard them outside. That is how she knew.'

Zoe returned inside and decided to go straight to the kitchen. She had lunch to prepare. Besides, the TV blared loudly from Mirela's room. She was not needed, nor did she have to explain who was not at the door.

At half past noon exactly, Zoe entered her patient's room with a full tray in hand.

'Lunch is ready,' she announced as she closed the door behind her with her body. The salmon smelled divine, cooked in virgin olive oil and fresh lemons. Asparagus, broccoli, and carrots gave the dish color. A tall glass of lemonade filled with ice cubes crackling at its top, a small plate with a square piece of milk chocolate and an array of pills in a see-through plastic cup made up the gang occupying the silver serving tray. The glow on Zoe's face revealed how proud she was of her presentation. A short-lived glow as Mirela looked startled.

'What? Who are you? What the hell are you doing in my house? Where is my daughter? Alice? Alice? Help!' Mirela raised her voice with each word until her cough strangled her words and silenced her. Zoe quickly placed the salver on the bedside table and rushed to her patient's aid.

'Relax, Mrs. Mirela. It's me. Zoe. Your nurse. Zoe.' She repeated her name, hoping for a memory jolt. She stroked the old woman's hand and smiled widely. Mirela's eyes trembled and watered up. 'My nurse?'

Zoe shook her head. 'I am here to take care of you. I am Zoe. You have nothing to fear. Everything will go just fine. I have cooked your favorite. Salmon. Alice, your daughter, sent me a list of foods you enjoy.'

Mirela's heavy breathing relaxed. 'Where is that ungrateful bitch? Her mother is in pain, prisoned upon a damn bed. Where is she? Partying with men and drinking and dancing...'

'She is in Athens, Mrs. She is a... businesswoman.' Zoe was not exactly sure what her profession was. 'I am sure she would love to be here with you, but people must work. She loves you very much and cares as much as to hire me to...'

Mirela closed her eyes and turned away. 'Just feed me and be quiet, child. You know nothing. Lesson two. Keep your opinions to your bloody self.'

All forty-eight spoonfuls were served in silence. The pills followed, helped down by a gulp of lemonade. The chocolate was there to remove the nasty after taste of the drug cocktail. 'Now quickly leave. I need to take a shit. Come back in twenty minutes to change me. Out!'

Zoe obeyed in silence. '*What a vulgar, bitter old witch!*' she thought on her way to the kitchen to clean up. '*I hope I never end up as lonely and angry as she.*'

Zoe went about with her chores and duties for the rest of the day without speaking much. To Mrs. Mirela that was as she drove herself halfway to crazy with all her inner chatter. Nightfall came as a relief. Her ankles ached -too much for a twenty-three-year-old woman. '*Must be the long journey here.*' Her eyes felt heavy. She saw them staring back at her in the hallway mirror. Red and puffy. The expensive antique did not lie.

'Goodnight, Mrs. Mirela,' she wished as she gave her the last pills of the day. The old woman swallowed them without water, grunted and turned to her side. Zoe switched off the lights and gladly returned to her room for a much-needed shower. Zoe had never seen an en-suite before. 'All mine.' She showered without rush, enjoying the hot running water and essence shower gel. A young soul deprived of any sort of luxury in life, Zoe often dreamt of a life where she was not an orphan but the daughter of a wealthy family. She dreamt of island breaks and visits to the hair salon. Dining in fine restaurants and wearing designer clothes. 'Reality is a harsh bitch.'

Zoe dressed in the bathroom, a habit of a child growing up with communal spaces. Underwear and a white gown that fell all the way to her knees, covered her body as she stepped back into the room. Her eyes sparkled at the large bed that was waiting for her. She leapt on it and fell back into the soft pillows. She exhaled and released her anxious-ness of the first day. 'One down, a thousand to go,' she joked. 'If the old bat lives that much.' Her jaw clenched at the sight of 'no new messages' on her phone. Her ego needed contact from Leo. She wished him to be the first to cave in and reach out. She missed him. His green eyes, his dimples, the warmth of his naked body. He was her first lover and so far, her only.

Zoe was glad that the light switch was just above the bed. She raised her arm and off the light went. Darkness settled and only green screen light shone upon her from her phone as she scrolled through social media looking at her favorite influencers and stars. Their bags, their jewels, their boots, their happiness.

Her morning bus journey out of town, her ferry ride from the port, the taxi to the village and a day of work ganged up and a ton of exhaustion spread on her body. She lowered her phone and as its screen went dark, Zoe noticed the thin line of light below her door.

'Didn't I turn off the corridor light?'

Zoe remained in bed. She had just gotten comfortable; her head having created that ideal positional dent in her pillow. *'What if the old lady wakes up before me and shouts about the electrical bill? Nah, with her strong meds, she wakes up after the sun, surely. She will see no light.'* Zoe persuaded herself to stay in bed. Just as her eyes closed, she heard a faint noise coming from the hallway. Her eyes reopened. She focused her attention. Did she hear right? Footsteps? Her heartbeats raced into the hundreds, and she quickly sat up in bed. And there it was, a shadow cutting the slim line of light in half. Someone was standing outside her door. Zoe never imagined herself as the type to freeze. A woman of action, she disappointed herself with her inaction. *'Could it be one of her children?'* Cold sweat formed on the back of her neck and below her hairline on her forehead. A new terrifying thought. *'A thief. A rapist. A murderer.'* She finally got her feet to obey, and she crept up to the door and as quietly as possible she turned the key. The locked door offered her a sense of security. She let out a soundless sigh. She placed her ear on the door and waited. Nothing. Silence had returned to the house.

'Michael? Michael?'

Mirela's calls grew louder.

'Who the hell is Michael? Great. The old lady now thinks the burglar is someone she knows.' Zoe walked over to her night-

stand and picked up her phone. 'I'm calling the police.' She whispered the words, but her fingers never moved. '*And if it was a trick of the light? A shadow from outside? My sleepy eyes playing tricks? I am not going to embarrass myself on my first day…*'

Zoe had a talent for driving herself crazy in thought.

'Michael? Michael?' Where are you, my boy?'

'*Could she have a dog and forgotten about it? The daughter did not say such a thing, but she never visits much…*'

Zoe's tongue ran along her dried lip. A sign of deep thought, of coming up with a plan. She wore her white trainers and opened the window. The air outside was clean and cool. '*What's the point of air conditioning?*' With the power of her youth, she jumped and landed with ease on the dying grass. She tiptoed up to Mirela's window. It was open just an inch for fresh air. Zoe slid the window aside and climbed in. Faint light was provided by a single lamp placed on the floor in the corner of the room next to a porcelain pot featuring a shrub too green to be real. Thankfully, the old lady's bed faced away from the window. She was still mumbling the same name.

'Mrs. Mirela? It's Zoe. Your nurse. I am here. What's wrong, ma'am?'

'My son. My son, Michael came to visit. Where is he?'

'Your son is Theodore. He is off studying, remember? Mrs. Mirela, do you own a dog?'

The old lady quit her tossing and turning and looked straight at her with an icy gaze. 'What are you on about, you damn fool? Michael is my youngest. He is here. No, I don't have no bloody dog. They smell and shit all over the place and need attention. Go out and look around. See who is here.'

Zoe's facial and neck muscles clenched. 'I… I am scared.'

Mirela's sinister laugh made her skin crawl. 'The little orphan is scared of the night! How much worse can happen to you, child?'

Zoe held back tears gathering below her trembling eyes. She closed Mirela's window, tucked the old lady in, wished her a good night and exited her room. *'I'd rather be out here with the burglar than with that evil witch.'* The corridor was empty. Zoe headed straight into the kitchen and opened the top drawer. She picked up the biggest knife and began switching on every light. Room by room she checked the massive mansion. Locked and empty. The cellar door was locked with no key in sight; the only room she could not enter. She knelt and looked through the keyhole, flashing her mobile light through it. It appeared deserted. Zoe went upstairs to the closed-off upper floor. When Mirela could no longer use stairs, her bed was brought downstairs.

Zoe kept the knife by her side that night. And just before finally managing to close her eyes, she picked up her phone and sent a text over Messenger. 'Leo, I wish you were here. It is one of those nights. I need you. When can you visit? Good night, x.'

Achilles' Heel: Chapter Four

'Sounds like an awful first night.' Damien spoke as Zoe had stopped retelling her first day and turned for water. She shivered as she tried to reach the water bottle. 'Here, let me.' Damien walked over and poured her a glass. The woman looked tired and pale. 'Shall we continue?'

Zoe pulled down the white sheet that was covering her body. She wore only a hospital gown and multiple stitches on her right thigh. Her eyes focused on the wound. It seemed smaller than she expected. When the knife slid through her, she thought she would lose her leg. The excruciating pain was like no other. She remembered the amount of blood that oozed out of her. And now, all it caused her was a mania to scratch. An itchy long red line upon her leg, taunting her. Taunting her about all the different choices she could have made and changed the deadly outcome. But what was done, was done and the detective was waiting. Yet, the Lieutenant had walked over to the window and was staring outside. That is when Zoe realized how see-through the cheap, thin gown was. She had made him feel uncomfortable. She pulled up the sheet and wiggled to get back into a cosy position. 'I need some sleep, officer. I promise I won't forget anything. How could I? This will loiter in my nightmares until my final breath. It will be morning soon and the light and the nurses will invade my room in a couple of hours.'

Damien scratched his right eyebrow and continued down to his unshaved cheek. 'Yeah, yeah. You're probably right,' he agreed in a reluctant tone. 'I'll be back in a few hours then.'

Zoe's eyes seemed to be sparkling. They had watered up. Damien wondered if the meds were wearing off or if the pain was from the memories of the night. 'Please, turn off the light. It's burning my eyes. I've been awake for twenty-two hours straight.'

'Sure thing, Miss Zoe. Have a much-needed rest. We will talk in the morning.'

Damien's two-bedroom apartment was not far from Corfu's main hospital. He chose it as it was one of the only blocks that provided underground parking. A luxury in the small town where there seemed to be more cars than humans, if possible. Wherever you went, it was a struggle to find where to park. Now, the gate opened, and his allocated spot was there waiting for him. It was the only one that was empty. No other tenants out at four in the morning. For Damien, it was the norm.

At least this time he was not stumbling in, drunk into nirvana, intoxicated into an oblivion of thoughtless heaven.

He always returned alone. Any time he *got lucky*; a cheap hotel owner *got lucky* as well.

The only female his home needed woke up as he closed the door behind him.

'Hey, Jolie,' he said as the canine rushed towards him, her nails scraping along the white tiles. He knelt and let the German Shepherd lick his cheek as her tail whipped the floor. 'Who's a good girl? Huh? Who's the best? You are. Yes, you are,' he said in the same tone most used on babies. His fingers ran through her thick coat and white and brown hairs scattered around them. 'Not built for a Greek island, are you dear? Too hot, who's too hot?' He stood up and looked over at her two bowls. Both were half empty. Her water and food were probably the only things in his daily routine that he worried about. He filled up her water, stroked her head and stepped on the envelopes that had been thrown under his door as his mailbox below had been overpowered by super-market and kebab shop flyers. 'Final notice!' He mocked the words. 'I will pay you Mr. Electricity. I think I haven't gambled away all my wage yet.' Jolie wiggled around him as he continued speaking in the tone that he only used with her. Damien sighed, kicked the envelopes to the side and headed into the kitchen. The light scared a rather large cockroach that was standing on top of his leftover microwave mac and cheese with chunks of chicken. Damien did not care enough to chase it. The air was stale, carrying an odor of fried eggs and milk gone bad. Damien opened the window an inch and ordered the night breeze to cleanse the room. He then grabbed a packet of paprika-flavored chips from the cupboard on his left and kicking off his shoes, he trotted to his bedroom. He undressed to his underwear and rubbed his lower back. That is when he noticed. His bedside table was empty. 'Where is...?' He did not manage to finish his sentence and his eye caught a glimpse of the Jack Daniels bottle that lay on the floor by the bed. Jack was a good whiskey for its price, but it was not his top choice.

He chose it for home due to its shape. Round bottles rolled away from him, hiding under the bed or among tossed clothes. Or worse, travelled too far than he could manage to walk. Jack with its square shape stayed where it fell. He raised the bottle and shook it, smiling at the half-full whiskey bottle. He took off the cap and brought it to his lips. He devoured his morning snack in a matter of minutes, sharing with Jolie who had jumped upon the bed and settled by his leg. He washed the chips down with the rest of the whiskey, set his alarm clock to go off in two hours and eleven minutes, and with a heavy head, he closed his eyes.

He could have sworn only five seconds had passed since he drifted off and the beeping sound echoing from his phone woke him. At least it saved him from the same dream. His nemesis. The repeating nightmare.

Jolie did not move a muscle as he threw off his boxer shorts, sat on the toilet playing Fruit Ninja on his phone, took a two-minute shower, dressed, made a frappe, served her beef from a tin, and exited the front door with a lit Assos cigarette stuck to his bottom lip. 'In my next life, I'm coming back as a dog. Or a cat born at a grandma's house.'

Last in, first out. All cars were still resting; his was the first to break the silence underground. He came up to the quiet street and squinted his eyes at the strong morning rays that welcomed him. He threw on his shades and turned left. Besides the bakery and the corner cafe, all shops were still closed. Few people, mostly elderly, wandered around at such an early hour. Soon, chaos, honking and swearing, would erupt. The straight line to the hospital took seven minutes while the scenic route by the sea took thirteen. Damien lit his second cigarette for the day and opted for a blue background than one of grey, dull buildings and weeds growing high in the sunburnt earth. The Ionian did not disappoint. It never did. A magnificent carpet of clear waters all the way to the horizon, sparkling as the sunrays danced upon the tips of short-lived waves. Some dying upon sandy beaches, some upon austere scintillating rocks. The seagulls provided the lyrics to the music of the sea. Damien drove with his window down and his radio off. You never got any decent songs anyway at such an hour. Just mellow tunes interrupted by snippets of depressing news. At least, that was his conviction.

He arrived at his destination, finished off his coffee and lit a third cigarette as he walked up to the main entrance, shaking off bad memories from the depressing hospital. He stood by the side, near a climbing ivy until he smoked it all down to its bud.

'Hard to quit, huh? Maybe you should switch to vaping,' a lanky nurse said as he exhaled a large cloud of smoke. It smelled like forest fruit. Damien stepped on his dying bud, and without eye contact, said, 'I guess you're a vegan and always politically correct, too, huh? Vices are meant to harm you. If you like wild berries and strawberries, just buy yourself a fucking croissant, muppet.'

A bunch of sickly-looking people and worried relatives waited for the elevator. Damien opted for the stairs. *'And the captain says I never work out.'* His mind journeyed to the pretty girl with the stabbed leg. The image of her wobbly teary eyes as she tried to run towards him replayed in his mind. *'Poor thing.'* As he pushed back the heavy fire exit door, he wondered if she had gained his sympathy due to her looks and how she reminded him of *her*.

Outside of Zoe's room, a short male doctor was asking two nurses in spotless white robes about his patient. '...she woke up a bit disoriented. We told her specifics about her leg and condition, and she just lay there staring at us.'

'She did smile though,' the other one, the older one, commented. 'She seems sad. She's only a child really. Twenty-something and to live through such an ordeal.'

'She seems older, though...'

'Ladies, concentrate,' the doctor said and chuckled. He knew his staff well. They always gossiped and even though he never admitted it, he rather enjoyed it.

Damien walked over and introduced himself. The morning doctor was far more welcoming than the one from the night shift. In her defense though, Damien did realize he was well more presentable at that moment. The black circles below his reddish eyes could be seen as a sign of an overworked public servant and smelling of cheap cigarettes compared to cheap booze, made a huge difference.

'She is doing just fine. That one is a fighter. She may not seem it, but she has a strong spirit. The wound will heal, leaving just a thin scar behind.'

'All wounds leave us with scars. Depends how much we let them get to us.'

The doctor was not expecting a philosophical reply. He nodded his head. 'Yes, yes, of course,' he said and walked off to check up on his next patient. A boy with a broken arm, a worried mum, and an angry dad. The expensive brand-new bike was totally wrecked.

Damien knocked and entered the room, wishing Zoe a good morning. The nurse had just finished drinking a glass of milk. Zoe quickly wiped her white lips with her right hand and sat up straight. 'Good morning, Lieutenant.' She waited for him to turn and pull near a chair, before running her fingers through her messy hair, hoping the hairs would comply and form a semi-decent style. '*Vanity*,' her inner voice told her off.

'You sure you don't need more sleep? I could return later?' Damien wished for no such thing. He needed her statement as soon as possible. His itch to investigate was growing. He wanted to go up to the house with his partner, talk to the forensics team, go down to the morgue, and sit in on the autopsies. But he had a survivor. Just one. Why gather disperse pieces of a puzzle when the woman before him had the box with the image on it?

'Don't you?'

'Sleep and I have never been friends.'

'I can only sleep in complete darkness and silence.' She raised her hands as to present the environment. Strong sunlight rode in from the window overseeing the East and above them four powerful fluorescent lights were switched on. Voices and footsteps made up the commotion outside her doors that had a gap between them, allowing every single sound to journey through.

'If my mind offers me silence, then I sleep.'

'And if it doesn't?'

'I silence it.'

Zoe chuckled but controlled her laughter as she noticed that the Lieutenant was not joking. She wanted to ask how, but knew the question was far too intrusive. There was something about the man though that stirred her pot of curiosity. She kept trying to order herself to behave, to remind herself that she had just lived through a massacre, saw dead bodies for the first time in her life, yet her mind blurred the blood and focused on the officer with the badly ironed clothes sitting by her bed.

'Shall we pick up where we left of? After your first night?'

'Eager to purge my memory, detective? Do not fear. I have forgotten nothing. Every single detail has been burnt into my brain.'

Grab your copy...
vinci-books.com/AchillesHeel

About the Author

Luke Christodoulou is an Amazon bestselling author, a poet and an English teacher (MA Applied Linguistics - University of Birmingham). He is also a coffee-movie-book-Nutella lover.

His first book, *The Olympus Killer* (#1 Bestseller - Thrillers), was released in April, 2014. The book was voted Book of the Month for May on Goodreads (Psychological Thrillers). The book continued to be a fan favorite on Goodreads and was voted BOTM for June in the group Nothing Better Than Reading. In October, it was BOTM in the group Ebook Miner, proving it was one of the most talked-about thrillers of 2014.

The second stand-alone thriller from the series, *The Church Murders*, was released April, 2015 to widespread critical and fan acclaim. *The Church Murders* became a bestseller in its categories throughout the summer and was nominated as Book of the Month in three different Goodreads groups.

Death of a Bride was the third Greek Island Mystery to be released. Released in April, 2016 it followed in the footsteps of its successful predecessors. From its first week in release it hit the number one spot for books set in Greece.

Murder On Display came out in 2017 and enriched the series.

Hotel Murder, the fifth and 'final' book in the series, followed in early 2018.

In 2018, his box set of mysteries became an international bestseller.

Luke Christodoulou has also ventured into 'children's book land' and released *24 Modernized Aesop Fables*, retelling old stories with new elements and settings. The book, also, features sections for parents, which include discussions, questions, games and activities.

In 2019, *Twelve Months of Murder* came out, his first collection of shorts.

His first novel outside of the Greek Island Mysteries collection came in 2020, maintaining his love for a Greek theme. A supernatural thrill ride with the name of *Beware of Greeks Bearing Gifts*.

Pandora's Box followed in 2021. A mind-twisting whodunit set in his favorite Greek town, the seaside resort of Parga. The following year saw the release of the highly anticipated *Achilles' Heel*.

His first YA murder mystery, *Senior Year Murders* was released in 2024, hitting the charts for young adult thrillers.

He is currently working on various projects (which he is secretive about).

He resides in Limassol, Cyprus with his loving wife, his chatty daughter and his super-energetic son.

Hobbies include travelling the Greek Islands discovering new food and possible murder sites for his stories. He also enjoys telling people that he 'kills people for a living'.